DEVIL'S LANE

BY
ELLWYN K. COLLINS

Order this book online at www.trafford.com
or email orders@trafford.com

Most Trafford titles are also available at major online book retailers.

Printed in the United States of America.

ISBN: 978-1-4120-6468-2 (sc)

Trafford rev. 07/07/2014

 www.trafford.com

North America & international
toll-free: 1 888 232 4444 (USA & Canada)
fax: 812 355 4082

Acknowledgement

To my wife, Constance, her love and support all these years are a source of joy.

To Ken Dobratz, friend and a great golf partner!

CONTENTS

Character References!

Uke: Not as slow-witted a hero as he appears to be, learns success is where you find it.

Sis: Uke's domineering sister whom he relies upon, (far too much).

Otto: Uke's brother-in-law. A fast buck artist whose greatest skill is avoiding honest labor.

Father Aloysius: He finds it's easier to join the clan than fight them. He has connections. It helps.

Abe: Uke's identical twin. He strikes out trying to pinch-hit for Uke at Uke's wedding.

Ruth: She deserves better, but settles for Uke.

Higgie: Window washer/peeper, the wealthiest in town except for Fred Studey, the lawyer, who controls grand dad's estate. Sure he does. Fred Studey cares for grand dad's estate, yeh.

Albie Nostrov: Why don't we just forget him, his mother and brother? They operate the world's second oldest profession.

Herman: An ancient catfish, wise to the ways of fishermen, especially Uke, Otto and Higgie.

Then there is the character who whittled decoys for a living, also the game warden whose only ambition in life is to catch Otto poaching.

Where would you hide a 17 foot high statue from the city fathers in broad daylight? Uke knows.

The boys over at the capitol need a state rep to replace the one whose wife did some dentistry on her husband with his shotgun of all things!

Ben Hibbs: One of the states finest troopers. He has the chore of deciding whom to believe, Uke, Abe, Sis or Ruth? If I don't know why should I tell you? Guess who finds the gold mining stock?

Judge Bower: His financing power makes up for his high handicap golf by nailing anyone caught in his court with "costs."

Archibald Hobart:" Owner of Hobart's Funeral and Furniture emporium hides down on the corner waiting for his crew to deliver Otto. Instead they mistakenly deliver furniture to the house.

Frenchy:The town drunk knows valuable junk when he sees it.

McNammara's Hill: Steep, with a curve, a freight train, boulders, and other stuff it collects at the bottom of the hill.

George: Uke's best man. They both spent most of their schooling in the fourth grade on sums.

Cuke Cumber: Druggist. Unknown to most, he's the county coroner the most powerful dude in the county.

Gadflies: Other characters that slip into the story unnoticed.

Will Uke ever consummate his marriage?

Who polishes off Otto?

Why does Uke feel responsible for Higgie's misfortune?

A freight train and a squirrel help Uke turn his life around.

CHAPTER ONE
THE TRIANGLE

"Gol Dang!" Uke swore softly to himself.
Otto was right and that's what hurt. Uke,he
insisted,didn't have a full deck. True, in
politics,he could do no better than to hold a
pair, but this time his two pair of aces were
better than the royal flush public office
dealt him. Unlike other politicians Uke was
different...he was honest. Dumb perhaps,like
Otto always insisted, but honest, even for
the late 1920's.

None of the county's good burghers could
deny his two political attributes. Some wondered about him before he became the county's
most important elected official. The only
problem was Uke just couldn't seem to earn
respect. But how could he be expected to
solve problems when most of the civic woes
took care of themselves if left alone.

"Yer the best damn sheriff this county ever
had," Otto always insisted and for good
reason. He promoted the saying that behind
every good man was a good woman. However,
Otto, his brother-in-law,was the real power
behind the office, not Sis.

The voters were amazed that Uke had become
sheriff. It was relatively simple: finding an

empty space on the nomination papers, he
filled in his name. Only after the registra-
tion deadline had passed was it discovered
that Ulysses S. Compton had embroidered the
top of each sheet. There wasn't a shyster in
the crowd that could dispute his legal right
to the job, no matter how much hot air they
blew. The intended nominee's name could be
found no where on any of the papers.

Sis took care of most of Uke's personal
difficulties when she wasn't consumed with a
couple of problems of her own. Otto handled
Uke's political maneuvering. It was one of
the few things he was good at: petty crook
that he was.

Sis could be counted upon except when she
was busy with Mihich Nostrov, seer extra-
ordinaire, her damn fool statue, or when she
was tracking down and putting a stop to shady
dealings of her husband, Otto Granley.

"Yer brawn an my brains kin go a long
ways," Otto assured him.Uke appreciated this.
He had learned to rely heavily on his sister
and brother-in-law almost from the time he
was born. Ma took off with a drummer about
the time he and Abe, his no account identical
twin, were four years old.

Uke knew that lately Sis was busy with
Mihich who had predicted a dire future for
Otto. When her crystal ball clouded up,
Mihich's hand flashed out palm up and the
ball cleared enough to pocket another dollar.
It bothered Uke some that he suspected Sis
squandered divvy money (the interest proceeds
from Grand Dad's estate), on Mihich.

"Rootville," Higgie Jones, whom some insisted was the wealthiest man in town, observed, "would not be safe if the scheming
Otto and Mihich ever teamed up together."
Higgie, the towns only window washer, had
good reason to know.

Uke knew Sis and Otto had marital problems, but seldom bothered to think about them
or much of anything else for that matter. It
was none of his business he always told himself, but never admitted he'd like to know
what the problem was.

He prided himself on his juvenile delinquency program. When he caught Lester Simp-
son's kid, George, smoking corn silk wrapped
in cigarette papers he had stolen from "Kuke"
Cumber's drug store, he marched George out
behind Johnson's Lumber Yard.

"How old are you, kid?"

"Fourteen, and please let go of my ear."

"When I do, you'll wish I hadn't." Uke let
go of the jug handle and at the same time
spun him around. With a cuff up side the head
and a kick in the slats, George was sent
sprawling in the dust.

"If your old man is of any value he'll beat
the hell out of you when you get home," Uke
advised him. At the same time he doubted it.
Lester was one of those do gooders always
messing into other people's business instead
of taking care of his own.

"Don't tell him, I won't do it no more,"
the kid whined as he limped toward home.

None of this went into a sheriff's report
since Uke never bothered to write one. He
came upon young Dick Armbruster in the shrubs
behind the church with the young Wilson girl.
Uke dragged Dick through town in his long
underwear and tossed him in the river to cool
off.

"Can you swim, kid?" Uke shouted over the
bridge railing at the floundering romeo. Uke
only had Dick's welfare at heart. He never
gave the girl a thought.

Once word got around among the kids about
Uke's effective counseling, there wasn't much
juvenile delinquency to speak of in the

county. The towns social worker left for
greener pastures.

His alcoholic program produced like results. Revelers who had too much cheer were
allocated the same spot behind the lumber
yard and allowed to sleep it off. Why mess
up the county jail? It smelled bad enough as
it was. When the souses recovered, they
picked up their valuables at their local
watering hole. The county had voted "dry" in
the last election. Otto, with the help of
unknown sources, kept the lid on prohibition's investigative efforts.

Uke's version of social justice worked
well. The victim never complained, the system
was never burdened with needless paper work,
lawyers did not have to expend any gasoline
or oats chasing ambulances, and Uke had not
much to do except to stay out of the taxpayers' sight.... and his sister's.

It was hardly any trick to stay out of
Sis's sight. He knew she could always be
found in one of two places, out in the shed
pounding away on the statue, or in Mihich
Nostrov's parlor staring into a crystal ball.

Uke did suspect Mihich knew two things: Sis
had a family inheritance coming, and it was
no trick to get Sis to part with a sizeable
amount of it. Why people would believe the
nonsense Mihich concocted was beyond Uke. She
tossed out tid-bits of things she knew and
her customers gobbled it up. Half truths,
lies and promises full of greed were her
tools of the trade.

Why smart, thrifty Sis fell for Mihich's
fortune telling was beyond his understanding. Mihich, he was certain, had Sis's
measure. "Every word comes true." Sis
defiantly defended Mihich.

All told, for a city of sixty-five thous-
and, Rootville was well behaved, except maybe

at the Fourth of July parade.

There were plenty of pool halls, honest poker games, social amenities, parks, athletic fields and places where a young stud could entertain a lady undisturbed. Three taverns surrounded each church in this legally dry town.

Uke was aware of all these establishments (and the good they accomplished). He had to be aware of them: his brother-in-law, Otto, frequented all of them except the churches, and some places Sis would not appreciate. But what the hell, it was her fault if she didn't keep Otto satisfied and happy. Too late, Uke saw Otto heading in his direction.

"Uke, we got problems with that bunch of swindle artists down at city hall next to the band shell." He waited for Uke to absorb this announcement.

Uke had no authority over the mayor or city council. If he had, both Otto and Sis would never let him rest until he ran them out of town. All three had their own reasons for wishing city hall did not exist.

"What's the problem?" Uke wondered. At twenty five, six feet four and 240 pounds, he was big and powerfully built.

"Higgie says they're gonna' make me buy a license for my popcorn wagon down to the park." If Higgie said it: it was true.

"Why tell me about it?" Uke wondered. He knew full well he had no authority in Root-ville, only in the county.

Otto paused, shrugged his shoulders and hurried toward his truck without waiting for a reply. Uke knew he was heading for the empty poker chair at Lil' Joe's Saloon & Emporium. The flat bed Model-T truck dis-appeared up Devils's Lane in a swirl of dust. He knew Otto would find a way to avoid buying the license.

With few exceptions, life was as good
as it was ever going to get without having a
wife to look after him. Sooner or later he
knew Sis would create this problem for him
with Ruth. Like all women, Sis seemed to think
men had to be miserable.

Rusty blonde hair escaped from under his
sheriff's cap in unmanageable directions.
Uke's grey eyes were said to have come from
his mother's side of the family. It was the
extent of any inherited traits that could be
detected by a casual observer.

Word had it Grand Dad had been hung as a
horse thief or shot in a poker game. The page
in the Historical Society's journal was missing making it difficult to know how Grand Dad
had cashed in his chips. At any rate, people
gave Uke a wide berth in case some of the
dirt had rubbed off on him. When possible,
they steered clear of Otto, too. At times,
Sis also shied away from Otto, other than to
go through his pockets each night.

Unease brewed deep in Uke's soul, or maybe
it was in his stomach. This was where he felt
it the most. His problem, he knew, had to do
with Sis, and her husband, Otto and the fair
city of Rootville.

Down in the middle of town, near city hall,
the city claimed a small plot of ground. They
had papers to prove it. Sis also had papers
to prove it belonged to her, or rather to the
Compton estate. Uke, Sis and Abe, were the
only heirs.

The courts were reluctant to step into the
fray, simply because they knew the Comptons
owned the ground deeded to them by Grand Dad.
Nor would they rule against the city when it
came to money.

Times were tough and an appointed judge
never knew where his next buck was coming
from. The buck was more important than jus-

tice. Everyone was aware of the Compton estate and the fact the Compton's attorney drove a new Packard every year and used his brother-in-law as his chauffeur.

The lawyer had taught his chauffeur how to wash windows. It appeared to be a profitable business until the fool had fallen off the ladder, broken his leg and almost drowned in the soap suds. Worse yet: it had dried up the black mail business. Around town, it was understood that the Comptons were a power.

The tiny park, filled with a grove of trees and grass, was too small for much of anything other than a drinking fountain, perhaps a popcorn wagon might fit. Trees sheltered the area just large enough to hold a picnic if too many people didn't attend. The city felt there was no sense in putting a fountain there: no one would know about it and besides, someone would forget to shut it off in the winter and it would freeze, break, and cost money to fix.

Mayor Wendell Clauson brought the subject up at nearly every council meeting, "What should we put in our park?" He had an answer in mind.

The city council dressed in their black business suits to match the mayor's garb, collectively shook their heads. They also knew the honest and legal answer and it wasn't a statue of the mayor decorating the park.

The property continued to lay idle due to the loggerhead in the council so they did the reasonable thing: nothing. Each one secretly desired a statue of himself (at the city's expense) to be erected there.

Sis, however, knew exactly what had to be done with the hallowed ground as well as Mayor Clausen and his covey of black birds. Due to the dispute, no honor ever befell the park.

The courts had validated Grand Dad Compton's will and honored almost all facets of it long ago. The ancestral home was put into a trust so no Compton would ever be without a roof, but the old geezer had dropped a bomb into the will. His statue had to reside in the park before the will could be probated.

Sheriff Uke and Otto spent a good deal of Uke's spare time, which was considerable, trying to find ways to subvert the legal nonsense in the will. Why waste time when the money was there for the taking? Their real problem was getting past the shyster with the Packard. They expected no help from Abe. For good reason Abe hadn't been seen for some time.

The demands of the will had become an obsession with Sis. She spent her free moments out in the shed banging away at the sheet copper encasing the statue's wooden framework...and wondering what Otto and Uke might be up to.

Grand Dad founded Rootville and had been the first and foremost citizen for some time. He was on the way to becoming the wealthiest and politically active until destiny, a sturdy tree branch, and a stolen horse interfered with his livelihood. There was no doubt about his guilt: it was said he was riding the nag when accosted. The only real fact was that since that time, all the Comptons had exceptionally long necks.

To show its appreciation for Grand Dad's lifetime efforts, the fair city of Rootville stole his property a piece at a time in the name of back taxes. The exceptions were the homestead and the tiny plot near city hall which they figured was already theirs.

Several times the city attempted to break the will and failed, so they simply assumed title to the eighth of an acre of ground by putting up a couple of "No Trespassing" signs ignored by one and all.

Like Uke and Otto, Sis knew the only way to beat city hall was to shit on the steps and run like hell. Uke knew she had no intention of running. He also knew that her concern at the moment was that she needed another sheet of copper. Each large sheet was always the last she would need in order to complete the statue. Buying and hauling it home fell to Otto and his flat bed truck.

Uke was surprised to hear Otto's Tin-Lizzie returning. By now he thought Otto would be half way to Lil' Joe's.

Otto leaped from the open cab and strode toward him, "Keep your damn big mouth shut about my winning the deed to Maloney's farm," Otto barked. "The old fool shouldn't have stayed in the pot with two pair."

He shook his finger in Uke's face and wheeled back to the idling truck. Uke wondered why he was so concerned about a chunk of paper: other than the fact that they both knew Sis would demand he give the deed back. He hadn't known about the paper until this moment when Otto threatened him.

He felt anger rising. Otto's concern was a leak in the family security giving Sis all her information. He was blaming me as the informer!

Only one person in town would know and profit from secrets. Higgie Jones, window washer, no longer had job competition. With a little leverage applied down at city hall, he could under bid everyone. His profits were in peeping, not washing windows.

CHAPTER TWO
THE TRIP

"Sis wants another sheet of copper. I'm busy, so you're going to have to run to Middletown and get it by yerself." Otto informed Uke the next morning.

"Got a really big poker game going today?" Uke grinned, trying to hide his pleasure and excitement. Otto had never allowed him to take the truck alone before. He wiped the peanut butter from his fingers onto his leg unmindful that most of it had just decorated his .38 holster.

Otto gave him a sly grin. "Yeh." They both turned uneasily to watch Sis bearing down from the shed where she kept her almighty statue.

She maneuvered to keep between them and the building. No one was allowed into either shed except when Otto backed the blue Durant out for a Sunday drive. The tires were always soft and needed pumping up. Somehow Uke always wound up with this chore, but never with an invitation to ride along.

An old blanket protected the seats from chicken feathers. The car had to be washed before Sis would consent to grace it with her presence, since it provided a convenient place for the hens' eggs. Otto's old Model-T flat bed truck provided the major portion of his transportation. Uke walked or hitchhiked for the most part.

Sis seldom strayed far from the old house other than her twice weekly visit to see Mihich, the old witch, doing her mumbo-jumbo trance worth a dollar (to Michich).

The homestead, as it had been referred to ever since Uke could remember, lay on the edge of town alongside of Devil's Lane. One of the two impressive things on their acre was a huge oak tree blocking the sidewalks on one front corner.

Instead of removing the tree, the city had chosen to curl the concrete walk around it. Tree roots had forced the cement walk into an abbreviated roller coaster design. The other thing was the rumor that Devil's Lane had been renamed after either Otto, Grand Dad, or Abe.

A worn tire from Otto's truck hung on a length of heavy rope from a high limb and served as a swing. Some snitches proclaimed it was the same rope that caused Grand Dad to gasp his last breath. Passer-bys were welcome to stop and swing on the tire. For adults it was a moment to regain their childhood. For children: a novel experience.

"Don't forget to air the tires on the Durant," Sis, legs spread wide apart and hands on hips, reminded Otto. She pointed to the rusty hand pump on the running board. "And wash the car." she snapped, eyeing the decorations the chickens provided.

Uke knew he'd wind up with the chore.

The two storage sheds lined the drive near the middle of the acre. The chicken yard was farthest from the street and closest to the house. It was inconvenient when the wind blew from the wrong direction, but when breakfast eggs were needed and there was no ice in the ice box to keep the eggs, or the Sunday menu

called for a supreme sacrifice: the chickens
were handy. Sis usually popped their heads off
from the back porch with her trusty .22 short
rifle.

Out behind the sheds, almost hidden in the
weeds and wild sun flowers, lay an assortment
of items rusting in disuse.

An old wheel barrow and the cab from an
ancient truck poked through the weeds. The
truck cab had been discarded when the rest of
the vehicle was converted into a tractor and
then lost in a long forgotten poker game. The
other item showing above the high grass was a
sulky rig with one wheel missing. No one would
allow it into a poker pot. None of the
residents knew where the sulky came from.
Likely a horse trainer mistook the area for
the city dump.

Items not showing were many and it was a
dangerous place to try to take a shortcut.
Abe, Uke's no good identical twin, had thrown
two fox traps into the weeds one night when
the game warden closed in on him. Uke didn't
know for certain if they were still set.

Especially dangerous was a small, wooden dog
house sometimes used by stray badgers or
raccoons seeking shelter from rain or snow.
He had learned early in life not to corner any
animal, especially wild ones. It was a handsome doghouse, but Uke could never remember
their having had a dog.

The home was a two story frame structure
that defied antiquity. It looked like two
houses pushed together, and in fact it was.
Old Grandma Compton had purchased both of them
and had them rolled in on window weights to
their present location.

The window weights, round and about a foot
long, were made of cast steel. If installed
inside the window frame, their normal use was
to counter balance against the windows to keep

them open. This was a novel idea from Grand
Dad Compton: most people used sticks to keep
their windows open when they weren't using
them to straighten out the kids.

Grand Dad had never been able to convince
anyone to substitute the weights for their
wooden props, so he had them stacked in the
farthest shed with an array of other seldom
used items, like Abe's forgotten box of dynamite. The floor had long since buckled from
the window weights.

Grand Dad Compton was to have contributed
his fair share to the home by installing the
weights into the window frames. He never did,
neither did Pa Compton, and Otto always managed to avoid the project. A half hour per
window would have accomplished the feat. Abe
used the propped up windows to sneak off to
avoid Sis. Uke smashed several panes of glass
trying to install the weights, and gave up
after Sis's foot stamping demand.

The half case of dynamite remained from when
Abe used it to blow up the excess chicken guts
and manure for farmers. An assortment of other
used items were piled haphazardly in the dark
shed and held together by spider webs. The
near shed contained Sis's royal blue Durant
and the statue.

The house was spacious in the tradition of
large farm families who discovered child labor
was much more profitable than paying hired
hands. Except for the sleeping quarters, the
kitchen with the huge wood burning stove saw
the most use. The upstairs was heated through
a lattice work design in the kitchen ceiling
allowing the stove heat to rise. In summer it
was too warm to sleep up there and in winter
it was too cold.

Uke was aware of every minute detail in
their acre of ground and would have known if
much more than a pebble had been missing,

although theft of any kind was unusual.

Sis stalked off, but wheeled and was bearing down on the two of them once more. Uke
maneuvered to keep Otto between him and his
big sister. Cripes, she couldn't even wait
until she got near them to start her bossing.
He relaxed, she was looking at Otto, not him.

Something was on her mind. After she left,
he'd catch hell from Otto who was probably
responsible. Not at all the way a sheriff
should be treated. Someday, he promised himself, I'll put a stop to this game. Suspic-
iously, she shifted her glance from one to the
other.

"Are you ready to go get the last sheet of
copper I need?" She waited for the answer
hands on hips, legs spread apart, a favorite
pose.

Without replying, Otto gave Uke a shove
toward the truck. "Come on, Uke, sooner we get
away from her, the better," he growled softly
so she wouldn't hear.

"I didn't spill the beans about the deed to
Maloney's farm." Uke complained.

"Nobody twisted Maloney's arm ta stay in the
pot last night," Otto insisted. "The rumdum
shouldn't have tried to buy the hand with two
pair."

It was the first Uke knew that choice tid-
bit. Uke waited for him to climb into the
truck and adjust the spark and gas levers on
the steering column. When Otto nodded, Uke
kicked the front tire before moving to the
front of the truck. He grabbed the crank and
spun the engine to start it. The engine fired,
caught and danced violently while Otto fever-
ishly jerked at the timing and spark levers on
each side of the steering column with both
hands in an effort to smooth the vibration.

"This tire kicking has got to stop," Uke
muttered. The truck lurched violently as he

put his weight on the running board and
climbed in. He didn't openly rebel because
riding beat walking all hollow. He was aware
that while Otto insisted the truck could not
be started any other way, Uke never saw anyone
else kick a tire.

In fact, some of the newer cars could be
started from inside just by pressing on the
floor board. It didn't occur to Uke to wonder
how Otto got the damn thing started when he
wasn't around. When a cranked vehicle back
fired, it scared the chickens, and cats, half
to death.

Also, a broken arm was the result and the
only ones happy about starting engines in this
manner were doctors.

Uke twisted around in the seat. He could see
Sis watching through the dust churned up by
the truck until they disappeared from sight.
She was probably thinking they had better remember to get the kerosene can filled or else
was wondering what mischief they'd been up to.

He often saw her going through Otto's pockets after Otto had dragged in late and was
trying to catch up on some sleep after an all
night poker game. Uke was willing to bet she'd
use the copper sheeting excuse to spend the
afternoon and a lot of our money down in
Mihich Nostrov musty old shack absorbing
incantations.

"She's watching us," he informed Otto.

"To hell with her," Otto growled. "Damn,
she's getting her three squares, why is she
such a bitch?"

They both knew she trusted neither one for
totally different reasons. In her mind, Otto
was incorrigible, and Uke was still such a
boy. She told Uke once that he was showing
some small signs of maturity. What she meant
was he no longer insisted she comb his hair
for the weekly Wednesday or Saturday night

dates with Ruth.

Sis often told him since he had taken up with Ruth in the fourth grade that she was an empty headed thing. Sis often wondered aloud what chance Uke would have with the girl if Abe hadn't decided to trade her to Uke. Sis never did find out exactly what Uke gave Abe in return. Knowing Abe, Sis knew full well that Abe had extracted something in return.

After his mother, Ma Compton, ran off with a peddler, Sis had raised the twin brothers and always said that while they were identical, Abe never turned out like Uke. She meant it to be a compliment to Uke. Sis's admonition constantly rang in his ears,

"Ruth couldn't tell the two of you apart, and I doubt Abe has ever really given her up," she cautioned Uke.

No one had seen Abe after he tried to get rid of Luke Beyer's manure and chicken gut pile with dynamite. If it had worked it would have been a quick and dirty way to solve the huge pile smelling up half of the county. Trouble was, his method wasn't quick, just dirty.

Abe had left town before things settled down and Sis insisted that she would go along with Uke and Otto to make certain they cleaned up the mess. They spent four days picking chicken entrails out of the nearby trees and sweeping manure from the roofs of all the buildings on Luke's property. Worst of all, Abe had been paid in advance. All he left behind in his hurry was the half a case of dynamite. Luke's place looked like a cat farm for several weeks.

The truck struggled up Main street past the grocery store and filling station combination. Otto slowed to a halt when they were opposite Lil'Joe's Saloon & Emporium and stuck his head out the open window to study the

tavern. Light peeked through a crack in the
drawn upstairs shades in the clap board building. He made a mental note to tell Joe to tape
up the slit so the cops wouldn't see it.

State police often raided the poker game and
Emporium. They left without molesting the
players after discovering Otto at the table:
they figured the others would get what they
deserved with Otto in the game. He could do
tricks dealing cards with one hand. He learned
the trick from an old gent who had mashed his
paw in a farming accident and had to find
other sources of revenue.

Paying the old gent to teach him was one of
the best investments Otto had ever made. He
made it a point to never sit in a poker game
with the old guy. It was likely he hadn't
taught Otto everything he knew.

The police always left the Emporium with a
satisfied smile on their faces. In all prob-
ability, the poker table was the only place in
town Otto was warmly welcomed, except when he
left with all their money.

Uke meant to enjoy the three hour drive over
to Middletown once he had dropped Otto off at
Lil' Joe's.

"You go ahead and get her sheet of copper,"
Otto ordered, sliding out from under the
steering wheel. "We'll get the kerosene at the
store before we go home."

Uke eagerly scrambled into the driver's
seat. The truck was a pleasure and an honor to
drive. It didn't bother him that Otto forbade
him to drive by way of McNamara's hill.

"The Hill" as it was known, shaved an hour
off the driving time, but since Uke so enjoyed the rare privilege, he cared less about the
distance and time saved. It was a beautiful
day and a nice drive. With gasoline raging
around seven cents a gallon Uke knew Otto was
torn between McNamara's shortcut and the cost

of extra gas by going the long way around.

"The Hill" was the highest in the county and what with tall trees and a hidden railroad track curling around its base more than one driver came out second best with a freight train.

He pulled away without a backward glance at Otto. The fresh summer morning had hardly begun and there wasn't a better way to spend the day. He waved to Father Aloysius puttering in his garden among the stations of the cross. He liked the old fogey, although Sis, who claimed to be a Latter Day Saint, never would allow Uke to enter a Catholic church.

Sis would have him fried in eternity if he did. She claimed her church upbringing would never permit it. He could never figure out why everyone else except the Comptons had Saturdays and Sundays mixed up.

He continued on through the downtown section not yet busy with automobiles or horse and wagons. Once out into the country the fresh air filled him with the sweet smell of freshly cut red clover and alfalfa.

He had the copper plate tied down and was on the way home before twelve o'clock. One thing bothered him on this otherwise wonderful day...he couldn't remember what Otto said about stopping for kerosene.

Better be on the safe side, he decided, and get the can filled and lashed down on the rear of the truck. Otto had warned him never to keep it near the cab: if it spilled they'd have an awful time keeping the stuff from creeping all over the truck's upholstery. Kerosene had that trait of creeping like a blotter besides having an awful smell to it.

Otto knew about those things. So Uke followed instructions and filled the can before leaving the outskirts of Middletown. He tested the ropes, satisfied the can was secure over

the left rear wheel. Relaxed, with his left
foot out the side window he continued his
journey homeward singing at the top of his
voice. He had filled the order. Now there
nothing for anyone to get sore about.

At the turn off by Dell's Woods, just above
McNamara's hill, he pulled the truck from the
road. It was Otto's favorite spot to rest. The
bees hummed in the heat of summer. Grass-
hoppers chimed in with their soprano melody.

Too bad Ruth didn't come along. She loved
the rides, but her pa was feeling poorly the
past few days, and Uke hadn't seen much of
her.

He closed his eyes and visualized Ruth, soft
and sweet, not at all hard and cold like his
sister. Ruth was smart, too. She knew about
things that needed knowing about, like fixing
meals and making ice cream. She was far from
empty headed like Sis always maintained.

He stretched out in the shade on the warm
ground, I don't really envy Otto, he mused,
but I know him better than other people do. He
had a peculiar feeling Otto would never arrive
at a ripe old age living the life of a fast
buck artist. His string of pop corn wagons
never supported Otto's life style. Sis was the
one person Otto could not outwit.

Sis lived by the Bible, but seldom went to
church. I can read and think for myself she
insisted many times to anyone who would listen. She helped the Widow Jenkins and her
seven kids. It was Sis who saw to it the
Jenkins' had food and coal on the holidays and
not the old biddies at church who rustled
around cackling about each others beautiful
new hats and dresses.

Uke enjoyed taking things to the widow. It
made him feel good. Sis always ordered Otto to
take the gifts, but Uke wound up doing it.

"Ain't got no time," Otto would explain, or

"I'm pretty busy."

The statue consumed Sis. After many false starts, she began to fashion a likeness in her mind of her dear, departed old grand dad. No amount of persuasion from Otto could deter her from the likeness she thought she was fashioning. After several comments from Otto she simply forbade him or Uke to enter the shed.

He wondered many times where Abe was and what he was doing. He hadn't seen him for several years. Abe was similar to Otto in many ways with one notable exception: Otto was not vicious like Abe. At least he didn't think so.

Then there was Ruth. Springtime, roses in bloom, sunshine on a rainy day. A strange, uneasy feeling filled the pit of his stomach when he thought about her, and it wasn't hunger pangs, either. He knew the difference.

She was a small girl, and appeared smaller when near Uke. When he took her hand (the most advance he had ever tried with her,) his thumb reached almost to her elbow. Over the years he had met prettier girls, but none any nicer. The moths flitting around right now in his stomach caused him to quit thinking about her. Her quick smile and flashing eyes always did this to him. Why, he didn't know.

He rubbed his eyes and played with two questions he couldn't answer. One, how did I get where I am, and two, where am I going? It had been surprisingly easy to become sheriff. The pay was low, but the work was easy. While he did not pretend to understand politics, he knew he was a success.

One morning he woke up and everyone congratulated him on becoming sheriff. All he had to do was kiss babies, listen to complaints, promise anything, but do nothing. This was Otto's advice and it worked fine.

"Stay on the good side of the county coroner," Sis had advised him, "he's the only one who can arrest the sheriff."

Uke discovered this was true. It was a part
of the checks and balances built into government he learned over coffee with Higgie Jones,
window washer and window peeper. Higgie would
know. How, Uke had no idea.

Higgie toured the town at night throwing
dirt and dust at interesting windows, thereby
assuring they would need cleaning the next
day. He also learned many profitable things in
the process. Most of it while cleaning the
windows.

In his three years since he became
sheriff, Uke had never met the coroner. While
he took Ruth to the movie at the Bijou every
Wednesday which was date night, and he always
said "Howdy" to the theater manager, Mr. Elvin
Hotchkiss, he was unaware this small, docile
man was the county coroner.

He could go on being sheriff indefinitely,
Otto had assured him. Many people felt he was
a "natural" politician.

"Natural" to Uke meant an easy job to hold.
To Otto it meant a person who could be manip-
ulated without his being aware of it. Others
were aware of this fact, and it became one
advantage that could cause Uke to go far in
politics.

Uke stretched and yawned and caught himself
dozing off. His eyes felt heavy for lack of
sleep. The afternoon sun bore down with an
intensity the morning sun did not have. His
head dropped down on his chest.

CHAPTER THREE
THE FIRE

Uke shook himself awake with a start. Many times he had rested in this spot with Otto, but the shade of the small elm tree had never cast its long shadow over that gray boulder before.

He scrubbed his eyes with his knuckles and glanced up at the sun. "Lordy, it has to be near four o'clock! Otto will skin me alive unless I can cook up a good story."

He pulled his giant frame from the warm earth and paused for a moment to allow dizziness to evaporate before rushing to the front of the truck. He grabbed the crank and spun it before remembering to turn on the key.

The truck refused to start. Frantic, he returned to the cab and readjusted the levers on the steering wheel. He fought to control panic rising in him. Once more he charged to the front of the truck and reached for the crank. Several spins produced no results.

He had only a vague understanding of the spark, gas levers and the choke, but nothing about the fact that all the gasoline had evaporated from the carburetor while he slept.

Otto always insisted the real secret was in the kicking the tire. He paused, shrugged and then wheeled around and gave the right front

tire a swift kick before reaching for the
crank. Unknown to Uke, the previous cranking
had replenished the carburetor bowl. One spin
and the engine roared into life.

The truck lurched under his weight as he
stepped on the running board and hurriedly
clambered behind the wheel. He fooled around
with the levers and choke knob until his steed
settled down to a steady rhythm. He paused long
enough to wipe the sweat from his face with the
large red bandanna from his back pocket.

How to make up the lost time? McNamara's
hill! It would save almost an hour. He was
aware that Otto avoided the downhill run for
the most part. It was long, steep and had a
sharp curve at the bottom. Worse, a hidden
railroad track circled the lower reaches of
the hill. He pushed for speed, the turn off
point loomed before Uke and he did not have the
luxury of spending much time on a decision.

"Otto doesn't think I can handle the hill,
but I'll show him," he muttered into the
rushing wind. Pressing his foot down on the gas
pedal, he waited patiently for the truck to
speed up to its capabilities. The speedometer
indicated sixty-five. The face plate said it
could go seventy-five. Otto always said it
wouldn't go that fast when new.

The turn off flew past and he regretted his
decision on the steeply sloping route It was
too late now. There was no way to turn back.
The first part of the hill began with a long,
twisting glide. Too late he realized when Otto
chanced it, he had gone into this part much
slower.

He pushed down on the brake pedal to slow the
truck down, but the pedal pushed back at him
with no effect. He did not understand inertia,
only that he had a problem. Panic welled up.

All he could do was continue to hold the
pedal down. With a sigh of relief, the bottom

of the hill came into view. It was a long way
off. His powerful leg was tiring from the fight
with the brake pedal. He gasped in relief. He
could see no train smoke near the crossing.

His headlong flight continued. There was
nothing he could do other than to keep his two
hundred and thirty pounds pressing down on the
brake pedal. The truck continued to thunder
toward whatever destiny had in store for it.

He felt his cap fly off when he made the
mistake of trying to look back out the side
window for a peek at the copper sheet. At least
it was in place. The cap on the kerosene can
was missing. That could easily be fixed by
stuffing a rag into the spout.

Hope sprang up momentarily as he glanced at
the speedometer, it was slowly unwinding.
Horrors! The truck was speeding up. The gage
had quit working, he had to be doing all of
seventy-five, maybe more. For now the road was
straight, but he heard a rear tire blow out and
the truck began skittering like it was on ice.
Despite this, confidence was building and he
felt pleased that he still had control.

He could smell the brakes beginning to heat
up due to the pressure on the brake shoes. Do
I take my foot from the brake pedal? Another
smell came to his nostrils. Kerosene? No. He
sniffed the air trying to identify the odor. He
pressed harder on the brakes to try to slow the
rig down. Keeping control was becoming more
difficult. The bottom of the hill drew near.

Someone is burning some pretty acrid garbage
way out here. It must be my imagination, he
decided. A glance told him there was no smoke
or fire on either side of the truck. Otto had
often talked about swiping a mirror from Sis
and mounting it on the windshield so he could
see the back of the truck without twisting
around, but he had never gotten around to it.

He heard another tire blow out: the truck was

becoming almost impossible to handle. Only his
sheer strength held it on a straight course.
Fortunately, there were no other vehicles on
the hill, other than a horse and wagon.

Unknown to him, the kerosene had gushed from
the spout like it was trying to imitate Old
Faithful and even now was seeping through the
truck bed. Nor could he know the vile smell was
from the over heating brakes.

The volatile liquid dripping through the
wooden truck bed headed unerring down to the
only brakes the truck had, directly under the
kerosene can. The wind insured more than enough
oxygen for a good marshmallow roast.

At first only a plume of white smoke trailed
out from behind the truck as the fluid searched
for the hot brake drums.

But the temperature of the brakes was too
great for the kerosene to cool them and sub-
mitted to temptation. The smoldering combination suddenly gushed forth in a burst of
flames, tracing its way back to the source like
the fuse on a stick of dynamite.

Unaware of the changing events behind him,
Uke squirmed in his seat. "Gosh," he muttered,
"I didn't realize how hot it is out today. A
cold beer would be nice right now." Now why
would I think of that? While the country was
dry, most of the residents weren't.

The truck lifted off the road as it flew over
the railroad tracks giving him an empty feeling
in the pit of his stomach. The flames parted
the rope holding the kerosene can, tipping it
over. The liquid gushed forth over the truck
bed. The truck became a mass of bright red
flames and oily, black smoke.

Uke twisted around and peeked through the
small oval window at the back of the cab to see
if he still had the sheet of copper after the
truck bounced over the tracks. If it landed on
the tracks a freight train would ruin it for

sure.

The blood drained from his face. He felt
faint as his face turned an ashen white. The
back of the truck was a mass of flames! How
could this be? Panic surged through him.

"I got to get help," he screamed into the
rushing wind. But who? Otto? No, he'll rip me
apart for this. "I had better get Sis, she'll
know what to do." Somehow he felt better for
his decision.

He could see Root City glimmering below him
in the late afternoon sun. The river shimmered
in the distance as it snaked toward Lake Mich-
igan. His thoughts turned to heading for the
lake to quench the fire. The river was closer.

The truck roared through the open countryside
into the view of many of the good burghers.
Word of his impending arrival spread rapidly
through town.

The fire department, playing cards in front
of station number three, was alerted by several
screaming civic minded souls pointing toward
the highway. Putting their cribbage boards
away, they raced to their trucks and hurried
out to meet Uke.

The speedometer needle leaned on the pin
nearing seventy-five as he passed his rescue
escort headed toward him from the opposite
direction. Uke counted two pumpers, two hook
and ladders, and a utility truck and the
chief's car streaming out behind him as they
roared by. The wind bounced off the trucks
fanning the fire.

"My luck," Uke fumed, "I got all these
troubles and they decide to go out for a Sunday
drive like some volunteer fire department."

He breathed a sigh of relief when the truck
careened around Frenchman's curve, the only
banked turn in the county. He was aware of the
city limits as he raced into town.

Helplessly he ignored the stop signs and the

only stop light in town which only recently had
been installed. He ruled out trying for the
lake or the river, Devil's Lane, Sis and home
were closer.

The fire department, except for the chief,
lost ground. They were instructed to get to
fires safely. Instructions came from the chief
who had a habit of not following his own rules.
His Dodge auto was able to do a 360 spin out
and lost little time. The fire trucks had to
stop, back around and turn toward their goal.

The speedometer backed off the stop pin and
began to register before Uke careened onto
Devil's Lane throwing up a cloud of dust like
an explosion. The truck headed for the house
much as a homing pigeon to its roost. The
brakes, he knew, were useless, he'd have to
find another way to stop, and find it fast.
Stomping on each of the three foot pedals
seemed to help some.

"Twenty-five," he muttered to himself, glancing again at the speedometer as the truck lifted up on its two outside wheels and threatened
to roll over as he skidded into the driveway.
With brute effort he leaned against the force
threatening to throw him out of the cab and
willed the truck not to tip over. It acceded to
his demand and settled back on all fours bent
upon other destructive possibilities.

Before he could gain complete control, the
truck managed to take out the peony bushes Sis
had been nursing, brushed the second shed,
continued through her vegetable garden and
headed for Mr. Fred, a Plymouth Rock rooster,
and Fred's eminent domain, the hen house with a
fenced chicken yard.

Chicken fencing wire wrapped itself around
the vehicle and ripped the cab off, slowing it
down considerably. Moments later it slammed
into the hen house. Mr. Fred, greatly agitated
by this invasion of privacy, headed for the

peak of the house protesting vociferously.

Uke managed to untangle himself from the flaming wreck with a burst of energy he didn't know he had and jumped free before the flames could consume what little was left of Otto's pride and joy.

His leap caused him to fall over the half hidden doghouse. In this he was fortunate, landing on his face, he rolled over slapping vigorously at the conflagration beginning to engulf him. His clothes were little more than dust rags by the time he had extinguished the flames.

The fire chief's car skidded to a halt on the remaining peony bushes followed by the first engine, a pumper, announcing itself with a deep throaty roar of confidence.

Sis and Otto appeared simultaneously at the kitchen door to investigate the disturbance.

Rising to his knees, Uke parted the weeds and wondered how come Otto was home. I was supposed to stop and get him. "Damn, now I'll get it for sure."

Flames shot skyward to the height of the poplar tree marking the back corner of their acre. The other fire engines began arriving in droves, firemen jumped free and began unrolling hoses on the run before their trucks had halted. The chief motioned toward the house and sheds indicating that they were to protect them rather than Mr. Fred's prize hens. The horse drawn fire wagon was the last to arrive.

Uke cringed when he saw the angry look on Otto's face and ducked just in time to miss getting hit with a piece of sod Otto had torn from the edge of the garden in his fury.

"You fool, you absolute fool." Otto had had that truck for over three years and it was the most important thing in his life. Poker and his pop corn wagons paled in importance to it. Now it lay collapsed and sighing its last breath in

the remains of the chicken yard amid scorched
hens rushing around with their tail feathers
smoldering. Mr. Fred was still attempting to
reach the safety of the peak of the house.

"We'll get you another truck," Sis snapped
over her shoulder as she hurried to examine Uke
for injuries. "Just leave the poor boy alone."

She tried to pull down the strap on Uke's
overalls for a more detailed examination. He
struggled to stop her.

"We best get those guys to squirt some water
on that shed," Otto whispered recovering from
his shock.

Uke nodded vigorously, trying to contain Sis
at the same time, she was intent on her close
inspection under his scorched overalls.

"Leave the shed be," Sis turned on him dis-
gustedly. "The statue is in the other shed by
the Durant. A few sparks can always be drench-
ed." Next in line behind the statue was the
Durant, Sis loved to be taken for a ride.

"But there is almost a whole case of dynamite
in there," Uke hissed and waved toward the
other shed with his free hand while he gripped
his overall straps to protect himself from
Sis's probing.

They all took an involuntary step backwards,
although each knew full well one step wouldn't
help much.

Otto spoke first, putting his anger aside.
"Let's mosey over and ask them to wet down the
shed as a precaution, casual like, 'cause if
they find out there's dynamite in there,
they'll pinch us fer sure." He shoved Sis
gently forward and nodded to two firemen near
the shed.

Sis shrugged, releasing her firm grip on Uke'
overalls and walked over by the firemen playing
a hose on shed number two. With Sis out of the
way, Otto turned on Uke bent upon venting his
wrath with some choice invectives. Uke braced

for the onslaught. Instead, at the last moment, Otto pushed him out of the way and strode toward the road.

Uke's eyes followed him. Another truck, a model newer than the one smoking in the chicken yard, all shiny and in much better condition than the old one had caught his eye. Love at first sight. Despite the crank hanging out the front below the radiator, this one would have a self-starter on the cab floor.

He watched Otto examine it patting the hood, and then the fender. Otto was in love. Uke knew about all Otto had to do was wait for the owner to appear. By the look on his face, it was a foregone conclusion that Otto would have this truck. Good, he had already forgotten the smoldering ruins in the chicken yard.

"Some fire, huh?"

Otto wheeled to confront the speaker. A big fellow, about the size of Uke, offered his hand and Otto grasped it warmly. Big people, he had always told Uke, were easy marks.

"Jim Arnold's the name, saw the guy wheel up the road an fer a minute I thought it was the devil his self here on Devil's Lane." He laughed loudly at his joke.

Otto shook the hand again for good measure. Whenever he did this, Uke knew he planned an easy time of it with his mark.

"Otto Granley's the name, an it was my truck the fool burned down the chicken coop with."

"Too bad," Jim patted his truck's hood fondly, "I don't see how they can ever make a better truck than this one."

"Mine was just like yours" Otto continued as if he hadn't heard. "I was planning on going down to that new place and get one of those beautiful yellow ones with the red wheels first thing in the morning. They got it all over these Model T's."

"Oh, yah, how do you figure?"

"Color for one thing, more power, a better gear shift and they're bigger. Otto waved his hands enthusiastically to prove his point. He had often cursed the planetary clutch system in his old truck. At times, three pedals on the floor were confusing.

Uke smiled knowingly: he had seen Otto at work many times before.

"Get better gas mileage and are a lot easier to handle," the mark insisted.
Otto wiped the back of his hand over his mouth to remove some drool.

"Really? Maybe I should go down and have a look see," Jim decided, half way convinced.

"Let's go down together," Otto suggested with a friendly slap on the back, "we'll both look at those beauties, say, whyn't we go right now!" He looked back over his shoulder, glad, Uke supposed to be removing himself from the vicinity of the fire and the box of dynamite.

* * *

The fire department and the crowd were long gone when Uke heard a truck and peeked out the kitchen window to see Otto returning about dusk driving Jim Arnold's truck. On the back of his newly acquired love was a roll of chicken wire.

Uke ambled out to inspect it with a peanut butter sandwich in hand. A new fence for the hens would be easier than rounding them up. Although it could be done except for the rooster. Mr. Fred refused to leave the peak of the house and looked like a weather vane up there. Why should he return to his domain? The hens were still rushing around in the sun-flowers avoiding Hofner's three legged cat.

When Sis came out to inspect the nearly com-pleted fence, Uke knew she would hang around insisting on improvements until she was satis-fied. If she didn't, the job would remain just that: temporary. She did not voice her sus-picions on how Otto had obtained this truck.

Uke didn't need to ask, although he suspected Sis wanted him to broach the subject. Best, Uke thought, to let well enough alone. Otto would only lie about how he acquired it.

He was surprised that Otto labored harder than he could ever remember and seemed gracious except when Uke headed for the kitchen to get another sandwich. He could feel Otto's eyes on his back. He fought the urge to look back. Should he or continue on for a sandwich? The peanut butter won.

"I need your help towing the old truck remains down into the weeds behind the sunflowers back of shed number two," Otto advised when he returned.

They used a length of window weight cord and hitched it to the rear axle of the new truck and to the front axle of the old one and dragged it squealing and protesting to its new home. Several uprooted peony bushes helped improve the appearance of the area.

Uke turned toward the house intent upon another peanut butter sandwich.

"Wait a minute," Otto called.

He paused and turned back to where Otto was waiting in the cab of his new truck nestled among the sunflowers.

"You owe me thirty-five bucks, Uke." Otto reached into this pocket and withdrew a pencil stub and a scrap of paper. He wet the tip of the stub. "It's what it cost to replace the truck. You're lucky I found this fella willing to part with about what I'd settle for in a truck."

"Yeh, I guess," Uke agreed and followed the truck through the weeds back to the house and caught up to Otto on the back porch.

He noticed Otto had been careful not to park the truck too close to shed number one. Smoke wafted up from weeds near by. He surveyed the scene of the disaster. Only a few hours before

it had been a total mess. Sis, no doubt had
been busy.

Otto continued to suck on his pencil stub
while scratching on an old envelope. Uke
guessed Otto delayed going into the house to
be confronted by Sis.

She would want to know why Uke and not Otto
had made the trip to Middletown and how Otto
had come by the new truck so easily. Uke knew
he ought to go see Ruth or go to the sheriff's
office. Things would get pretty hot around here
when Otto tried to lie his way out of this
mess.

He stood on the porch trying to decide what
action he ought to take, while Otto continued
to calculate his finances.

"Let's see now, I had fifteen bucks when I
left the house this morning to get the sheet of
copper and I still got it. My poker winnings at
Lil' Joe's for the day about pay for most of
the new truck. Once you pay for the damages to
the old truck, I'll be about ten bucks ahead."
"Maybe Sis would kick in?" he continued.
"After all, I never charge her taxi fare."

Otto's threat to leave her had always been
enough to get Sis to hide her foolish pride and
buy him off. Sis, they both knew, didn't want
anyone in town to know she might be having
domestic problems.

Uke patiently watched Otto until he stuffed
the stub safely in his vest pocket. "What are
we going to tell Sis? She's waiting for an
explanation, you know."

"Tell her?" Otto pause, "Oh, how come you
got into this mess? We'll tell her the truth...
we stopped by one of the popcorn wagons and you
got impatient and took off all by yerself ta
get the sheet of copper."

Uke reflected upon this. Otto did have a lot
of popcorn wagons around the county, but other
than to pick up the dimes in the till, he knew

he never went near them. Nickels and pennies
were left for wages and seed money. About once
a month he made the rounds with more baby white
popcorn and filled his pockets from the till
with loose change, if he didn't forget.

At length Uke agreed for lack of a better
story. "Yah, does sound pretty good." He knew
Sis wouldn't take him to task. She seldom
scolded him. Not even for the damages when a
stray dog bit Uke. He had tried to befriend it.

He retaliated by catching the dog by the
throat. With a crushed windpipe it would never
bite anyone again. Abe tied a half stick of
dynamite to the dog's tail and lit it to put
the poor thing out of its misery. The dog hid
under Maloney's machine shed. Sis never said a
word about it after paying the damages.

"Yeh, we'll tell her the truth," Otto
decided. Now that they had their story agreed
upon, they approached the kitchen porch.

"One good thing came out of all this," Uke
grinned and reached for the door knob. Otto
gave him a quizzical look.

Uke waved a huge hand at the pall of smoke
hanging over the neighborhood behind him. "We
shouldn't ought'a be bothered much by
mosquitoes this summer."

CHAPTER FOUR
THE STATUE

"Cripes," Uke whispered, glancing at Otto, "What is it?" He scratched his head, lifted his huge frame from the fender of Otto's new truck and moved closer for a better look.

This didn't seem to help him fathom the conglomeration of distorted metal before him. He reached inside his over-alls and scratched his favorite spot just below the back pocket. The fire may have, or may not have disturbed Sis's original design of the statue, it was hard to tell.

Sis was nowhere about when they pulled the shed door open to sneak a look at her labors. The last either had seen of her she was hiking down Devil's Lane scuffing up dust on her way to visit Mihich Nostrov.

Otto shuddered and did not attempt to disguise his contempt. "That's the statue Sis has been hammering on and which her and the town are gonn'a have one hell of a battle over when they find out what she's up to."

Uke knew Otto was no fool...he was a lot of other things, but no fool. He could only agree with Otto's assessment.

The copper figure held an outstretched hand to the sky with a garish shaped bird house in it. Sparrows were already fighting for eminent domain. The sputsies didn't mind that it resembled a tipped over two holer.

The statue's other hand held what at best guess could be a Kentucky long rifle. A great felt hat with a wide brim covered the head. The coat had been shaped by fire from the salvaged copper sheet instead of by a hammer before the truck was towed down into the weeds. A large metal hair comb served for an attempt at a moustache. It hid the mouth which had a sneer on it despite Sis's best efforts.

"Sure looks like Andy Gump," he grinned at Otto. Andy was his favorite funny paper character. "But what's that thing he's holding in his hand looks like an outhouse?!"

Otto agreed. "Couldn't look no more like it if'n it had a half moon over the door. Ought'a make the politicians feel right ta home."

Uke tried to reflect on what might happen now that Sis had almost completed her statue of Grand Dad. Now what? His sister had been pounding away for a good long spell all taken up with this thing and not even allowing him to see it. He was aware that anything a Compton wants...this town doesn't want.

It rankled all of them that the family's choice property had been lost in court battles and taxes. They continued to receive tax statements despite the long and winding trial of endless court procedures designed to keep lawyers happy and wealthy.

"Keeps a lot of ambulance chasers from winding up digging ditches fer a living," Otto insisted.

Sis was rightly proud of their genealogy. Grand Dad had been the first citizen and original founder of the city. He had discovered bootlegging was profitable, was an adventurer and had stretched rope over ownership of a horse. Neither Otto or Uke's identical twin,

Abe, were impressed. They ridiculed and sneered
at Grand Dad Compton's deeds, all except the
inheritance money.

In Uke's mind, the old duck was entitled to
a place in the park, and in the archives with a
bottle of whiskey in the statue's hand, instead of a bird cage, would be fitting. He
agreed with Otto on one thing: a lady or a
deck of cards in the other hand would be more
appropriate than a rifle. Only thing Grand Dad
ever hunted was loose women.

Uke desperately wished he could be more like
Otto or Grand Dad. Instead, he shrugged and
gave in to an intense yearning for a peanut
butter sandwich and headed toward the house
while reflecting upon the old coot.

The story was that Grand Dad nearly starved
to death the first winter and was saved by
pigeon soup and a horse. This, Uke had to agree
with Otto was hardly an excuse for an outhouse
in the statue's hand. He had been forced to eat
the horse, but since he had been hung as a
horse thief in later years, Sis wisely decided
not to have any reference to horses in her
memorial.

History never recorded which end of the horse
Grand Dad had eaten first. It made no difference to Uke and Sis didn't want to know.

"She'll get her statue into the town square
despite the mayor, town council, and all the
citizens," Uke assured Otto. "There ain't
enough of them to keep Sis from it." He refrained from adding that with a husband like
Otto, she'll probably have the town standing
out there on Christmas Day in their underwear,
cheering her on."

With the slab of peanut butter bread in hand,
he hurried back anxious to learn what Otto
might have in mind. All he knew was that they
were soon going to move the statue. Whenever he
broached the subject, Otto would grin, shrug

his shoulders and either walk away or change the subject.

"The town ain't within yer authority," Otto assured him. Despite political shenanigans periodically causing discontent, the citizens somehow tolerated the current office holders who permeated the town.

Otto only nodded at Uke's quizzical look and ventured, "You have your own reasons for keeping the status quo?" Studying the statue had whetted Uke's appetite even more. He hurried back to the kitchen for another peanut butter sandwich. He returned with it in one hand the other clutched his holstered .38 revolver. The pistol kept slapping his leg.

Right now he was having a problem taming the .38, since it was smeared with peanut butter. (It was not the first time peanut butter had interfered with the law.)

Uke made a better sheriff than Higgie Jones who was financially well off, but wanted the job since he was tired of washing windows. They both knew smiling at people and cooing at babies was not hard work. Higgie's window peeping gave him an edge over any other candidates as well as the town's string pullers. He left Uke alone, however, not wishing to get tossed into the river.

Sheriffing was easy. There were never any prisoners to feed since Uke could hardly write, other than his name, (a secret Otto had warned him never to divulge). Uke couldn't arrest a speeder. This, however, was no problem. The county, in an effort to get him to resign, had never provided him with transportation. Uke walked or hitch-hiked on all official business unless one of the deputies was handy and willing to provide taxi service.

All he had to do was holler, " Otto, hey, gimme a lift," and then explain what his excursion might be about. He knew full well

Otto would be trying to figure an angle. The ride was more important to him than any doings from Otto.

Depending upon why and where Uke might want to go, Otto would provide taxi service if it was in his interest to do so. He had long since appointed himself Uke's official advisor. It kept him aware of city and county business and he knew more of it than most officials.

While the county was officially dry, liquor flowed freely when and where necessary, women were willing and poker was a favorite pastime. But, of course, there were always do gooders out there trying to upset things, and so far, Otto had out foxed them on the dry part. If a raid was deemed necessary, all parties were forwarned and it came to nothing. Neither Otto or Uke would ever divulge their twenty-five cents source....Higgie.

"Sis wants to see you before you head up town," Uke panted hurrying in response to Otto's call. He did not get too close to Otto while informing him. Otto had a temper when either of them interfered with his planned pleasures. He had forgotten to tell Otto until now and Sis was already headed up town to have Mihich read her palms.

Since Sis controlled the family purse strings, she decided any and all issues, and there were always issues. She kept Otto and Uke under control, much like the government bribing the states with their own tax money.

Old lady Nostrov was buzzing Sis about coming into some money soon, but never told her from whom or from where. Uke guessed it was because the fortune teller didn't know. The only one making any money on the deal was the old lady so far. Phony old Nostrov managed to create issues in order to milk Sis. Why Sis continued to be exploited mystified him.

"Come on along," Otto invited Uke, ignoring the citation from his wife. He considered it was safe to do so since she wasn't home anyway.

Uke knew Otto would say he had never told him, and Uke would say he forgot, and Sis would shrug or throw up her hands and forget about whatever it was she wanted. And besides, Sis was capable and if there was any real problem, she would deliver the message herself. They both knew right now all Sis was concerned with was the finishing touches on the statue, moving it and trying to figure out old lady Nostorv's latest bit of skullduggery.

Uke eyed Otto warily, but fell into step beside him, waiting to be taken into his confidence. He did not worry about Otto not responding to Sis's demand, it was not the first time Otto ignored her. How could he possibly know it was Mrs. Mihich Nostrov's deep dark warning Sis was upset about?

Uke remained silent as they rattled their way up town in the new truck. Otto had something up his sleeve, and even now Otto was casting about for any suspicious characters before confiding in Uke. Otto pulled up in the shade of a huge Oak tree and jerked his head indicating Uke should follow him as he left the truck. Herding Uke toward the town square, he headed for the privacy of one of his string of popcorn wagons spread strategically throughout the town.

"Uke, I'm going to let you in on one of the biggest deals ever."

Uke studied his slippery brother-in-law out of the corner of his eye. Uke always listened to some kind of scheme shortly after he had been paid his monthly stipend for his sheriff duties.

"Yep, gonna let you in on the ground floor on his terrific opportunity, tomorr'a it'll cost you twice't the amount." That's lucky, Uke thought to himself, trying not to show too much interest. When he gets done, I'll ask why the price would change the next day.

"The seventy-five bucks the county pays you is chicken feed and will never handle what I have in mind," Otto continued.

"Yah, I can't get along on the money I make," Uke agreed. Two days from now he would probably be flat broke.

They halted in front of a popcorn wagon, and the attendant nervously watched them, hoping Otto wouldn't notice the corner with the broken frosted glitzy glass where the popped corn piled up. Otto fully expected income from it to soften the blow of a bad night at poker. Right now he was mentally calculating Uke's income and did not notice the broken glass caused by an irate customer. The biggest sign proudly proclaimed butter. In the finest marketing tradition it did not, however, say there was any butter on the popcorn, (that was a penny extra.)

"I'm going to buy another wagon," he whispered conspiratorially to Uke. "Where I put it will dramatically increase the profits." His gaze shifted warily to the people roaming through the park before continuing. "But yer pay and yer divvy will never cover your end of the cost."

Uke had no idea how much a popcorn wagon could cost. He had a strong feeling it was going to cost him something. 'Divvy,' was when Sis announced a dividend from Grand Dad Compton's will. It was the interest the lawyer assured her had accumulated over a month's time. Had any of them known how to figure interest, it would have been simple matter to determine the money involved.

Neither the lawyer nor the banker would tell them the devious arithmetic used to figure interest...it was not the way arithmetic had been taught in school.

Suddenly Otto's face brightened, "I have an idea! Have you ever heard of 'up payments?'"

"Up payments?"

"Yeh," Otto grunted, excitedly, "You pay me a bit at a time and when yer paid up, own what you want." He rubbed his jaw in order to hide behind his hand, which gave him the opportunity to see if Uke took the bait. He wasn't going to give Uke the time to figure out whether he wanted part of a popcorn wagon or not. He had long since learned greed was a selling point.

"Nobody has ever done 'up payments' afore. Gosh, you'd be the first one! Man, you could buy anything you want with my system. All you gotta do is pay up one dollar a week for say 100 weeks and you'll have seventy-five bucks invested and the use of the product." He clapped Uke on the shoulder.

Uke stopped short, "What do I want with a popcorn wagon?"

"You don't," Otto snapped, "I do." He remembered to turn on a smile. "You'll collect half the profits if you keep up the down payments, so it's likely it won't cost you nothing."

"But I thought they was 'up payments'?" Uke questioned.

"Up payments', 'down payments,'" Otto shrugged, it made no difference, just so the money came in. "Right now I'm expected at Lil Joe's. You come along and stand around out front and keep things on the quiet side."

They hurried back to the truck and Otto pulled up in front of the swinging doors of Lil'Joe's Saloon & Emporium and disappeared into the darkened recess, but not before looking up and down the street for police.

A thought came to Uke, he might just know

where Otto planned to place the new popcorn
wagon. The park where Sis planned on planting
her statue was an ideal spot for it...if however, both the wagon and the statue didn't fit:
well, there was room in the grove of trees for
the statue.

He yawned and settled comfortably against the
warm side of the building and studied the sky
and the few people on the street. Wish I could
make money the way Otto does, especially the
part about not having to work for it, he fant-
asized. His reverie was interrupted by Higgie
carrying his bucket and long handled squeegee.
He claimed to hold no malice toward Uke for
aceing him out of the sheriff's job.

"Hey, Uke, staking out the poker game in the
upstairs room, or you keeping a look out for
your shyster brother-in-law?"

Uke paused a moment before answering. In so
far as he knew, shysters were lawyers, not
brother-in-laws. Normally he didn't want Higgie
around because he knew too much, but right now
he was glad to see him. "Hi, Higgie, say, you
ever heard of 'up payments', or maybe 'down
payments?"

Higgie studied him. "Uh, hmm, I'd say Granley
has been working on you. There ain't no such
things."

"Yes, sir, there is so. If I pay him a buck a
week, I can own a chunk of one of his popcorn
wagons. An the best part is, the money I earn
will pay the 'up payments'."

"How big a chunk?" Higgie asked softly, kicking at an imaginary spot with the toe of his
shoe. Higgie loved popcorn and he was concerned
his free treat might dry up if he didn't handle
things right. He had money.

Few people knew he made more money looking
into windows than washing them. He was believed
to have more wealth than any fast talking
lawyer in town. The difference was by keeping

his eyes open, his mouth shut and his palm up,
Higgie had acquired an excellent cash flow.

"Half the profits," Uke certified with a
smile. He couldn't tell what was going on in
Higgie's head. Higgie would broadcast his
version of something all over town in short
order if he thought there was profit by it.

"He makes a lot of money on those wagons,"
Higgie nodded, "an he don't pay those kids
nothing to run them and popcorn don't hardly
cost nothing. I've never known him to put a
wagon into a poker pot, no matter how good a
hand he's holding."

"He's thinking of buying another wagon," Uke
confided. Higgie thought this over. "Wonder if
he'd count me in?"

"Naw, you know he doesn't like you, Higgie,"
Uke paused like he had seen Otto do when bait-
ing the hook, "but maybe I could sell you half
of my share?"

Uke was smiling pleasantly when Otto came out
of the saloon several hours later. He clutched
the five silver dollars in his pocket careful
not to let Otto hear the jangling. Standing in
front of the saloon, waiting for Otto, he had
managed to sell five half shares in the profits
and his half share remained in the venture.

It wouldn't do to tell Otto about it, somehow
he'd find fault with his arithmetic. They
hurried home and he was pleased: standing in
the sun selling 'up' or 'down' payments sure
beat anything. "Get any more good ideas, Otto,
let me know."

Otto was engrossed in deep thought but cast
him a quick glance. After three hours in the
poker game, Uke knew he had broken even, unless
he counted the useless gold mining stock Archie
Dover had foisted on him when he refused to let
him bet light.

He was certain the stock was worthless, it
was so old. The only reason he took it was

because Archie was a dollar light in the pot.
None the less, Archie's luck was running
against him. Otto now had property, all he had
to do was plan how turn a profit on the
worthless stock.

CHAPTER FIVE
McNAMARA'S CROSSING

With her hair in a severe up sweep topped
off with a bun, Sis appeared taller than she
really was. The effect was dangerously close to
the town's perception: Sis looked like she had
had her neck stretched. A throw back perhaps
to Grand Dad? Her small, tight mouth had a
faint hardness about it. When she spread her
feet apart and folded her arms, her glare cut
clear through you.

Uke, trying not to be obvious, watched the by-
play between Otto and Sis. He knew Otto was
judging her mood and temperament.

"Me and Uke's going over ta Middletown fer a
wagon," he offered at length. "Anything we can
bring back for you?" He combed his pencil thin
moustache with a toothpick as he spoke.

Uke wished he could manipulate people the way
Otto could. Otto never gave up trying to test
his wife. What a man demanded of a woman Otto
rarely received. Conversely: what Sis, a woman,
looked for in a man, she never found in Otto.

"No", she snapped. "I want you to give Maloney
back the deed to his farm. You can't keep it
'cuz of a poker game." She assumed her favorite
pose. A lesser man would have cringed. Uke
marveled that Otto didn't fold.

Uke admired his brother-in-law for this if no
other reason. He had no way of knowing that Sis
secretly wondered if Maloney's farm deed was
Mihich Nostorv's idea of Sis's possibly new
found wealth.

"I plan to give it back," Otto gave her his
most innocent grin. "Never intended to keep
it." He shot a sour glance at Uke.

Uke knew how she knew about the stock. He saw
her going through Otto's pockets again last
night. He watched as Otto's hand involuntarily
started to reach for his back pocket. It wasn't
for the deed. It had to be for the gold mine
stock. Apparently Sis thought it was the deed.
How, he wondered, had she missed the stock?

If I ever get married, Uke silently vowed,
I'll copy Otto's methods concerning a wife:
agree to everything, but follow through on only
enough promises to make her believe you. He
knew he could bank upon Otto accusing him of
telling her about the deed. He would have a
time getting Otto to believe he knew nothing
about it.

Sis had questioned him early this morning. He
knew better than to tell Otto that Sis got her
information from Otto's back pocket. Sis didn't
know what Uke knew....Otto usually put really
important things like money and gold stock
under his pillow while he slept, unless he
forgot.

"Another thing," Sis paused. She had seen him
reach and made a mental note to remember to
check his pockets again tonight. "The mayor and
the council refused to give me a permit to move
my statue."

"They didn't give you a permit to install it
either," Otto laughed. "When ya gonna learn not
to try to get permission? Just do it!"

"That park is my....our property," she spat,
glaring around like she half expected some of
the city fathers to come crawling out of the

woodwork. More often than not, Sis was about as exciting as watching the grass grow. Her venom surprised both of them.

"We'll get your statue onto your property, don't worry," Otto assured her.

Uke wondered why the fool park had to be right in the middle of town and just across the street from city hall? One good thing, the city thinks it owns the park. They won't have any idea where she wants to put it, unless, of course, one of them can think. It would be a new experience for a politician, Otto always maintained.

He also knew he was in for a tongue lashing from Otto, who had snatched his hat from the back of the kitchen chair. With a snapping motion of his head toward the back door, he commanded Uke to follow him. They left the house before she could press Otto for details about moving the statue.

He grabbed his hat and followed Otto outside after giving his sister an apologetic look. "Gotta date with Ruth tonight. We best shake a leg if we're going to get back on time." He said it loud enough for both of them to hear. He gave Otto a glance. When Ruth was concerned, he tried to be forceful. He had to be. More than once he saw Otto mentally undressing her.

Otto ignored him as he climbed into the truck. He set the timing and spark advance on the steering column and switched on the key. Uke waited in front of the truck for a nod.

He gripped the crank and gave it a healthy spin. Nothing happened. Unaware that Otto had turned the key off, he continued to crank until he remembered the front tire. He dropped the crank and gave the tire a vicious kick unaware that Otto had turned the ignition back on. The engine caught after several more spins, back-fired a few times and then settled into a comfortable rumble.

"Beats me how a tire will start the engine,"
Uke panted climbing in beside Otto. "Yer a
genius to have figured that out."

"Yeh," Otto smiled, busily backing the truck
out the driveway, "it took a lot of figuring.
Don't never tell nobody, I plan to patent it
and we'll be rich."

He hoped Otto would decide to play poker and
let him have his new truck for the trip. He was
disappointed when Otto raced past 'Lil Joe's
with only a glance at the pulled down shades on
the second floor.

They drove silently until they approached the
railroad crossing at the bottom of McNamara's
hill. The truck slowed and Uke jumped out on
the run nearly toppling over his "sitting
boulder." Otto backed down the road away from
the crossing until he was a speck. Climbing on
top of the huge grey boulder at the edge of the
tracks, Uke's position afforded an excellent
view to watch each way for trains.

Freight trains coming down the long grade
used the hill to make up for any lost time.
Blowing wind and trees sometimes hid the
billowing black smoke gushing from the engine's
stack at the blind crossing. At times the
whistle could not be heard, either.

The flat bed gained speed and grew larger as
he watched. Uke jerked his head from side to
side and waved an arm in a come-on signal. Otto
gave him the thumbs up sign when he flew past.
The truck bounced safely over the tracks.

Uke slid down the rock and mopped his face
with the red bandana hanging out of his back
pocket before beginning his long, warm trek.
The red flag was necessary in order to wave
down Otto should a train appear. As Uke trudged
along, he squinted up the hill. The Model-T
was just about at a critical spot on the road.

Momentum had helped keep the truck moving
until it reached the half way point. The carb-

uretor, had to rely on gasoline provided from
the tank under the front seat and gravity to
feed the engine had drained of gasoline. The
truck slowed to a halt alerted by the struggling engine. The truck turned around and slowly
began to back up the hill. This was the univer-
sal solution to a vexing problem. Gasoline
couldn't run up hill, so far no one had found a
solution to the problem.

The latest models had the fuel tank located
under the hood right in front of the windshield. The extra eighteen inches of height
helped, but didn't entirely correct the problem
on steeper or longer hills. McNamara's was long
and steep.

Unhappily, Uke watched the truck back up
until it reached the crest of the hill. It
disappeared among the grove of shade trees
where it could cool its steaming radiator. He
envisaged Otto eagerly climbing from the cab
and stretching out on the grass to wait for him
with his hat over his face, probably asleep.

He was only now rounding Frenchman's curve,
twenty-five minutes away from a chance to rest.
Otto was snoring when he arrived tired and warm
and his shirt was soaked.

Uke grabbed the old towel reeking of gasoline
from beside the seat and wiped the perspiration
from his face before cleaning radiator steam
from the windshield. He wiped the dust from his
shoes with the towel and then stuffed it back
into its hiding place. Salt and gasoline from
that old rag had made his face itch. He
shrugged and walked over to wake Otto.

He would like to stretch out on the soft,
green, shaded shoots of grass and red clover
with Otto, but this was date night. Ruth and
time were at a premium. He waved a honey bee
away from Otto's ear and placed his foot just
below Otto's hip. The force of his motion
rolled Otto over on his stomach.

Otto awoke spitting grass and dirt as Uke
quickly stepped backward and innocently looked
at him. From past experience he knew Otto was
refreshed and also none the wiser. Otto made
for the driver's seat ignoring the sweat running from Uke's face and his soaked shirt. He
took his place behind the wheel and nodded,
once again allowing Uke several extra cranking
attempts before switching on the key. They were
several miles closer to Middletown before Uke's
breathing returned to normal.

When he felt able to speak, Uke broke the
silence, "Boy, it's a long way up that hill, I
swear it gets longer every time." He pulled the
large, red handkerchief from his back pocket
and mopped his face for the fifth time.

"Wore me out," Otto laughed, "waiting for
you." Otto was peering at mailboxes as he
searched for the popcorn wagon house.

Uke spotted the wagon parked between the
house and the barn and silently pointed at it
and waited for Otto to realize what he was
pointing at.

He made no effort to join Otto while he
completed his bargaining for the popcorn wagon.
He overheard bits of the conversation and knew
Otto didn't give a rip for the lady's pleas for
a better offer. It was her problem that her
husband had died leaving her near to penniless.
He heard Otto explain almost tenderly the care
he promised to give the wagon.

The wagon was a magnificent thing with red
and gold wheels and a scalloped matching top
sure to attract any popcorn lover. Despite the
glass etched in ornate flowers, a wind-up
victrola and a speaker to blare out melodies,
Otto felt he paid a long price for it.

The frosted designs hid enough to allow a
customer to see only the corn and the
proprietor in action. But for that, he would
have refused to buy it. He convinced the lady

over and over that he would take good care of it before she would sell her dear departed husband's livelihood.

Uke knew that it was a finer piece of equipment than any of Otto's wagons.

Otto wired the whipple tree to the truck's rear axle with some bailing wire. Satisfied it was secure, he climbed behind the wheel and waited for Uke to complete the starting ritual. He was impressed: twice in a row Uke had remembered to kick the tire before grabbing the crank handle. The truck cab lurched under Uke's weight as he took his place in the cab.

Once the parade began to move, the wagon weaved from side to side. It was impossible to tow it. Otto stopped the truck and jumped out, his eyes searching on the bed of the truck.

He shook loose a long length of rope from the odds and ends and tied one end of the rope to the front axle of the wagon. Next he fed it through the ring on the whipple tree and fastened it to opposite front axle after measuring the distance to the flat top of the wagon. He tossed the line up on the roof of the wagon.

Uke guessed what was expected of him. He lumbered over and listened impassively to the instructions before climbing up on the roof. He dangled his legs over the front end and picked up the reins.

"O.K.?" Otto shouted over the noise of the engine. "Remember, it steers like a horse and wagon, but with no horse."

"Go slow," Uke entreated.

He appreciated Otto moving out slowly at first, so he could get the feel of how the wagon would handle. In reality, it was no different from driving a stage coach except it had a truck instead of four horses in front of it. He sensed Otto picking up speed. The experiment was proving a success.

Uke felt comfortable with an excellent view

well beyond the front of the truck. When the
wagon swerved slightly Uke managed to keep it
on the correct side of the road with a gentle
tug on the reins. The only danger was leaning
out far enough to see the angle between the
singletree and the ropes. His concern increased as the truck began to hurtle along.

He tugged wildly on the reins and pleaded in
vain with Otto to slow down. The rush of wind
made it impossible to be heard. It came to him
that this was the last thing Otto intended to
do: the wagon had to be steered and he was not
about to sit up there and trust Uke's driving.
And besides, Uke suspected, he had a hot poker
game he intended to sit in on tonight.

The miles wore on and Uke's cries diminished
as experience came to him. He began to feel
comfortable and confident and to enjoy the
challenge. Letting go of the reins with one
hand he managed to wave at a startled farmer
working a field with a two horse team.

He doffed his hat to a farm lady bent over
tending her vegetable garden. He grinned when
she waved back. He would have been concerned if
he had been aware that the left rein was
rapidly fraying on a sharp corner of the foot
board.

The violent swerving diminished as he learned
to hold the wagon in line with the truck. Despite McNamara's Hill and the railroad crossing
to come, Uke found the ride exciting and the
breeze refreshing. He refused to concern himself with the hill. He knew Otto wouldn't stop
anyway. Hopefully Otto would select the long
route and avoid McNamara's.

If Otto decided on the hill, a long plume of
black smoke lifting over the trees would warn
him long before they got into Frenchman's
curve. It'll be too late to stop if I don't see
it in time, he thought. He consoled himself in
knowing his perch was probably high enough to

give warning of a freight train.

The truck veered around the remaining curve
at the crest of McNamara's Hill and swept into
the clearing. Moments later Uke's worst fears
made him feel like he was wetting his pants.
They were in the final approach to the long
down hill run. "Otto, Otto," he shrieked trying
to make himself heard, but the wind pushed the
words back into his mouth. "Otto, I see smoke,
a train is coming!"

Distracted by the fool noises Uke was making,
Otto growled, "You better take care of my four
and a half dollar popcorn wagon an' quit
worrying about this grade." He pushed the
accelerator harder to the floor. "Wait'll we
get past Frenchman's curve, then we'll get some
real down hill."

The wagon began to weave and pitch violently.
Uke tried to control it with one hand and get
Otto's attention with the other. He slapped the
side of the wagon hard enough to break the side
window glass trying to make a warning noise.
For the first time he could see a freight train
already in the crossing.

The wagon swerved erratically behind the
truck. Why doesn't he slow down? Why doesn't he
come up here and handle this? He promptly dismissed the thought. Otto would never place himself at the mercy of Uke's driving ability and
judgement: especially on McNamara's Hill. Especially after what happened to the last truck.

Uke was unaware that Otto was having trouble
slowing the truck down with its added weight.
The swerving suddenly stopped and the truck
began to slow in response to the brakes.

Uke didn't know whether to laugh or cry at
the look on Otto's face when he glanced out the
side window to see Uke and the wagon passing
him. Uke's red handkerchief in his rear pocket
whipped wildly in the breeze like a warning
flag. The popcorn wagon picked up speed as Otto

smoked the brakes struggling to get the truck under control.

The wagon left the truck behind. Uke jabbed at the air and pointed toward the crossing making Otto aware for the first time that a fast freight train was rumbling over the crossing.

They both tried to calculate the timing now that the end of the hill and the end of the train were in sight. It would be close.

Small consolation that they could see the freight's caboose bringing up the end of the train. Uke prayed that he would miss it. Otto would never forgive him if he lost his invest- ment.

The caboose, last in line, and just ahead of a gondola filled with coal cleared the cross- ing. At that moment Uke's frayed left rein broke due to the sawing motion. The wagon veered to the right as if it planned to chase the freight train.

It was closing fast on the caboose, but before it could catch it, the wagon swerved violently onto the roadbed and cut a swath through the weeds. It came to a shattering halt against the large boulder Uke had sat on only hours before. The sudden impact catapulted Uke from his perch into the air as the wagon exploded into bits.

He rose majestically up in a beautiful arc.

The truck came to a grinding halt near the remains of the demolished wagon. It was only a matter of timing as to whether Uke would be ground to hamburger under the gondola's wheels or land on top of the caboose.

Otto forced himself to look. He had to concoct a story for Sis. It would take practice to make the facts sound like the truth. "The last I saw, he landed in a coal gondola in front of the caboose, right on top of a pile of coal...

Not a lot I could do." He practiced shaking his head sadly. Four and a half bucks shot to hell. Well, if Uke ever finds his way home he'll have to pay for it: he wrecked it.

He reached into his back pocket to check on the gold mining certificate. The way things were going, first the old truck, and now the popcorn wagon. He wouldn't be surprised if he mis-laid the worthless but impressive looking gold certificate before he could drop it into a poker pot.

He felt his back pocket. It was empty.

CHAPTER SIX
THE HIDING PLACE

"Fer cripe's sake, it's about time you got back," Otto snapped. Uke could only glare as he straggled up the drive toward the back door. Food and a bath were his only concerns.

He paused leaning heavily against the porch railing. "Least you could'a done was to follow along and give me a lift back. It was forty miles before the freight stopped for water."

"You could'a used some on yerself," Otto laughed. The whites of Uke's eyes, in contrast to the soot blackened skin made him appear like he was fresh out of a minstrel show. He blinked often, struggling to keep his eyes open and to maintain his composure.

"Ya ever flew off the top of a popcorn wagon into a coal car and rid forty miles out of yer way, been chased by railroad dicks with two overcoats on when you didn't have any? You ever had mean dogs snapping at your heels, mad bulls charging you, gone without sleep for two days and two nights eating nothing but mushrooms and fresh cow's milk? A farmer's wife came out with the shotgun and caught me in the watermelon patch. Her aim was bad." It was the longest speech of his life, but he was upset. "Melons weren't ripe, either."

He could see that his anger increased Otto's delight. The soot added color to his red lips and mouth. He stomped off to put the wash tub on the old wood burning kitchen cook stove to heat bath water. He thought better of it. It would be quicker to fix a peanut butter sandwich, grab a bar of soap and go for a dunk in the river.

"I need help with this statue," Otto called after him. "Say, you didn't see a worthless piece of yellow paper laying around, did you?"

Uke paused inside the screen door, and kept it from slamming with his foot. "Gonna move the statue tonight?" He wondered why he was concerned about a useless piece of yellow paper. Otto wouldn't tell him anyway...at least not the truth. He debated about getting cleaned up. This moving job could be interesting. A half dozen peanut butter and jelly sandwiches on some of Sis's fresh, home made bread would revitalize him. He would appreciate it if Sis would fix a chicken.

"It ain't going to sit here inta' driveway fer ever," Otto growled, jerking his head toward the statue. He disappeared into the shed almost falling over a large box. Uke grinned and turned toward the cupboard for the jelly and peanut butter.

Uke supposed he was angry because he hadn't been around to help him drag the statue out of the other shed.

Nor was he certain about Otto's last statement. He had seen a couple of aldermen nosing around last week and whenever anyone from city hall showed up, he figured it's one of two things: there's trouble or he wants votes.

Uke couldn't see how the statue was going to win any votes, especially when the two men were from other wards. One bird, as Otto referred to them, was a downtown alderman who was naturally mean, having to listen to merchants whining all

day long. The other he did not personally know,
but recognized him as one of the city hall
pigeons. One of those "birds" someone always
had to clean up after, Otto claimed.

He decided to let the bath wait, settling for
a quick washing in a soup kettle before ambling
outside with his hands full of sandwiches. He
eased himself down on the large wooden box that
Otto had fallen over. He wasn't certain if it
was the box of dynamite. In the half light he
couldn't read the printing despite the fact it
was in large red letters. His only concern was
that it was strong enough to hold his weight
while his eyes adjusted to the darkening
evening sky.

"I might as well give Otto a hand before he
starts hollering," he decided. Brushing a large
cobweb out of the way near a stack of window
weights, Uke picked one of the four pound
weights up in each hand. He lugged them out of
the shed, examining the foot long cast steel
bars before dropping them in front of the
statue.

Looking up, Otto ordered, "I want at least
six weights under the skid at all times. Ya
pick up ta others and drop 'em in front ta'
kind'a steer it."

Uke nodded. Maybe this won't be much fun
after all?

"Shouldn't be any problem moving it," Otto
continued. "Just so's ya keep two weights in
front of those two by sixes at all times." He
pointed to the two beams stretching the length
of the skid like rails. The front of the beams
had been beveled to allow them to climb up and
over the weights.

Depending on the angle that the window
weights were dropped, the skid could be
steered. Uke felt proud that Otto would trust
him to steer the statue. In fact, he was rather
pleased that Otto would ask his help.

They both heard the quick, short steps on the gravel drive.

Without looking up, Otto said, "Hello, Sis. "I'm about ready ta move out, soon's it gets dark." It was obvious to Uke that Otto wasn't pleased having her along.

"Excellent," she nodded. Uke wondered if she had told him about the special council meeting this afternoon. Probably not.

Uke watched the two in silence. Otto had told Uke the problems and responsibilities were a pleasure now that the statue was ready. He guessed it was because Sis was easy to get along with lately. She admitted to Uke that she admired Otto's planning. It was her first compliment about Otto that he could ever remember.

He guessed that they had a pretty good fight about whether Otto should go and find him. He also knew what Otto's response probably was when Sis demanded that he do so. It didn't really matter now that he was back home.

"He'll show up when he gets hungry enough," Otto had tried to assure.

Uke marvelled at the change in his sister. The completed statue had to be the reason she was so friendly.

"I'll need your help and Uke's." Otto said still without looking at her. One of you on each side. Fetch the weights rolling out the back and then toss them in front." He noticed Otto refused to call it a statue.

Sis straightened up, hands on hips, a warning signal not to cross her. "Uke has a date tonight with Ruth and I'm not going to run up and down the street with ten pound weights." She pressed the wrinkles in her apron...as if the thought had messed it. "Get Higgie to work one side and Ruth can ride along while Uke handles the other side."

"Not Higgie," Otto objected. His face brightened at the mention of Ruth.

Uke knew that Otto thought Ruth was a great idea. Higgie, Otto always knew was a nosey little bastard, useless other than to keep windows clean or to be pumped for information. He was so stupid he drew to inside straights. Worse, he often filled the hand.

"Higgie," she insisted, " we'll give them all a bag of popcorn when we're done." She walked away, the subject was closed. Uke watched her eyeing the new chicken yard and knew she would get out her .22 rifle and pop the heads off a couple of chickens to fix for supper. "Uke," she wheeled around and confronted him, "Head for the river and don't forget soap."

He waited, but just as quickly she glanced back at Otto over her shoulder. She took Otto to the wall often. Uke knew it was due to a gambling debt years ago and she had no intention of letting Otto forget it. Despite the fact that she had kept Otto from getting his knee caps smashed over a fifty dollar debt he couldn't pay off, Otto didn't appreciated her.

* * *

After settling for another cold water sponge bath in the rain barrel, he hoped that they would have rain to replenish the meager supply after he finished slopping around. Sis relied upon the barrel for soft water to do the laundry. He hurried into the house careful not to slam the screen door.

Uke tore into a half a chicken, sucking it out of his teeth with a hissing noise. He wiped the greasy remains on his overalls. He could hear Otto backing the truck up to the statue.

The sun had given up on another day and twilight decorated the sky like the pink inside of a clam shell.

Otto had steadfastly refused to ask Higgie for help. "Ta' whole damn town'll know about it a'fore we get to Main Street," Otto demanded. He gave Ruth an appreciative glance as she materialized out of the gathering dusk.

Uke helped secure the rope firmly to each front corner of the skid. The disaster with the popcorn wagon was fresh in both their minds. He waited for Otto to complete a tour around the statue giving it a final inspection.

Ready?" Otto shot him a glance and headed for the passenger side of the truck.

He watched Otto open the truck door and offer his hand to Ruth. She hitched up her full length skirt and hiked it up almost to her knees in order to reach the running board with her foot.

Otto often said she was a gossamer web, fragile, beautiful, exciting and inviting. Uke understood it to be a compliment.

He agreed in part, she was a hard working girl that could be appreciated for that trait alone, but he was not at all certain he knew what else Otto was talking about. Webs were a product of spiders, maybe gossamer webs were different? She was tough as nails from all her housework and taking care of her old dad.

Uke knew her shining, innocent, brown eyes with a mischievous twinkle lit a spark in Otto. She paused longer than necessary climbing into the cab, he thought. Some thigh was visible.

"This is exciting," she exclaimed to no one in particular. She turned backward, kneeling on the seat in order to watch the proceedings through the tiny oval shaped rear window.

Sis discovered Ruth and hesitated before crowding in on the seat. She reached in and carefully pulled the girl's dress down to cover as much of her bare legs as possible, but not as much as she would have liked, before squeezing in beside Ruth.

Uke knew Otto was well aware of the bare legs so close, so inviting, but for him, yet far away. Sis had threatened him once with her .22 short rifle which she kept hidden in the rafters of their bedroom.

The engine roared and then shrieked and groaned struggling to overcome inertia after the slack came out of the tow lines. The statue moved forward with a quick jerk and nearly toppled while Otto was concentrating on the young legs beside him. He came back to reality when Uke shouted a warning.

"I thought you weren't going along?" Otto leaned over the steering wheel and shouted above the roar of the engine, discovering Sis for the first time. Ruth wiggled closer to Otto to make room. "We can watch things all right," he growled.

Uke thought he saw a surge of passion well up in Otto as Ruth snuggled closer. He smiled grimly as Sis satisfied her authority over seat space with a sharp glance at her husband.

"You watch the road, Ruth can watch the statue and Uke and I'll watch you." Sis advised her husband.

Uke picked up the first set of window weights and considered throwing them at the truck. Ruth was laughing with delight at the conversation between Sis and Otto. When they both fixed their eyes on her, she clapped her hands and pointed excitedly at Uke.

The distraction served it purpose: neither would remember what they were squabbling about with the statue grudgingly on its way.

Uke wondered why Ruth was determined to land him. Was he her hope of foiling spinsterhood? No, that couldn't be it. They had been dating since the eighth grade. Despite her beauty, she had no idea how to attract a man. She had hinted at marriage almost every night at the Bijou. They always went to see romantic movies on Wednesday night. He went alone on Friday nights to see the cowboy and adventure movies.

She suggested several times that he was as slippery as "Rock River Herman", Otto's old

catfish nemesis. Uke almost wished Otto would
think about Herman. He'd forget everything, get
his tackle box and poles and head for the Rock
River. The weights were getting heavy.

He found it impossible to keep up unless he
tossed the cylinders over the hitch to the far
side. This saved time. He soon learned to drop
the first one near his foot leaving him free to
aim the far weight. Once he almost dropped the
near weight on his foot and another time nearly
had his foot run over. Luckily, Ruth had shouted at him. This was like pitching horseshoes
while running. The sponge bath was a poor substitute for a dip in the river. The coal dust
and accumulation of dirt was rubbing his skin
raw and slipping and falling in the pile of cow
duty in the dark while trying to escape a bull,
was none too savory, either. The statue had not
as yet cleared the end of the drive.

He took heart when the statue gained the
road. Devil's Lane was dustier, but firmer. By
dropping a weight at the desired angle of
travel under each skid he managed to get it to
follow the truck past the sharp turn of the
drive onto the road. This initial test gave him
pride and confidence.

The first few blocks were slow until Otto
managed to get up enough speed to slip the
truck into second gear, but by now the radiator
began to boil. The windshield was wet from live
steam billowing out from under the brass screw-
on pouring cap. Otto was finding it difficult
to see and began cranking the hand operated
windshield wiper high up in front of him.

Uke wasn't too busy not to notice Otto pre-
tending to be tired from working the wiper.
Otto kept glancing at Ruth and taking time out
to wipe his sweating forehead. She would have
to lean over him to operate the crank. Instead,
Sis reached across Ruth and began cranking it.
Uke smiled, until now he had considered tossing

a weight over the cab onto the hood.

Since second grade, Uke had kept Ruth on a pedestal. He knew Otto had no such reservations about her fresh innocence. He couldn't fault Otto because Sis was granite hard. Otto would attempt to gain Ruth's favor if he had the least opportunity, but with Sis present, the most Otto could gain was small compared to what he had in mind for the little vixen.

At the foot of Hillcrest, Otto called a halt to allow the laboring engine to cool down. "Take a rest," he called to Uke, "you've been working hard. Take the bucket and go find water."

"I'm going with him," Ruth crawled past Sis. "This is better than going to the movie house," she called, disappearing into the dark.

"Tell Uke to be quick about it," Otto called to her as she danced off. Sis moved over to filling the spot that Ruth had vacated.

"Tell Uke to keep his eyes open for a place to hide Grandad while yer at it," Otto called, "We won't make it to the park afore sunrise."

Ruth bobbed her head in reply to Otto's instruction. Uke laughed, it was too dark for Otto to see her nod. The two disappeared into the night holding hands while Uke swung the water pail happily. It banged against the holster with each step.

Had they kept moving they could make it to the park, Uke knew. The park wasn't that far away. He guessed Otto didn't want to arrive at the park with Sis along. She wanted the statue in the opening among the trees. He was pretty sure Otto planned to move the popcorn wagon located at Ninth and Dunmore into the park where there was much more foot traffic nearby. Since there wasn't room for both, the statue would be placed on the edge of the park in plain sight of city hall.

He wished again for a quick dip in the river

to work out some of his weariness. But for the
chickens Sis had shot from the back porch with
her .22 short, he would have liked to quit. He
was warm and uncomfortable from the heat of the
night and the labor. He wondered if Ruth would
like to chuck this adventure and join him for a
midnight dip? It would serve Otto right to
leave him in the middle of Hillcrest street.
But no, he couldn't do that to Sis and he
wasn't sure if Ruth would agree. He had never
asked her anything like that before, in fact,
he had never given it a thought before.

Sis would never forgive him if he abandoned
the statue. He would have to sleep out in the
shed for the next several weeks in the tiny
back seat of the Durant. She would also keep
him too busy to see Ruth. Sis neither liked nor
disliked Ruth, but tolerated her. He asked Otto
why once, but didn't understand his response
about "bitchy" and dropped the subject.

The ache in his body eased as Uke felt no
need to hurry. He strolled along in silence
wondering about where they could find a place
to hide the statue. There were few places a
seventeen foot high statue could stand in the
middle of town without someone noticing it.

"Hey, Ruth," he nodded toward the Catholic
church on the other side of the street just
down the block. "It has a water spigot real
handy, I used to swipe a drink there when I was
little. Let's rest up there for a minute.

As he began to fill the can he wondered why
she didn't answer. He hadn't noticed until now
that she had been running to keep up with him.
He hadn't been hurrying.

Five feet tall, Ruth had a quality that excited men. All that mattered to him was that
she was his girl. He never questioned Why. Why
should he? While he couldn't prevent others
ogling her: he could discourage them with a
glance. His sheer size kept coveted looks to a

minimum. He veered toward the spigot.

He could tell by the sound of the water that the can was full. He straightened up, and turned the faucet off before seeing Father Aloysius in his black bathrobe, almost on top of him in the darkness. The good priest was fingering his rosary, muttering his prayers, fighting his insomnia, and deep in thought with a half finished glowing cigar clenched between his teeth.

"Evening, Father," Uke spoke softly hoping not to startle the man. "Saying your beads?"

"And getting some air," the chunky, balding priest replied. "Mr.Compton, I believe?" He showed no surprise at having company at two-thirty in the morning. Nor did he consider why the sheriff and this girl were in his garden at this hour drawing water. This would never propagate the faith. He remembered seeing her from time to time, but never in his church.

"How are you and what brings you out on so dark a night?" He felt safe asking the question since all they were doing was filling a bucket with church water.

"Yes, sir," Uke replied, mustering up respect for the man of the cloth. "I do have a problem, otherwise things are fine."

"A few minutes on your knees with the Lord and perhaps He may help you resolve your problem," the good priest suggested. He refrained from prying into exactly what Uke's problem might be. He wasn't sure he wanted to know.

"I don't quite see how the Lord could help me out," Uke spun the bucket of water absently and watched the reflective glow of moonbeams on the surface. The fire from the priest's cigar added to the colors in the bucket.

"He works in wondrous and mysterious ways, you need to take the time to talk to him," the well meaning priest assured Uke. "The door to the church is always open." He briefly regretted his suggestion, then dismissed it.

"Thanks, we have a few minutes," Uke laughed.
He decided it won't hurt any, and besides Otto
said to get some rest, didn't he? He groped for
Ruth's hand as they walked carefully through
the tall hedges and stations of the cross in
the garden.

"Remember, son," Father Aloysius called after
them, "He works in mysterious ways. He may not
resolve your problem in the way you ask, but He
will solve it." He watched the pair stroll hand
in hand toward the church door. The glint of
the moon reflected upon the water slopping out
of the pail.

Father Aloysius had never known any of the
Compton crowd to go to church. He did remember
the little mouse with Uke. He suspected she
only went to church on special occasions.

Perhaps she or Uke had heard the clarion call
of the Lord?

On the other hand, he wasn't certain he
appreciated two young lovers alone in his
church in the dead of night. He shrugged and
continued on his way through the stations of
the cross. While he didn't really know Uke, he
had voted for him for sheriff. He had the feeling he was a whole lot more honest than many of
his parishioners who might cherish the job.

Uke paused before entering the church and
placed the bucket on the top step. He hoped
nobody would come along and swipe it while he
rested. "Would you stay out here and watch the
pail while I rest?" he asked of Ruth.

Disappointed when he didn't ask her inside,
she nodded and watched him disappear.

Uke felt better as he strolled slowly toward
the altar. In the tranquility and darkness of
the church an idea came to him. He rushed out
the side door in his eagerness to convey it to
Sis and Otto. Ruth caught sight of him in the
moonlight and hurried to catch up lugging the

heavy pail.

The radiator cap was cool enough for him to unscrew. He remembered Ruth and reached out for the pail. She surprised him by jerking it away angrily and standing on her tip toes, poured the water into the spout. He ignored the tongue lashing from Otto for being so late in returning. Once Ruth finished pouring the last drop of water, and Otto had finished complaining, Uke suggested his plan with some hesitation.

Both Sis and Ruth in a moment of pride, applauded his idea. Otto shrugged and climbed back into the truck, anxious to get on with the chore. "Gotta think that over," he growled.

"Ready?" he called back to Uke.

"Yep!" His weights in readiness. Uke noticed happily that Ruth found no room on the seat and had to be satisfied with dangling her legs off the rear platform of the truck. Removed from Otto, she now had a better view and could watch the statue so it wouldn't topple over.

* * *

It was almost dawn when Uke returned to the sanctuary of his bedroom and pulled off his cowboy boots. He smiled. It was one of the rare times Otto had admitted he had had a good idea. He wondered what Father Aloysius' would do when he discovered Grand Pa Compton standing in the garden among the stations of the cross. I have to agree with the good padre, Uke admitted, the Almighty works in mysterious ways. He was asleep before he could finish chortling.

Late the next morning he awoke to Sis's banging on the ceiling with the end of the broom handle. He agreed to see if the statue was all right. She expressed having second thoughts when they had left her work of art. He agreed since he had nothing special to do today.

Ruth was angry with him anyway. He didn't know if it was over the bucket of water she had to carry or because he hadn't walked her home

last night. He was just too tired. He felt
refreshed now after four eggs, bacon, fries and
three slices of toast.

Otto and Father were in a heated conversation
when he arrived at the church. The good man did
not approve the addition of Grand Dad standing
among his collection of religious statues. Uke
had to admit in the light of day it did look
out of place among the stations of the cross,
but was well hidden from the street. That was
what was important.

Apparently Otto had arrived moments before
and without preamble, the priest turned demanding, "Mr. Compton, was this your problem last
night, by any chance?" Before Uke could reply,
Otto laughed slapping his leg, "Uke did manage
to find a suitable hiding place."

He was too shrewd to lay the blame at my
feet, at least for the moment, Uke judged. If
things got too hot he could be expected to take
all the blame. It wouldn't be the first time.

"You will remove it immediately. I can't have
it here," the priest growled in his best
authoritarian voice. An involuntary shudder
passed through the man as he gazed at the
monstrosity. Uke noticed it caused the pastor's
double chin to tremble.

"I can't move it until after dark," Otto
advised him.

"Did you steal it?" The good man hurriedly
revised the foolish question. Is someone paying
you to get rid of it?"

"Kind of, it's a long story," Otto began,
seating himself on the back step of the church,
out of sight of the statue. Uke knew Otto was
prepared to talk until dark, if need be. He'd
be confident he could stall until Father
relented and allowed the statue to stay.

The two finally acknowledged Uke who was
fishing his red bandana from his back pocket,
"It's going to be hotter than hell today," Uke

observed.

Otto cringed, maybe Uke wouldn't be much help after all.

"Sheriff," the priest ignored Uke's profanity and besides he had to agree: it was hot, "is it within your power to force this man to remove this monstrosity from my garden?."

Before Uke could answer, Otto jumped up and cut in, "Yes, he could make me do it, but he'd be sorry and so would you."

The priest was looking at Uke for a reply, but now sensing he was being threatened, wheeled toward Otto. His face turned red as he strode toward this person.

"Sheriff, make him move his statue right now." There was no doubt in his mind Otto, and not Uke, was behind the devilish plot to disgrace the stations of the cross. He had worked hard to get the congregation to shell out the money and one did not threaten him, a pastor, a priest, a man of the cloth and a servant of the Pope and the Lord. By God, they didn't.

"If he makes me move it, Padre," Otto half whispered his threat, "I'll see to it he pinches half your parish for selling lottery tickets all over town...and raids your fund raising card party next week. The rest of the parish will be in the pokey for playing bingo...that's gambling, you know."

The priest hesitated, shaken by the viciousness of the threat. Judging from comments by some of his parishioners, Mr.Otto Granley was no bluffer and he had heard legends of the tricks Otto could perform with a deck of cards. What if the man showed up at the card party? Horrors! The priest knew when to fold and let the pot go. The parish fund raising drive was close to his heart and nothing must be done to disturb this source of revenue.

Besides, not all of the stations were paid for. "Very well," he relented, "but get it out of here tonight."

Otto raised the ante. "Can't tonight," he declared, Grandpa peeked out from behind the third station. "I'm going duck hunting in the morning and I have to get up early."

"Duck hunting?" The priest wheeled around to see how well the statue was hidden before continuing. "Wherever do you hunt ducks around here?" He had never met a poacher before.

Cripes, Uke thought, doesn't this guy know ducks are out of season?

CHAPTER SEVEN
THE DECOYS

"Duck hunting?" The priest wheeled around to see how well the statue was hidden before continuing. "Why, I have never been duck hunting! Where do you hunt ducks around here?" He had never met a real live poacher before, although he suspected more than one in his parish.

"Ya know the big slew north of town just below the big bend in the river? Lousy with ducks 'bout daybreak," Otto asserted.

"Can I go along?" Uke knew without asking what Otto's answer would be.

"No," Otto snapped, "I bet you ain't been near the sheriff's office in two weeks."

"Darn it, have so!"

Otto turned to the priest, "Glad ta have ya join me. Boat sits two nicely. We kin be back a'fore noon."

Uke suppressed a smile despite the rebuff. Duck hunting companions out of season were no more welcome than holding a full house and getting beat by four of a kind.

Father Aloysius apparently having forgotten their dispute, clapped his hands together excitedly as the two turned to leave. "Where will I meet you, and what time? I do have a seven o'clock mass in the morning."

* * *

Uke dressed silently in the dark and crept
down the far edges of the staircase to keep the
steps from creaking. It wouldn't do to wake Sis
and Otto. He could hear Otto snoring on the
front room couch where he often slept to avoid
having to listen to Sis expound on the virtues
of honesty in marriage, or gambling, but most
importantly: to keep her from going through his
pockets.

He loped toward the river and the willows
where the duck boat was hidden. Shortly after
that he heard Otto's truck rumble to a halt. He
could not make out the priest and Otto's
conversation.

Peeking through the shrubbery, he could see
the priest making no effort to help Otto pull
the boat from the willows. Uke wondered when
and where the priest had ever used the hi-cuts
laced almost to his knees. He also had on a
hunting jacket with over-sized pockets. A
double barreled shotgun was cradled in his arms
like an old hand. This alone gave Uke cause to
wonder.

Otto used an oar to steady the boat while the
priest carefully entered the tiny craft. Otto
squatted on the deck and nodded to the
priest."You take her up to the pond, an' I'll,
ah, bring her back down."

Father Aloysius hesitated since the boat was
pointed on both ends making it difficult to
decide if it would make any difference which
way it would travel. He guessed correctly. Otto
nodded encouragement from his vantage point on
the deck. There was no room for him in the
cockpit and he looked just as happy sitting on
the deck with his feet in the bilge.

The warden would be playing golf, not out
stalking hunters, Otto had assured Uke when he
questioned him last night.

Uke eased himself out of his hiding place and

cautiously worked his way up stream. Since he couldn't use the worn path near the river bank he had to pick his way slowly in the false dawn. He could hear the priest grunt with every stroke.

Otto was humming, "Row, row, row yer boat."

Uke felt concern for the priest struggling to make headway against the slow moving current. The man could give out long before they reached their destination. Perhaps that is what Otto has in mind? Fortunately the wide beam of the shallow water boat kept the craft from capsizing as the priest lunged from side to side pulling on the paddle.

He knew about and used a short cut through a meadow, not wanting to have to account to Otto if he was discovered. His concern for the priest grew as he peeked out from behind tall cottonwoods at every opportunity. The man's face was bright red and he was wheezing.

Otto's words of wisdom rang in his ears. A boat, water, and two shotguns were a combination only the devil could love. Uke did not have to have it explained to him. He, Uke, as a hunting companion was the problem, not the boat, water or guns. The insult had hurt.

He arrived at the mouth of the drainage and chose a position where he could see the duck boat leave the river. The pond, to the left of him, was by nature, shallow and an ideal place to test decoys. He could see wooden mallards rocking gently as they drifted about bumping into Lilly pads and changing direction with whatever breeze appeared.

Old Ed Crowley did a lot of bragging about his ducks. A perfectionist, he claimed his decoys were as perfect an imitation as could be made. Ducks were pretty high on the "smart" list, much smarter than dogs, but not as smart as pigs which he raised to support his overbearing wife of 47 years. In his mind he and

his decoys, not the pigs, kept them in vict-
uals. His birds were near perfect and were a
good excuse to stay a way from his wife.

Uke could distinctly hear the good priest
reciting "Hail Marys" as the boat slowly moved
into the channel. He dropped the paddle and
crossed himself in thankfulness that the end of
the voyage was near as the duck boat coasted
toward Uke.

He could see Otto put one finger to his lips
to demand silence, cupping the other hand to
his ear. The duck boat continued to glide
smoothly up the narrow passageway. Uke could
see by the look on his face that Otto was beginning to admire the priest. Otto winked and
smiled wickedly at his henchman.

"What is it?" Father demanded loudly in an
excited voice. "Do you hear any ducks?"

From his perfect spot behind a huge Willow
tree hardly ten feet from the two culprits Uke
suppressed a snicker. He realized that he could
arrest them both right now, but Otto would make
the rest of his life a living hell.

"Shush," Otto whispered, attempting to hide a
look of disgust at this amateur hunter for
making so much noise.

From his vantage spot, Uke could also see old
man Crowley moving around in his duck blind at
the far end of the small pond. At times he
could hear him grunting and wheezing as he
shifted his weight in the confinement. The
blind was well selected. Tall grass and reeds
surrounded it right at the water's edge. Old Ed
had woven a small window into the front of it.

Otto's plan became clear. Otto never allowed
anyone to best him. He was about to make the
priest pay dearly for threatening him at the
Stations of the Cross.

Otto had a score to settle with Ed, also.
Nearly everyone in town knew old Ed would be
out at his blind almost every morning except

Sunday, field testing his decoys. Last fall Otto wanted Crowley to sell him a couple of decoys on credit. Old Ed refused. Said his credit wasn't any good, in fact, he insisted, Otto didn't have any credit with anyone.

It was getting even time.

Otto motioned for the priest to raise himself out of the cockpit and sit on the deck opposite him. It would be more comfortable and would allow both of them to place their legs in the cockpit well. Once they were settled down, Otto handed the priest his shotgun.

Otto placed his gun into the well and took the paddle. Uke glanced at the dozen decoys floating around on the pond.

Many a Mallard had lost its head trying to woo one of Ed Crowley's wooden ladies. As he watched, two ducks circled overhead and then glided down to join Crowley's crowd.

Uke turned as he heard Otto whispering instructions to his cohort.

"Just around the bend you're going to see a whole flock of ducks like decoys in a shooting gallery. When I move in fast, you have the shotgun aimed and ready to fire. Give them both barrels," he ordered trying to restrain the excitement in his voice. "We'll have a feast for dinner!"

Otto eased the boat to the entrance of the pond, set the paddle into the mud bank for leverage and half rose from the deck to insure a mighty thrust that would propel the boat into the open water.

Uke strained to help Otto force the boat toward the opening. "Ready?" Otto whispered.

The priest nodded, excitement rising in his face. Otto leaned against the blade and the tiny boat shot through the opening.

He heard Otto hiss, "Now!"

Uke covered his ears just in time. Both barrels of the shotgun blasted almost in unison. Birdshot whistled over head. Why, the priest hadn't even come close to the decoys!

"Oh, boy, oh boy, oh my!" Father Aloysius exclaimed.

Uke was amazed at his agility. The priest leaped up and scrambled over the boat deck nearly submerging the craft. As he passed Otto, he shoved the shotgun into his hands and made shore in one bound.

Otto fell backwards roaring with glee. The seat of his pants dipped into the water along with the rocking boat deck. He lifted the shotgun high to keep it from getting wet.

Otto wiped his eyes as old Ed charged out of his blind. Not far behind him was another man. Uke recognized Jim Hoskins, the game warden. Jim strode purposely toward Otto. Uke was surprised, he had no idea Jim had been hiding behind the blind.

"Caught you red handed," Hoskins growled. We'll end your poaching for a time."

Otto abruptly ceased laughing and slid down into the wet cockpit.

Uke thought old Ed might have a stroke he was laughing so hard. Then a thought came to him. Old Ed was a member of Father Aloysius' church. Maybe the warden was too.

Otto pointed a finger at the priest. "He done the shooting, not me!"

"Seems like to me you're the one holding the gun," the warden snapped, sniffing the barrel. "Let me see your license."

Dumb request, Uke thought, if anyone in the county didn't have a license, it would be Otto. From past experience the warden also knew it. He had seen enough. Silently Uke moved away. It was best none of them were aware that he was observing them.

"He doesn't have a license, neither," He heard Otto shout angrily, pointing at the priest.

Uke paused, seeing the priest turn to the warden, "Do I need a hunting license to row a boat?" He held up his hands as evidence. The delicate white palms were swollen and red. Blisters had appeared on his palms and thumbs.

Warden Jim, struggling to keep from laughing, placed his hands on his hips and turned to the Father "If I asked you if you shot at the ducks, you wouldn't lie." He paused for effect before turning to Otto, "but you would."

* * *

Uke trailed the boat at a safe distance, guessing what was going through Otto's mind. He had been had! No, it wasn't possible. No one ever got the better of Otto. His biggest concern, if he was correct, was that Otto was worried about Higgie finding out. The lousy window peeper and washer was scheduled to wash courthouse windows today, Sis had mentioned last week. She kept track of Higgie for her own good reasons. Not only for information, but as her chauffeur when Otto couldn't be found.

The duck boat rocked gently in the brown water as it drifted down stream. The sun peeked over the stately cottonwood trees while Otto sat studying the fabrication of charges. No license, hunting out of season, profanity to an officer in the line of duty, poaching, trespassing, and intent to do harm to another's property. He wadded the sheet up, intent upon tossing it overboard. He thought better of it and stuffed into his shirt pocket.

Uke wondered about the conversation between the priest and the warden just before they left the pond. He distinctly heard the warden offer the priest a ride back to his parish house.

Warden Jim guided his Hupmobile out of the secluded spot reserved for young lovers and ground gears as the car struggled to get back up the hill to the road.

Father Aloysuis chuckled, "Imagine him trying
to pull a kid trick like that when my own
brother-in-law is the game warden? I doubt if
he will ever threaten the Lord's helpers
again!"

"Think he'll get that statue out of your
garden today?" The warden asked.

"I'll do you one better," the good padre
grunted struggling to unlace the borrowed knee
high warden's boots that were beginning to
pinch his toes. "I'm going to keep him from
moving it for a while.... and thanks for the
loan of the hi-cuts and jacket." He wiggled his
toes in relief.

CHAPTER EIGHT
ROCK RIVER HERMAN

The duck hunting incident was forgotten. Uke hurried into the house, waving an envelope in front of his sister's face before planting himself in front of Otto. "I got a job to do. Just think, after two years I got an official job to do!" He was unaware the papers had been waiting in his office for over a week.

Sis looked up from the wash tub she was filling with popcorn in the middle of the bare wooden kitchen floor. Popcorn, heated over a wood fire in the cook stove with a lid removed, sufficed for meals on Sunday afternoons. They served as a supply depot for unexpected guests. Otto did not disapprove of the free loaders: he hauled the leftovers down to one of his popcorn wagons turning a one hundred percent profit.

Uke often wondered why he was so nice to Higgie when he showed for a free feed. Nor did he realize how much gossip Higgie fed Otto for future use. Unknown to Uke, Otto could barely tolerate the useful Higgie.

"You got a job to do, go do it," Otto growled, flicking ash from his Sunday cigar on the worn wooden floor. He licked his thumb and deftly turned the page of the funny papers.

Uke knew he'd have a time getting Otto to pay

attention. Barney Google, Bringing Up Father, and the Katzenjammer Kids, Hansi and Fritzy were important. Whenever Otto caught him reading Orphan Annie he made fun of him. Annie reminded him of Ruth. Uke did prefer Andy Gump.

At the moment, Uke cared less whether he appreciated being interrupted while reading the Sunday funnies. Otto was still mulling over how to beat the duck hunting charges leveled against him.

Often enough he had told Uke justice had nothing to do with justice after the shysters got done with it. Nor was it a matter of right and wrong, but who did it. Money was the root of justice, the more you had, the more justice you could expect, and besides, he concluded: the only winners were the shysters.

"It ought to scare hell out of anyone knowing that guy up there on the bench with the black dress on used to be a shyster," Otto insisted.

* * *

Otto, Uke was certain, couldn't tolerate the feeling that the priest had bested him. Moreover, they had not heard a word about the statue. They both checked on it again late last night and it was sitting at the third station of the cross like it belonged there. Why wasn't Father Aloysius raising holy hob?

"Must be at least a hundred parishioners this afternoon down at the church," Uke advised him.

"I wonder why the ole geek's parishioners ain't raising hell?" Otto wondered. They had lavished a goodly sum on that garden.

"Ain't no vegetables in it, either." Uke offered.

The statue troubled Otto far more than it did him. He now had Otto angry because he had interrupted him with the funny papers.

No use delaying this unpleasant duty. Uke moved closer and drew his .38 revolver from the holster and leveled it at Otto. "I'm taking you his official tone of voice.

Otto put the funnies down carefully and
looked Uke coldly in the eye. "Put the gun
away, you damn fool."

Uke stepped back and lowered the pistol.
"Aw, it ain't loaded," he explained. He handed
him the envelope with his gun hand before jamm-
ing the pistol back into the holster. The safety caught the heavy leather tooling on the side
of the harness. Uke, as was his customary practice, had his finger on the trigger. The pistol
discharged....

The roar startled Otto who had begun pulling
the papers from the envelope. The funnies flew
off his lap and the legal documents shot into
the air. Sis, who was in the act of swinging
about to dump a just completed hopper into the
wash tub sprayed the kitchen with a hail of hot
popcorn.

The deadly missile pierced the tub making it
skid over the floor scattering the contents.
The kitchen filled with the acrid odor of gun
powder and smoke. Sis waved a hand in front of
her face to clear the air. A glance told Uke
she was all right. He was afraid to look at
Otto.

"Otto are you all right?" Sis demanded,
flailing her apron in order to see clearly.
Could Mihich's foreboding prediction have been
meant for her instead of her husband?

Uke froze. Fright at the mayhem he caused was
the least of his problems. Otto would destroy
him for this.

The last time he had accidentally fired the
pistol, he had shot himself in the toe and was
laid up during the entire fishing season. Something warm trickling down his leg. He forced
himself to look. A dark stain had slowly spread
to his knee. I shot myself in the crotch!

Trembling with fright, he pushed his hand
down inside his overalls and made contact with

the warm liquid. He forced himself to draw his hand back out of his pants and examined his wet fingers. It wasn't blood.

Otto glanced at him before picking up the summons from among the funnies. He stuffed the papers back into the tan envelope and tossed it on the table. Next he brushed popcorn from his pants, shook some out of his hair and carefully picked an old maid out of his ear before sitting down.

Uke realized he was dangerous when silent. He had no fear of Otto when he was raising hell and throwing things. Now his eyes were glazed over, like when he had a winning poker hand and knew it. No sign of surprise was evident. He began picking up the scattered funny papers.

He watched Otto scoop up a bowl of corn from what remained in the tub as if nothing had happened. Sis, he noticed, busied herself sweeping up the mess from the floor. She dumped it back into the huge tin wash tub after tasting a handful.

"I'll have to throw this out, it's tainted," she declared.

Otto arose and drifted over to the cook stove and scooped fresh corn from the tub. He poured a helping of hot butter from the tea pot on the back corner of the stove, picked up the salt cellar and went out on the porch with the corn.

Uke forced himself not to laugh as he watched Otto through the window. Otto spit out the first mouthful. He wondered if it was the gunpowder or the dirt from the floor. Otto leaned over the railing and dumped it into the peony bushes for the squirrels to enjoy. Uke heard him mutter, "Dumb bastard."

He should have offered to carry the wash tub out to the chicken yard for Sis, but decided not to stir her wrath by offering. She swept a large fresh chunk of ceiling plaster off the stove, threw some split logs into the fire and began to pop more corn muttering.

"What?" Uke asked.

"Nothing really, Mihich Nostrov's predicted this." Fortune telling was such an unreliable thing, Mihich constantly reminded her. Sis reminded herself it was also expensive.

Otto let the screen door slam returning to the table. He picked up the official looking envelope. "This here summons ordering me to go to court and explain how come I am moving things through the city streets without a permit, trespassing, storing things on somebody else's property without permission, and the last one is to be served if I refuse to accept the rest of them. How do you like that? Contempt of court and resisting an officer." He added two shakes of salt to a fresh bowl of popcorn and eyed Uke with obvious distaste He turned and stood looking out the screen door.

With Sis around, Uke knew Otto would save his wrath for later. Besides, none of them had anticipated this summons in addition to the duck hunting arrest.

Sis elbowed Otto out of the way, letting the screen door slam. She stepped over to the porch railing and dumped a load of old maids out of the long handled popper into the peonies. Four squirrels quickly scattered, but hurried back like they were on a rubber band. They showed up on Sunday afternoons with the blackbirds.

She marched back into the house and peered over Otto's shoulder at the documents. With a plaintive glance toward Uke, who hadn't moved since he had fired the pistol other than to check his pants, she demanded, "How could you do this to me?"

Uke hung his head. How could he explain it was Otto, not her, he was doing it to, but she would never understand. Typically illogical of a woman to be put things on a personal basis. He suspected if Otto was put up by the county

for a couple months and Sis lost her bed partner she wouldn't miss him. The last time Otto
found lodging in the pokey, she thanked Uke.

"Well," Otto observed, adding more salt to
the corn, "It's too bad you didn't find me
here, I'm going fishing."

"Can I go along?" Uke asked. Fishing was a
passion with Uke and he had a score to settle
with Rock River Herman. He scooped the documents into the envelope and stuffed it into his
back pocket Official business could wait.

Otto started to snap a sharp 'no' for an
answer, but realized Sis had paused in her
sweeping. "Yeh, I guess, but hurry it up.
We'll go up on the Rock River I hear the
channel cats are running over in Dane County."

"Got any money for the trip, Uke?" He stepped
on the Katzenjammer Kids reaching for a bowl of
fresh popcorn. Otto was difficult to understand with a mouth full of corn.

Sis stopped shaking the long handled popper
over the open flame, "What about the statue?
You're running away from trouble again?"
Despite her objections, she knew she needed
some relief from her husband and her brother.

"It's safe right where it is," Otto parried
what he deemed his wife's accusation.

Uke stifled a grin. It was not important is
what he meant. Besides, he knew that somehow
Otto figured a fishing trip would solve his
legal and financial problems if he got out of
town fast. Otto had the truck loaded and
waiting while Uke was having trouble finding
his tackle box and casting rod.

Sis was never included in fishing trips.
Someone had to man the fortress until things
cooled off. Besides, women couldn't shut up
long enough to let the fish bite. Uke agreed
with Otto's appraisal. It was one of the things
they agreed whole heartedly upon.

"Bring the summons along," Otto insisted.

"Why? It can't be served in a different county, it's out of my jurisdiction."

"I know," Otto leered, "and bring along a county voucher whilst yer at it."

Uke returned to the kitchen loaded with landing nets, fly rods, casting rods and a pair of waders, Otto stepped forward and raised his right hand. "Say to me, 'Do you swear to uphold the law and be my deputy?' Now then, pin the badge on me," he instructed the sheriff.

Uke dropped the gear and hurried to comply. The brief swearing in ceremony completed, Uke tried not to stick Otto with the sharp pin on the back of the badge. He broke into a broad grin when his official act had been completed and the badge was in place after several missed attempts that Otto suffered in silence.

"By gol, you are the one," he guffawed. Otto had an answer for everything. Of course, one of Otto's favorite sayings was 'county officials weren't wrapped too tight.' Uke never took this observation personally.

"Let's get going," Otto growled anxiously pulling a curtain open, he peeked out the kitchen window before opening the door.

He wasn't too anxious, Sis noted, watching the two through the kitchen curtain. Uke was kicking the front tire while Otto drummed his fingers impatiently on the steering wheel.

She made a mental note to find out exactly what this antic was all about. No one else kicked a tire to start a vehicle that she knew of. She had her suspicions. She intended to take this opportunity to check out the gold mining stock she had found in Otto's pocket. She guessed he had won it in a poker game. If she discovered the owner, she would return it.

* * *

The ninety mile trip to Indian Ford was made in silence other than when Otto stopped near a creek several times and ordered Uke to refill the steaming radiator from a bucket tied to the truck bed. He carried it for this reason. It also served as a minnow bucket. Uke wondered why Otto didn't get the radiator fixed.

"Higgie Jones claims a can of black pepper would seal the leak," he offered. "Said he saw the mechanic at Alfies' Dependable Dodge company do it."

"Wouldn't surprise me none, his mech is a crook," Otto observed.

Long after dark they arrived at their destination A wide spot of noisy rushing water below the dam. They both loved the quaint town of Indian Ford nestled in the hills of the Rock River that time had forgotten. The only boast the town could make was the power company dam located on the edge of town and the excitement a Greyhound bus created as it roared down the hill and through town once a day. Many of the people were tobacco farmers. They rode the bus to the top of the hill and then got off: if the bus driver chose to stop for them.

Otto selected the camp site for a special reason: it was difficult to get in or out of town without being noticed and the small clearing for the camp was in dense brush. The game warden would never scramble through all the tangle of blackberry bushes to check a fishing license. The rushing water below the dam drowned out any noises from the camp.

"Getting here after dark makes setting up camp kinda hard," Uke fretted.

"Also, nobody'll know we're here," Otto retorted.

Uke grudgingly agreed. This river was exciting and enchanting unlike the little old Root River at home. Perhaps it was the larger fish in it, or the yellow gravel river banks instead of mud, or was just being in a different place? Whatever the reason, the pleasure was doubled for him, Otto never objected to his company.

Uke knew fishing was a science and a serious business to Otto. Poker playing ranked right alongside of it. Part of the reason Uke did not always get to go along was Sis. She seemed to have jobs planned for Otto about the time a fishing trip was being hatched. Uke wound up getting stuck with these pressing chores. Or perhaps it was Ruth wanting something done.

"Drive those tent stakes in tight," Otto instructed, busy stacking his casting rods and set lines on the side of the truck.

Silently, Uke finished raising the tent and hurried to move the bedding and utensils under cover. He would have liked to help organize the fishing gear, but Otto was in a sour mood. He had to content himself to be along. He'd get his fishing in later, once he was certain the camp was set up. He didn't want Otto to send him hiking home for forgetting to do something, like the time he left the hand axe in the brush pile and Otto accidentally set the brush on fire with a carelessly tossed match. They saved the camp, but not the axe. Ninety miles would be a long way to walk home.

"Coffee ready yet?" Otto whispered. Uke nodded 'yes' in the dark, cracked a raw egg and tossed it into the pot to settle the grounds.

He found the sandwiches Sis had hurriedly prepared. He silently poured two tin cups of coffee from the fire blackened blue and white speckled enamel coated pot. They shared a seat on a fallen tree trunk and sipped the hot brew. He was always surprised coffee turned out tasting so good over an open fire. When he tried to make it at home on the cook stove, it wasn't fit to drink. Why the difference?

"Let's go do some fishin'" Otto decided tossing his unfinished coffee into the shrubs. "Don't forget the landing net." He slapped at a mosquito and grabbed his set lines.

Uke was reluctant to leave the coffee with

it's over powering aroma. He gingerly edged the
pot off the flames where it would keep warm,
but would quit boiling. "Yeh," he replied as he
heard him scramble off down stream.

It was about twenty feet from the camp to the
river bank and it would be no problem to find
the camp or the river in the dark despite the
tangled growth of bushes and trees.

"Right here," Otto whispered.

Uke carefully unloaded his burden, leaning
each item within easy reach against shrubs and
tree trunks. The flashlight and the landing net
had to be near, except he forgot the landing
net back at the camp. Oh, well, I can go back
for it while Otto places his set lines.

"Be back soon," Otto grunted disappearing
into the dark lugging his set lines.

Uke eased his bulk down and made himself
comfortable on the river bank content with his
own casting rod and swatting an occasional mosquito looking for a free meal. He heard Otto
swearing as he scrambled through the brush
looking for his favorite places to run illegal
set lines. Unless the game warden was looking
for illegal set lines, they could not be seen.

Otto was in too big a hurry at home to find
the canoe in the weeds behind the chicken coop.
Since he didn't have it, he had to be content
to heave the set lines out into the river and
let the current carry them down stream until
the sinkers caught on the river bottom.

He decided forgetting the canoe was a good
thing. If any city officials came nosing around
and saw the canoe, they'd know he hadn't gone
fishing.

Uke could hear a line splash and then a lull
before the next one. Anyone who might be within earshot would mistake them for a fish jumping. He counted four lines and then heard Otto
battling his way back to the first one to test
the bait. The mixture of cotton and cornmeal

had to be right. Cornmeal to tempt the cats and
enough cotton to hold the meal on the hook.

It was too bad they didn't have the boat,
then the lines could be anchored to the far
shore and no catfish could swim past the bait.

Fried cats were fine. Fresh smoked catfish
were a rare delicacy few people ever had the
opportunity to appreciate. Uke enjoyed the fish
since Otto did not rely on any of the many
commercial smoke houses around Rootville. He
had built his own out behind the number two
shed. The local fish tug proprietors produced
dried fish in their smoke houses rather than
smoked, Otto maintained. His hung out of reach
of cats, dogs and raccoons and provided smoked
fish all winter.

Fishing laws allowed two sets of lines per
fisherman. Uke counted four splashes, two lines
for each of them. Uke had, been instructed not
to claim Otto's two if the game warden interfered. He knew the only real reason Otto
brought him along was his fishing license. One
license was enough Otto insisted.

Otto would have preferred a loaf or two of
baker's bread in case the fish weren't hungry
for cornmeal. The nice, fresh, soft dough in
baker's bread could be worked into a ball between the fingers. The carp especially liked
the waterproof delicacy. Sis's bread wouldn't
do: it wasn't soggy or spongy and was much
better eating. It took some time before he
heard Otto crashing back through the brush.

A slight jiggle on his rod told him something was playing with his minnow. Between
slapping mosquitoes and watching his casting
rod, Uke forgot Otto. Rings of wavelets winked
in the moonlight around the end of the line
where it entered the water. Then a slight tug
on the line when the fish tried to remove the
bait from the hook.

He sensed something large had just taken his

bait. It had to be a good size fish, too big
for a slow moving Walleye, probably a cat the
way it was trying to run with the line instead
of fighting like a Bass would. He could feel
sweat begin to trickle down his nose.

"Kin ya move over?" Otto whispered in the
darkness. A full moon peeked out from behind
the clouds. Uke moved allowing Otto room to get
into position to coach him on landing the fish.

"Play him right, not too hard, Uke, he looks
like he could be bigger than Herman. Where's
the landing net?" He felt around for it.

Involved with the fish almost since Otto
first disappeared with his set lines, he had
forgotten it. Having tasted the bait, the fish
decided not to waste time and swallowed the
morsel along with the hook.

Herman was the name Otto had given to a
catfish, close to five feet long, about ten
years ago. The fish hung out once in a while
right in the hole where Uke was fishing.

"Might be Herman," Uke whispered. Otto had
forbade him to fish in that spot, but whenever
Otto went to check set lines, Uke dropped his
hook in the hole.

Herman had bent hooks, broken lines and
snapped poles. He was too smart for Uke, Otto
claimed. In a match up Herman always won previous struggles. This time it would be different
Uke vowed, digging his heels into the dirt.

Otto considered Herman his personal fish for
the past ten years he had challenged the wily
old cat. He had hooked Herman many times, but
he had never landed him.

Otto swore to all who would listen he could
hear Herman laughing at him on a quiet night.
He claimed he saw Herman thumbing his nose at
him in the flashlight beam once. He swore the
story was true, and admitted with delight he
always came out on the short end of the battle.
Uke had no doubt Herman was the one thing in

the world Otto admired and respected.

He could hear Otto fall into the tangle of bushes and low hanging limbs in his excitement before he found Uke's three cell flashlight in the bushes. Otto claimed that Rolf Baumgart had tossed it into a five card draw poker pot above Stockwell's Drug Emporium according to Otto.

Uke knew Otto had really swiped it at a drug store. Higgie Jones saw him take it while he was washing the drug store windows and told Uke, hoping he would arrest Otto, but it would have been Higgie's word against Otto's. Judge Milton Fishbain would be reluctant to believe either of them. Otto solved the dilemma by giving the flashlight to Uke for Christmas.

"I need help," Uke gasped. Otto was flashing the three cell around to best determine how to extricate himself from the blackberry brambles. They needed the landing net.

"Don't let him get away!" Otto hissed. Thought of the sweet, greasy, hickory smoked catfish which they would soon share spurred Uke on. He glimpsed Otto crawling on his hands and knees between the thorn bushes searching for the net. From somewhere nearby a rattle snake objected to being disturbed.

"Be quiet, Uke," Otto tried to whisper, "you'll wake up the dead." What he was really concerned about was waking up the game warden. The warden did not have a sixth sense, instead he had six kids who tattled to him.

"Hang on a minute, Uke," Otto spoke louder easing away from the sound of the snake, "where's the landing net?"

"It's," Uke shouted over his shoulder.

Otto fell over the minnow bucket, narrowly avoiding becoming impaled on the sharp metal end of the fish stringer. It was made from a piece of clothes line attached to a flattened copper tubing sharpened on one end. It worked like a leash on a dog except it slipped through

the gill and then out the mouth of the fish
without hurting it.

"Up," Uke gasped, deliciously fatigued,
spurred on with the thought of imminent help.

Otto frisked him with the light on the off
chance he might have the net.

"At the," Uke managed to say before Otto cut
him off again.

"Tell me, man!" Otto shrieked. This fish
would never come out of the water without the
net, it was far too large and would snap Uke's
casting rod and the fish would be lost.

With a final effort Uke braced himself and
gave a mighty heave on the pole. A moment before, the catfish, intent upon freeing itself
dove deeply and then surged toward the surface
in another attempt at freedom. It arched clear
of the water. Uke gasped "Camp."

"At the camp?" Otto screeched. He had told
him twice to bring it along. He was about to
take Uke and his ancestors back through their
spotty history when the beam of his flashlight
caught the catfish arcing through the air to a
resting place in the bramble patch Otto had
recently vacated.

It was too much for the rattler, who hurriedly left the scene, but not for Uke. He dove
head first into the briars unmindful of the
thorns, intent upon capturing his prize before
it could climb a tree or hide in the woods.

Otto was rooted in place, numb with disbelief. Collecting his senses, he bounded toward the briar patch and falling over a low
hanging branch, managed to lunge out with the
flashlight and catch Uke behind the ear,
knocking him cold.

"Ya dumb sock, ya caught Herman!" A sacri-
lege. Herman was his fish! Take him along on a
fishing trip and he catches my fish....again!

He stepped over Uke who lay with a smile on
his face and carefully picked up the aging

oversize fish and cradled it in his arms like a
small child. With care he released the hook
from its mouth and picked his way through the
shrubs and brambles toward the river.

Playing the beam of light on Herman he patted
him on the top of his head. One eye had turned
white since he had last seen him. With a final
pat, he kneeled and slipped Herman into the
river without a splash, old age was catching up
to him. With an after thought, he picked up
Uke's casting rod and tossed it into the
bushes. Uke could find it there in the morning,
he had done enough fishing for tonight.

Minnows in the bucket were starting to turn
belly up when Otto took aim with the brimming
bucket of river water. He caught the peacefully
smiling Uke in the face with the contents.

Uke sat up slowly and rubbed his head while
he brushed minnows from the bib of his overalls. "What happened? Hey, where's my fish?"

"Stay sitting," Otto grinned,"This is going
to be hard to believe, but your fish was none
other than Herman. He must have wrapped his
tail around the flashlight and flipped it,
catching you in the noggin. I told you he was
too smart for you to fool around with him."

Uke agreed, "You're right." He rubbed his
throbbing head."It's the third time he's gotten
away," he recalled, feeling the knot on his
head. "The first time he bent my hook and
slipped off the line, the second time he slapped me in the face with his tail and knocked a
tooth loose, he gets rougher each time."

Otto grunted in agreement. The rare times he
had ever had a good look at Herman was when Uke
had caught him.

CHAPTER NINE
THE GOLD STOCK

The hidden camp ground served them well.
But Uke knew the peaceful life would have to
end sooner or later. The river's music was only
interrupted by the one bus a day roaring down
into the valley, over the bridge and then up
the opposite hill. He also knew the game warden
would become aware of them before long. Also,
Otto became almost human soaking a fish line
most of the night.

They saw no more of Herman. Most of their
discussion was about him, however. In anticipation of having to leave this bit of heaven,
Uke busied himself filling the live box with
fish. He was rather pleased that he had contributed to the catch.

He pulled grass until a shock comparable to a
wheat bundle was ready to use. Humming absently
to himself, he layered it into the live box
along with the fish. Otto offered no help other
than to kick the flopping creatures away from
the water. The catch was crappies, blue-gills,
a northern, two walleyes and four small catfish
on the bank.

"These walleyes are too small," Uke observed.

"They're plenty big, stuff them in right on
the bottom," Otto instructed searching for his

pencil stub. He began to scribble on a scrap of
paper, pausing occasionally to suck on the
pencil's tip.

"An don't forget to souse them with lot'sa
water." Otto turned back to his paper and
pencil.

From experience he knew Otto wouldn't tell
him what he was writing until good and ready.
He turned away and studied fresh teeth marks on
the outside of the live box and debated if he
should disturb Otto in his figuring. He decided
against informing him of the marks. Otto had
just broken his lead and was angrily sharpening
a new point on the stub. The paper, he was certain, had something to do with him.

A leatherback turtle drifted right up to
shore and grinned at Uke. It was the powerful
jaws of the turtle trying to get to the fish
that had made the marks on the top of the stiff
wire box. Idly he wondered if he should try to
wrestle the wash tub sized reptile to shore. It
would make excellent soup. He took one step toward the edge of the river and it disappeared
with no discernible effort.

Otto was studying him again. It made him
uncomfortable.

"Whatcha doing?" He wiped his face with a
huge hairy arm. No breeze reached them in their
hideaway. The camp would test Daniel Boone,
secluded from the world like it was.

"Tell you when the fish are all packed," Otto
answered absently, sucking on the stub.

After the box was filled, Uke soaked it with
the minnow bucket and dragged it into the shade
and sat down on it. Nobody but Otto would think
to pack fish in this manner, Uke marveled. They
would be able to live on only the moisture for
several days.

Otto looked up from his sheet of paper and
rubbed his chin with the eraser end of the
pencil. "You think thirty bucks is too much?"

"Naw, I don't think so," Uke replied, "unless I owed it to somebody." He had the frightening thought Otto would try to stick him with the entire cost of the fishing trip. Then again, maybe he was talking about selling the fish to the farmers on the way home? No, this couldn't be it, usually he wound up with eggs, bacon and potatoes bartered from the farmers, not money.

"We each get three bucks a day for room and board," Otto continued figuring absently combing his mustache with the sharp end of the pencil. "We have each earned nine bucks and I get five cents a mile for the truck each way, that's ten bucks more, and then a special fee of eleven for being your Special Deputy."

"Wait, now," Uke objected, realizing what Otto was figuring, "we won't have gone a hundred miles yet when we get home."

"Not by the odometer," Otto readily agreed, inspecting his favorite casting rod. "The odometer doesn't register when we back up or when we're not moving."

"By golly, you might be right," Uke admitted. It was easier to agree than to argue with Otto's cock-a-mamey ideas.

"You bet I am," Otto responded. "If anyone should ask, you had to get clear over to the Wisconsin River before you caught me. Makes it a sight more than a hundred miles."

"Don't I get no special fee?"

"Yer the sheriff," Otto responded, "You had to swear me in, remember? A real special deputy, in fact. They don't come cheap." He laughed at the truth in his statement.

* * *

Sis studied the worn, odd looking piece of paper she had found in Otto's pocket. She had no compunctions about her method of keeping tabs on her pandering partner. She had long ago learned to put odd scraps of information to-

gether and come up with a realistic sketch, and
besides knowing his character helped.

She put on her wide brimmed straw hat with
the bouquet of flowers in the band, pressed a
wrinkle from her skirt with her hand, let the
screen door slam and began to walk down Devil's
Lane toward town. She knew where Higgie could
be found scrubbing windows unless he had
altered his schedule due to a bait of choice
gossip. She had his window washing schedule
memorized and she utilized the creature as a
chauffeur and a source of information. Who
better than a window washer would know what was
going on around town?

Higgie saw her coming and began putting his
equipment away. Sis never walked anywhere
except to find him or Mihich. She looked him up
when Otto couldn't be found, which was often,
and while she never said it, the job was too
important for Uke. Driving her around was
easier and paid better than washing windows.
Higgie was always glad to see Sis....if she was
afoot.

After exchanging pleasantries, Sis told him
the purpose of her visit. Higgie picked up his
full bucket of water, wheeled around and threw
it into the street. The dirty soap water just
missed Father Aloysius' open touring car
whipping past.

Sis climbed into the window washer's coupe
and waited patiently for him to pile his tools
into the rumble seat of the ancient bright
green Maxwell before telling him she wanted to
go to Middletown. Higgie was about to grumble
about the lost day's wages when Sis handed him
two dollars. It was greater than he could earn
washing windows and a sight easier. Mollified,
he waited patiently for information to spew
forth from the lady.

"What fer we going over there?" Higgie didn't
expect an answer, but it didn't hurt to ask.

Sis was stoic despite his efforts to pry.
She directed him to stop in front of a dingy,
small shop with dirty windows and three golden
balls hanging over the door. A sign proudly
advertised it was a pawn shop and the world's
second oldest profession. He wondered what in
the world Sis was pawning and why go clear to
Middletown when Rootville had three? He knew
she'd never get work there if it was what she
wanted.

"Ya wan'na stop here?" Higgie gasped in
disbelief.

Filled with apprehension, and without replying, Sis struggled from the car and pulled the
shop door open. She eyed the fat man sitting
behind the glass cage. He had on a green visor
hiding the dirty rimless glasses he was wearing. He gave no hint she was in his store.

She halted in front of the cage. Glancing
around, she was filled with misgivings wondering if entering this place wasn't a horrible
mistake. Masses of spider webs danced in a
draft from a broken window pane. Coatings of
dust lay on everything. All the items looked
like they had been there for ever.

"Excuse me, could you look at this and tell
me if it is any good?" She handed him the gold
mining stock certificate, trying not to get her
dress sleeve into the grime on the counter. She
could not perceive he had been doing anything,
yet he seemed affronted by her presence.

Hardly glancing at it, he made a face and
looked up at her, speaking for the first time.
"Bah, Comstock Lode? Played out years ago,
this paper is worthless." He stood up, a full
head shorter than she, "You want I should throw
it away for you?"

He reached toward a cardboard box apparently
serving as a waste basket by the looks of the
trash in it. Sis shook her head no, and reached
for the paper. He made no effort to hand it

back. Momentarily in panic, Sis's first thought
was to run out and get Higgie. She relaxed when
the fat man sat back down. She had the feeling
he was an adversary, instead of a helpful
merchant.

"I suppose I could check it out completely
for you." He pushed the certificate into a
cubby hole after giving it another look.

"I certainly want a receipt for it," she
demanded, wondering if she'd have to call
Higgie after all.

He scribbled on an old piece of scrap paper
and handed it over.

Sis scanned it and handed it back. "I'll
need a description of what I handed you and the
number up in the right hand corner, also date
it." She added "please" as an afterthought.

Alby Nostrov knew when to relent, the woman
knew what she was about. Would she notice if I
wrote down the wrong number, he wondered?
Better not, he noticed the man who had been
sitting in the sport coupe was now at the front
door watching intently, his nose pressed
against the window glass.

Sis scanned the receipt, satisfied, accepted
it, and started for the door. She reached for
the greasy door knob and paused. "How long?"

Alby adjusted his visor before replying, " A
day, a week, who knows?"

"I'll be back in three days," Sis asserted.

Alby had no doubt she would.

Returning to the car, Sis found Higgie waiting patiently behind the steering wheel unaware
he had a smudge of tell tale grime on the end
of his nose.

"Home," she ordered.

"Ain't gonna tell me what that was all
about?"

Her mouth set firmly, she sat stiffly upright
in the seat and looked straight ahead.

He knew Alby wouldn't tell him.

* * *

Otto helped Uke lug the heavy live box up
from the river bank and along the sandy road.
The first real effort he had put in for the
entire three days. They heaved it into the back
of the truck together before returning to check
the camp area for missing goods. Uke found the
frying pan sunning on a rock in the river shal-
lows where he had scoured it clean with sand
from the river bottom. He smiled inwardly, Sis
would raise almighty heck it they returned
without her favorite skillet. Otto had slipped
the flat pan into his shirt before he went out
the door and when she missed it....she'd know
why it disappeared and who had it.

They had eaten well, some fish, but mostly
spuds, fresh pork, green onions, and the like
from the farmers Otto had bartered and worked
over. When they refused to trade, he waited
until after dark and helped himself. One of his
prizes was an old onion sack filled with green
tobacco leaves. When the leaves dried out he
had several customers in Rootville who preferred them to any plug tobacco in the stores.

Satisfied that the area was cleared, Otto
climbed into the truck and set the two levers
on the steering column. Uke toyed with the
notion of refusing to go through with the tire
kicking ritual, but thought better of it. He
was no longer convinced it was necessary....he
saw no one else doing it. Otto would probably
do something to keep it from starting and worst
of all, he knew Otto... it would be a long walk
home.

He tried to refuse once a lot closer to home.
After Otto let him crank his arm off, Uke
finally relented, giving the tire a resounding
kick. The truck started on the next spin of the
crank. He did not see Otto reach for the
ignition key.

Uke straightened up to wipe his face with his

big, red handkerchief, and Otto had driven off
leaving him standing there. He did not come
back for him, either. Twenty miles and seven
pounds lighter, Uke arrived home in time for a
cold supper.

Despite the game warden's six kids, they had
not been discovered. Uke hunched in the front
seat staring through the dirty windshield while
the truck bounced toward home. The long ride
was nearly over.

Otto's ledger sheet lay beside them on the
seat. Without picking it up he tried to study
it. He was awed at his brother-in-law, amazed
at the way Otto could take command of any situation. What he would do without him? Otto was
thinking all the time. In fact, by the look on
his face, he was going at it right now.

He guessed Otto was trying to review the
events entangling his life, he always did on
these long drives. Otto kept his life simple
and free of complications. Now he had trouble
with the city council, a priest and his game
warden brother, with his wife and his missing
gold mining certificate. He did not know if the
stock was worthless or not. It could be worth a
mean fortune.

On top of all this, Sis was worried about old
lady Nostrov's foolish predictions and lately
she brought them up to Otto at each opportunity. She was obviously worried about some
terrible thing that that old lady had put in
her head.

But like Otto had often insisted, "Ya can't
last forever." Uke was more concerned about how
Otto would manage the county clerk when he
turned in his voucher for catching himself?
Once the county found out it would have to pay
the bill, they'd find a tame judge who would
try to make Otto forget the whole thing.

That's the way these things worked Uke had
learned. In his years as sheriff, he had dis-

covered things about government that would not
go down too well with most voters.

The newspapers, he was aware, seldom printed
the truth without embellishing it. Selling
newspapers was not their main goal: staying out
of troublesome law suits was their first
priority.

Shortly after taking office, Uke discovered
he should stay on the good side of the jackal
down at the bi-weekly Clarion Bugle who would
get into the act with one of his stupid edit-
orials on a subject he knew nothing about and
would try to stir everyone up with his drivel.
Like the last drive to clean the grass out of
the cracks in the sidewalks. Uke didn't understand the editorial.

Otto willing explained it. "Everyone knows
grass grows in the cracks when the Republicans
are in office, certain as green apples."

What wasn't certain to Uke was whether the
Republicans or Democrats were in office. He
never much cared, nor did he have reason to
care: both welcomed a winning incumbent.
Honesty and effort on behalf of the voters was
a matter of successfully fooling more than half
the population.

Uke had heard the old adage, "Things could
never be so bad but they couldn't be worse,"
but Otto said don't believe it. Things couldn't
be any worse. Sis was proof enough in Otto's
mind, and at times Uke had to agree.

With the first whine of the truck in the
driveway, Sis was on the porch tapping her foot
and pointing toward the hen house before they
had pulled the live box from the back of the
truck bed.

Uncleaned fish were not welcome. Nor were
fishermen until after the fish were cleaned.
All because Uke had forgot to clean a catch and
they had lain in the summer sun for a couple of
weeks until Sis got wind of them. Otto laid the

blame at his feet. He caught the fish, it was only right that Uke clean them.

When Uke appeared some hours later with the minnow bucket full of cleaned and salted fish did she speak. She suspected by the length of time it took, Otto hadn't helped with the project, but sat directing Uke. He had once told Uke he couldn't clean fish, it was against his religion. When Uke wanted to know what church he went to, Otto threw a handful of fish guts at him. They landed on Otto's favorite casting rod. It took two days for three stray cats to clean up the mess.

"Seems like some one in town and a few others have been looking for you, including a cemetery lot salesman who smells a sale," Sis said over her shoulder to Otto when he entered the kitchen. She was busily fixing a hot meal for the two filthy men in her life.

"What did the cemetery salesman want?" Otto wondered. "I don't need a plot."

It was one place you couldn't make a fast buck, although Nick Jansti tried to cover a poker pot with a deed to one. Otto allowed it in the pot and Nick won it back, which was as well: Nick was a switchman down at the railroad yards and slipped off a caboose he was humping the following day.

"The way people are aroused around here, you might need a lot," Sis replied grimly. "The town is up in arms, but fortunately for you, about half of them are rooting for you," she added holding out some hope for her tired warrior.

Uke pondered this for a moment knowing Otto couldn't count all his real friends on one hand, so something must be in the wind. Anybody knows city officials can give fits to people without half trying. You'd think the taxpayers were hired help the way the city clowns operated.

CHAPTER TEN
THE BIRDS AND THE BEES

Sis hesitated before turning to Uke,
"Ulysses, your twin brother Abraham is in town.
He blew in yesterday, but I haven't seen hide nor
hair of him. I fear he has his eye on Ruth."
She slid a plate of hashbrowns, corned ribs and
dandelion greens in front of Uke to ease the
shock when he understood what she was saying.

Uke was certain to be unhappy with Abe's
return or perhaps sad about losing his girl
friend, Ruth. Abe, his identical twin, had
bequeathed her to Uke way back in fourth grade.

Abe had split her head open with an icicle to
prove he knew who she was. After her dad had
caught Abe, he lost all interest in her and the
next night Uke acquired Ruth, one of her
mittens, and a lock of her hair with ink on it
from Abe with his compliments.

"Does that mean he wants her back?" Uke
asked, pushing his plate toward Sis for
seconds. "She's been my girl for a good long
time." The dandelion greens remained untouched
on the plate.

"A girl does get tired of waiting," Sis
replied, pushing the plate back at him and
pointing to the greens. "You'd better get over
and ask her tonight." Sis was not at all sure

Abe would leave a betrothed alone.

"Ask her what?" Uke started to rise to help himself at the stove, but sat back down, stricken, "Ask her to marry me?" He used the silence that ensued to refill his plate and wolf it down. A glance at Otto only produced a smirking grin.

"You wouldn't be the first nor the last." Sis offered, jiggling his chair until he got up and began wiping dishes. The greens lay untouched. "I've been meaning to speak to you about her. It's time you were getting married and settle down." She tossed him a dish towel.

Uke was aware Otto was trying hard not to notice the conversation. They both wondered how Sis always knew so much about things around town when she seldom left the house. Was it possible she knew where the gold mining stock was? While Otto rarely spoke on the way home from the river, it was always about the stock. But how could she know?

Uke settled into another chair away from his sister. "But if Abe wants her, I can't do nothin' about it." He wiped his perspiring face with the dish towel.

His older sister paused and fixed him with her coldest stare. "Do like I say. Chances are, knowing Abe, he's trying to pass himself off as you." She knew Abe used this approach whenever he hit town. Ruth knew it too, but always too late, - she couldn't tell them apart.

It was one of the reasons Uke was so hard pressed for money, Abe would run up bills in his name and the shop keepers would refuse to believe Uke when he told the truth. Was it really his fault they couldn't tell the two apart?

Uke shrugged and decided Sis knew best. He wiped his shoes with the dish towel, tossed it over a chair back and reached into the sink to

get some water to wet down his hair. He ran his
fingers through the wild stuff and reached for
his hat before Sis realized what he was about.

"Wait," she commanded, retrieving the dish
towel, "when you go to ask a girl to marry you,
you don't up and do it. You have to wash up and
put on your best suit and get some flowers and
candy and most important, you have to make her
feel romantic." Some rose water wouldn't hurt,
either, she could have added to kill the
lingering odor of fish.

"I suppose I can pull a handful of yer
Bachelor Buttons, but how do I make her feel
romantic?" Uke wondered aloud, hoping for some
hints. Otto would know, Uke was certain, but he
was strangely silent; all Otto did was cast an
apprehensive glance at Sis.

Sis ignored the question and busied herself
wiping dishes. She was positive if Ruth saw Uke
in a suit with flowers in his hand, she would
do the rest. She grudgingly had to acknowledge
Ruth was a sweet, efficient and capable girl,
perhaps too capable. Sis felt Ruth did not
need a man under foot any more than Sis did. A
lack of know how probably kept her from trapp-
ing a husband. Some girls couldn't catch a
husband no matter how alluring they might be.
Ruth was empty headed in this area of brains.

But Ruth of the dark brown eyes, light brown
hair and ready smile whose tinkling laugh sent
shivers up and down the spine of most men:
making them feel helpless. She could make
them feel like fools if they ever learned of
her talents.

Since Pa became infirm, Ruth had learned to
be self reliant. When the roof began to leak
she fixed it herself. She learned leaking
faucets were simple to fix. Electrical
problems consisted of changing light bulbs
since there was no other appliances in the
house.

While Uke could do none of these things, he was one of the few people who was aware of her talents. Especially her ability to cook. Her cherry and blueberry pies could have won prizes at the county fair if she could manage to get them there. Uke usually had them sniffed out and eaten before judging day. He had to be careful not to tell Sis he thought Ruth was the better cook of the two.

He had only a vague idea about the birds and bees and was content to let Ruth do whatever she set out to do. Since she hadn't set her mind to asking Uke to marry her, he was content to let the situation ride. Wednesdays and Saturday nights were date nights and he was satisfied with this arrangement. How could he know Higgie had dropped Sis off at Ruth's house for a short chat while he was fishing? Uke knew nothing of their woman to woman talks.

First chance I get, I'm going to ask Otto if I'm being taken in by scheming females. But Otto just sat silently throughout the meal enjoying the food. Uke guessed he preferred Sis's cooking to his, but why was Otto trying so hard to ignore the conversation?

Uke trudged upstairs to his bedroom and while he couldn't quite put a finger on it, other things in the conversation bothered him, but right now he couldn't remember what they were.

He came slowly down the steps a short time later clothed in his finest. Before he could disappear through the door Sis cut him off and straightened his tie and combed his hair. With a last desperate attempt she tried to press his hair down with her fingers after dipping her hand into the dish water. Uke tried to escape before she found the perfume bottle she kept handy in the kitchen.

"It is amazing how high a woman sets her sights," Sis paused for effect before glancing at her husband, "and how much less she settles for."

Otto shrugged, but said nothing. Uke pretended not to hear as he slipped through the screen
door letting it bang. Sis sounded like she was
looking for a fight. She didn't have it so bad
Otto often told him. The house and property
were estate. The furniture and Durant belonged
to her. She never missed a meal, Otto always
insisted.

She had a lot of things the biddies around
town couldn't crow about, he would add. Maybe
she did have to peel potatoes thin now and
then. The Sunday evening popcorn meals were her
own invention and the Sunday dinners kept the
chicken population down.

* * *

Uke trudged toward Ruth's home wondering how
to get 'romanticed up' like Sis had instructed.
She failed to tell him how. The holster slapped
his leg with each step and the bouquet of pink
peonies Sis had insisted on instead of bachelor's buttons, kept slipping from his hand
when he tried to adjust his gun. Wearing the
service revolver was his own idea; any official
act required him to wear it. Marriage proposals
might, or might not be an official act.

Sis had placed the flowers in his right hand
and not until he stopped to rest on the church
steps did it occur to him to shift them to the
left hand.

I should have asked to use the Durant, he
thought. No, then I would get to her house too
soon. Besides, Sis would refuse to let me
drive it. He didn't feel up to any rejections
right now. Perhaps worst of all, ants were
crawling up his sleeve from the peonies. He
could never remember seeing ants on Bachelor
Buttons. He laid down the huge flowers to give
them some rest.

Father Aloysius, annoyed with the city
council for insisting he had to have a liquor

license in order to sell beer at his garden
party, sought solace in the garden behind the
church. He avoided strolling past the monstrosity between the third and fourth stations of
the cross. With his head down and muttering
either prayers or invectives at the council,
he found himself on the front church steps and
in the gloaming discovered a visitor.

"Why it's Ulysses. How are you, my son?" He
peered into the gathering darkness never having
seen Uke dressed up. He hid his surprise at the
bunch of wilting flowers on the steps.

"Got trouble," Uke was receptive to any one
who would listen to his problems. He began by
telling the priest about Abraham being in town
and wanting to fool his girl friend. And then
Sis making things worse by wanting to head Uke
off at the pass with some flowers. Worst of
all, he had to get Ruth into a romantic mood.

He finished by asking, "How the hell-heck do
you get a girl romanticed up?"

The good priest had been around a long time
listening to other people's problems and advis-
ing them, but he could never recall having the
opportunity to advise anyone on this particular subject. He didn't have to hide his surprise; Uke had buried his head in his hands.

In a soft voice, he began to inform Uke about
the birds and the bees and Adam and Eve, and
after ten minutes Uke was well informed about
the weaker sex. Except what he really wanted
and needed to know.

"Go to her, my son," Father Aloysius commanded in his best pulpit voice. He helped the victim to his feet and gave him a reassuring pat
on the shoulder. "Oh, and tell your brother-in-
law I have a plan to put the statue into the
square without a murmur from the crowd of vultures down on the other side of the River
Jordan." He watched Uke trudge off, not at all
certain Uke would not get the two messages

mixed up, perhaps he should have used the words city hall instead of vultures?

Uke removed a wilted peony that had leaned over far enough to tickle his hand and ground it into the cement with his heel. Father had restored his confidence. This feeling grew on him whenever he had been in the company of the priest. Strange, how he could do that.

He approached Ruth's home in a less than attractive neighborhood but in much better spirits than when he started out. The peonies seemed to have taken heart from the lecture. I sure have to remember to tell Otto what Father said, he mused. Maybe sometime me and Otto can go fish this River Jordan and bring home a mess of catfish?

Ruth answered the door and the glint of mis-chief faded from her eyes. She recognized immediately that this shining gentleman had come upon a mission. It was partly the fruit of her own making and of Sis's.

She never really believed Uke would follow Sis's instructions. For the first time Uke realized Ruth had qualities he had failed to realize. The ready smile, humor, her hair was always neat and combed and the simplest house dress could suggested a party. The home she kept for her father was neat and clean. Her meals were a joy to eat and she knew the difference between gossip and chit chat. A man could hardly ask...or expect more.

Her great downfall was her efficiency and self reliance. But with middle age fast approaching and all the eligible men snatched up, at twenty-five, she had resigned herself to growing old with Uke on Wednesday date nights and Saturdays, until Sis had suggested a frontal assault to her.

She hated to think herself desperate, but if this is what it took, why not have a go at it? The fact Uke was now standing in her doorway

all spruced up was none the less unexpected.
She clapped her hands in delight, "Why I am
surprised to see you!" How had Sis pulled it
off, she wondered?

Uke hesitated a moment at the door, his
courage fast deserting him when confronted
with this vision. It was like seeing her for
the first time. She was tiny and couldn't lift
no where near what he could and she couldn't
move the boulder down at the square next to
the popcorn wagon, but then, there were few
people who could match his strength. He
couldn't hold it against her. He had no idea
where the birds and the bees fit into all
this.

He mopped his face nervously with a white
handkerchief. Ruth had never seen him with a
white one before. She stepped out of the door,
led him to the porch swing, sat down and patted
the empty seat beside her. He had meekly allowed himself to be led with no resistance.
Perhaps Sis knew what she was talking about?

"We'll sit out here. It's warm in the house
tonight." She smiled sweetly, taking the
flowers he thrust at her. She used them to hide
her face from the white lie she had told... in
truth her dad was up and fussing around and she
didn't want him to disturb this moment. She
peeked up at Uke from behind a pink peony,
taking some satisfaction in his plight. She
wondered how to shake the half dozen ants off
the flowers without altering his mood.

"Ruth," Uke stammered, "Ruth,"

Taking pity, she placed a soft hand gently on
his and Uke immediately felt like some one had
kicked him in the stomach.

"Ruth," he attempted once again, "I, you and
me, us, I mean will you," he hesitated in
frustration, "put them damn flowers down and
tell me if you want me to ask you if you will?"
He gave up in desperation and measured the

distance from the porch rail to the front gate and wondered if he could clear the rose garden in one leap.

"I will," she responded softly, and sank back into the swing for better or for worse. The proposal was obviously his best effort.

Uke swore softly to himself. Why did Sis and the priest have to go and spoil his relation- ship with Ruth? Until now they had been real good friends but now she wasn't the same girl. She acted different, she smelled different, no, it was the peonies. But she did sit there twinkling like the North Star on a dark night. What to do next, he wondered?

"You will," he finally found voice, "You will? Now, what the hell?!"

"The first thing you'll have to do is stop swearing," she reprimanded.

Uke ignored the order and pulled her to him, remembering how they always did it in the Wednesday night movies when the girl would either slap him or swoon in his arms. He wasn't certain what Ruth would do. There was one way to find out. Gently but firmly, he kissed her. Life, he realized with his first kiss ever, would never be the same again. He did not know why, but then he didn't care, either. Tomorrow would be soon enough to put a stop to her boss- ing him around. He'd swear if he damn well pleased.

They sat on the porch swing a long time, holding hands, not saying anything or doing anything. For one thing, Uke wasn't certain what was expected of him. Eventually she hid a yawn and he fidgeted and twisted the stems off the peonies before getting up and heading unsteadily toward the steps.

Once he was satisfied his legs were steady and would hold him he shouted, "So long," and vaulted the front gate.

"Sh, you'll wake pa," she scolded. With some

misgivings, she cleaned peony petals from the front porch and wondered why he didn't think to ask Pa for her hand, proper like. She giggled remembering when John Baker had asked Pa for her older sister's hand in marriage. Pa wanted to know if John fished? John said 'yes' so Pa agreed, he loved fishing. Well, Pa is too old to go off fishing and take my husband along. She quietly opened the door and then paused, the big galooot never even kissed me good night!

CHAPTER ELEVEN
THE SECRET PLEDGE

Uke dutifully brought Father Aloysius' message home to Otto who listened without comment.

"He got even with me at the duck blind, now what's he want?" Otto muttered, turning the kerosene lamp on the kitchen table lower. He let the screen door slam as he stomped out.

Uke couldn't blame Otto for not trusting the priest, but it wouldn't help any to remind him that he brought it all on himself. Uke guessed Father Aloysius hardly expected anything more from Otto.

He sat down on the running board of the truck alongside Otto and contemplated the situation. Otto looked like he might be doing the same thing. He could never quite be certain what was going through Otto's mind. All he could do was think about things and hope Otto wouldn't find fault with too many of his ideas. Most of the time he regretted saying anything. It seemed like Otto was always a step or two ahead of him with thoughts.

However, Otto and Sis and maybe Ruth embraced his idea about putting the statue in with the Stations of the Cross, although he could not be certain about Ruth. She was quite religious.

What disturbed him was his idea had created
this problem.

So far, the statue was still in the church
garden and the city was busy rigging complaints
against Otto. The statue could not be left
where it was, but the priest wouldn't let them
move it. Sis demanded action, Father Aloysius
demanded inaction, the city demanded action,
but refused to honor Otto's bills for visiting
Herman. The council was trying to pass a law
stating anyone owning popcorn wagons on city
streets had to have a license to sprinkle salt
on the popcorn. Uke guessed if he knew Otto,
the salt thing probably bothered him the most.

"You can tell that sky pilot I'll come and
see him when I get good and ready," he snarled
at Uke. He got up from the running board and
stalked toward the kitchen door to find out
what had detained Sis.

Sis was really the cause of all their
troubles, near as Uke could tell. Not only
that, but the feeling of impending disaster
which he had shaken off during the fishing trip
was now back in full bloom. I'll have to be on
guard tonight, he resolved. It would help to
know exactly what to be on guard against. Why
didn't Sis come right out and demand to know
what could befall her from that creepy fortune
telling old witch, Mihich Nostrov?

Otto returned with Sis and the three of them
climbed into the truck with Sis in the middle.
Uke enjoyed hanging one leg out the window. The
truck's cab was designed for two people, not
three and a half like Otto always implied whenever the three of them climbed in together. Uke
ignored the jibe, he was having trouble keeping
half of himself on the seat.

"Why we gotta go at night, I want to know,"
Otto made no move to start the vehicle. Sis
glanced at him. Otto stared straight ahead his
hands gripping the steering wheel so tightly

his knuckles were white. Uke shrugged and
reached for the outside door latch in order to
open the door and climbed back out. He had forgotten to kick the tire, much less spin the
crank.

The truck shuddered from the vicious kick he
administered. Next he stormed into position and
bent to give the crank a spin. The engine jumped into life with no argument. He straightened
up from the task and gave Otto a baleful stare
through the dirty windshield, but said nothing.

Sis, however, fixed a cold eye on Otto. "So,
you have been up to some of your devilish
tricks again with Uke?" She slid over on the
seat and stuck her head out the window and
called to Uke, "Get in. Otto, shut off the
engine."

Her orders obeyed, she instructed Otto to
start the engine again. Otto kicked the floor
starter and the engine spluttered momentarily
and then quit. The carburetor normally lacked
enough fuel when idle. Now, after its brief
roar, instead of not enough gasoline, it had
too much.

Defending himself against Sis's invectives,
Otto tried in vain to bring the balky machine
to life.

Uke shrugged and climbed out. He gave the
tire a resounding kick and then stamped in
front of the truck and spun the crank. "Now
start," he snapped. He wished his sister would
keep out of things in the world of men and
mechanical stuff.

The fumes had evaporated during Sis's tirade
against her husband and the balky engine
struggled to life. Otto tried to restrain the
grin creeping over his face. Sis sat with her
mouth open and her eyes wide. All her suspicions evaporated while the event she had witnessed crept into her comprehension.

Not so with Uke, "Isn't it the damndest thing

you ever saw?" he demanded of his sister. He
did not know why Otto was smiling while backing
his first love out of the drive. "We had the
same problem with the old truck." Uke asserted, ignoring his sister's faint objection to
his profanity.

Father Aloysius, waiting patiently for them
at the first station of the cross, had gone
through his beads several times. After
strained, but fairly cordial greetings had been
exchanged, he beckoned them back to the third
station hidden from the view of any passers-by,
where Grandpa Compton held out hope to all
stray pigeons and cats capable of climbing to
the bird house.

Uke felt nothing as he looked upon the statue
but he could detect a shiver of pride in Sis
and contempt for it wreathed Otto's face. The
good padre avoided expressing his opinion, Uke
noted.

The priest waited until they had gathered
around, and paused to gain the most effective
opening for the meeting of the minds. Father
studied the faces of each one of them before
reaching up and placing his hand gently on
Grand Dad's coat sleeve. Shrugging, he began
his sales pitch, hoping against hope these
people would agree, he desperately wanted this
monstrosity out of his garden.

The arch bishop's visit was soon and he did
not want to have to explain this, he had had
enough of a problem trying to explain the
statue to some of the parishioners. He had been
able to keep many more away by soaking the
entrance to the garden with water effectively
discouraging them from seeing the monstrosity.

"We are gathered here today," he began, before remembering this was part of his opening
harangue for next Sunday's sermon. "We are
here," he tried once again, "to get your statue
on its way to its final resting place." He re-

strained from the habit of making the sign of
the cross at this time. "The good Lord willing,
this fair city will turn out in the streets and
cheer when this statue passes by, preceded and
followed by marching bands in one of the most
festive occasions the dear burghers have ever
seen."

"Wot's he talking about?" Uke whispered to
Otto. Sis moved between Otto and the priest as
a precaution. Her face indicated excitement,
but she was perplexed, also.

Not so Otto. "You got an idea up your sleeve,
Reverend, cut out the damn Sunday sermon and
get with it."

"I am eager to be rid of this...this...the
statue just as you are anxious to move it,"
Father continued, choosing to ignore Otto's
outburst. He fished a cigar out from under his
robes, bit off the end and spat it at Otto's
feet. "I do have a plan, but it hinges on two
things. One: the Revolutionary War, and two:
absolute secrecy."

He dug around under his robes for a match
while they moved in closer. Each one drew in a
breath trying to help him light his stogey. He
sucked the flame from the match into his cher-
ished Havana, savoring the fine blue smoke
resulting from his effort. He allowed the aroma
to reach out and wreath itself around all of
them like a cloak, before continuing, satisfied
he now had their undivided attention.

"Are you prepared to swear to secrecy?" he
demanded. "I must have an absolute promise you
will never divulge to anyone who suggested the
plan to you, whether you agree to go through
with it, or not." From somewhere under his
black garment he withdrew a small Bible with
his left hand and then raised his right hand in
about the same position Grandfather Compton was
holding the bird house. He offered it to Sis
first and then to the others.

An involuntary shudder wracked Otto, but he placed his hand on the Bible. The few times he had ever touched one was when he was hauled into court for some nonsensical reason.

Once satisfied with the swearing-in process, Father examined the end of his cigar for a moment to allow them to get their inquisitive juices flowing and to enjoy the cigar smoke all but asphyxiating them.

"Brass bands? The Revolutionary War?" Sis asked, certain she was being put on.

Father Aloysius smiled, "In about three days it will be the Fourth of July. The town will have a parade. Each year it is bigger and longer than the last, and the entire town turns out," he paused allowing them to realize what he was saying. "In this parade will be a float called the Town Founder. A rather late entry, I might add," he grinned and flipped some cigar ashes at Grand Dad's feet.

"Now," he continued, satisfied they were beginning to grasp the enormity of the idea, "now I'll call a contractor who happens to belong to my parish and I'll have him set the statue on a flat bed wagon pulled by a tractor belonging a parishoner farmer who happpens to be a member of the parish. The contractor will then move his crane next to the park so he can pluck this thing off the wagon as it passes."

If I had thought of this, Uke reflected, they'd laugh at me. How come he can suggest a wild scheme and it is accepted by them? He was further upset by Otto's next question. Why couldn't he think of things like this?

"How do we get the float entered in the parade in the first place?" Otto demanded, "All entries had to be in months ago." He had tried to get his string of popcorn wagons entered, but had been refused. He could have made a killing selling popcorn along the parade route. His wagons, the Grand Marshall had decreed, were too commercial. Hell, everything in the parade was commercial.

Father Aloysius was equal to the task of putting Otto's thoughts into words. "My dear man, it so happens the Parade Marshal, Edgar Hughes, happens to be a dear and trusted member of my parish. He sits right up front with his wife, Bernadette, and their seventeen children most Sundays. Edgar will see to it the float gets entered, with no questions asked."

"How come you're so sure?" Otto was suspicious. Edgar sat on his right most Saturday nights at the poker table. He suspected it was Edgar who originally owned the gold stock he couldn't find. The stock entered the pot several times during the evening and it took a number of winning hands before he was stuck with it.

Sis nearly danced in her excitement. "I'm beginning to understand the beauty of the plan."

"Yah," Uke agreed, it had to be be a good plan if she approved.

"The whole thing sounds too smooth." Otto objected. Any projects he had ever been involved in never gained respectability, especially if he had confided them to someone else. He tried to think of some way to ensure the plan. It was a good one, but a priest capable of setting him up with the game warden had to be watched carefully.

"Edgar won't care, I'm sure," the priest assured them.

"But what if Edgar does care?" Sis demanded excited about the scheme. She saw great possibilities for the proposal. It was the one big chance they needed.

With a great show of patience Father tapped the inch long ash from his cigar and grinned, "Edgar has been parade marshal for seven years, nothing would suit him better than to lose the job."

He bowed low toward Sis and with a shuddering glance toward the statue stepped around it and disappeared in the direction of the fourth station. The glow of the cigar and the smell in the darkness was the only indication he had been there at all.

Uke was happy. The Fourth of July would give him a chance to shoot off a few sticks of dynamite and what with all the cherry bombs and fire crackers going off, nobody was ever the wiser. It was the safe way to dispose of Abe's cache. He had been ridding them of it little by little for several years.

CHAPTER TWELVE
THE GOLF COURT

Uke did his best to stay as far from Sis' view as possible. She was a terror, what with the wedding day fast arriving. He could hardly blame Otto either for making himself scarce. Not only the impending wedding had something to do with it, but Sis confirmed Abe was indeed in town, running up bills in Uke's name. What am I supposed to do, Uke wondered?

The last time Abe blew into town and ran up bills, Sis put an ad in the newspaper. Unfortunately for Uke, the paper got the information backwards and it took her months to get Uke's credit restored and besides, other look-a-likes appeared and managed to add to Uke's fast disappearing credit line.

"The wedding has to be on Thursday," Ruth insisted, "the Fourth of July is Friday." Sis helped Ruth make over her mother's wedding dress, and what with other wedding plans, Sis was unfit to be near and close to becoming untied.

"You'd think it was Sis getting married," Uke muttered half a dozen times a day to anyone who would listen.

"Aw," Otto finally informed him, "you're troubled because you ain't got nothing to say about the whole affair except 'I do'."

The wedding could hardly be postponed. They would have to let Ruth in on their secret agreement with the priest. Too bad she was not present at the swearing in ceremony in the church garden. Uke could see no reason for not telling Ruth and Otto thought it would be fine, but Sis was adamant. Ruth must not know, Sis's reason was simple: Ruth was a churchgoer and shouldn't be trusted.

Sis snapped and snarled and threw things whenever either of them came near. Her frustration was intensified with the knowledge that Abraham L. Compton was hanging around town the past several days, but had not put in an appearance at home. It did not occur to any of them to check out the run down boarding house by the river.

It was generally agreed among the family and endorsed by the town: Abe should have been named Benedict Arnold. He was a crook, a thief, and a liar. It would fit him much better than the misleading name he possessed. Black sheep would have hung their heads in shame to have him included in their numbers. Why, if all the things Otto was accused of were true: he'd be a petunia in comparison. Abe, in short, was skunk cabbage.

Otto said it best, "Don't trust him. He should'a been a politician."

"He's still riled over the legal mess with the popcorn wagons caused by the city council," Uke told Ruth, when she wondered why Sis and Otto were so short tempered.

"Seen anything of Abe?" Uke felt he had the right to know.

Ruth admitted that Abe came to see her and tried to pass himself off as Uke. "Sis told me she had told you to stay away until the wedding: so I knew it wasn't you trying to proposition me."

Uke was happy with this dictum: secretly he
favored the status quo, wondering how he had
ever gotten into this marriage mess? Life was
getting too complicated.

"I don't know what the big fuss is about,"
Ruth wondered. In all these years Uke had done
no more than hold her hand once in a while.

Uke worried about the prospect of having a
wife and responsibilities, but had no one to
confide this to, instead he listened to Sis and
Otto arguing. The three of them were trapped in
the kitchen, but because of Sis's irritable
mood, Otto refused to buy a new suit for the
wedding. He would not go down and look over the
Salvation Army's stock of used ones, either.

"My bright blue one with orange pin stripes
will do." He had purchased it second hand eight
years ago when Aunt Matilda Coonwright was
thoughtless enough to die when he was getting
ready to go fishing. He insisted it was the
prettiest suit he had ever seen and it would be
the one he would be laid out in, and if it was
good enough for that: it was good enough for
Uke's wedding, in this he was adamant. Uke
agreed. Sis threw up her hands in distress and
stormed from the kitchen.

Uke planned to wear his old suit since he had
purchased it for his swearing in ceremony four
years ago. He was surprised to discover a neat-
ly wrapped bundle delivered to the door. In it
was a new suit tailored to fit. It was almost
as if he had modeled it himself. A note peeking
out of the breast pocket was signed 'from a
life long friend'. The suit and the note
mystified him, but he gratefully accepted the
bright green present.

He laid the suit out on the bed and then recalled that Otto was due in court soon. He eyed
his fishing tackle longingly, regretting not
being able to go fishing down to the river. He
hadn't been able to find Otto and he was for-

bidden to see Ruth and Sis was horrible. Time hung heavily on him.

Otto claimed business was booming since word had gotten around he would have to get his wagons off the streets. The city had done him a big favor with their threats. The publicity was all free. He intended to continue to ignore their threats.

Uke had checked on Otto's claim in anticipation of collecting interest on his half share in the venture, he could use the money. People who had never given the wagons a second glance were buying popcorn when they found out they might not get it any longer. Strange, the minute they can't get it, they want it, he reflected. It was great that Otto's interest had been rekindled in the wagons. So far he had not received one red cent from Otto on his investment, although he had continued to make "up payments."

Uke couldn't blame him for flatly refusing to pay for a salt permit. What Uke didn't know was that Otto planned to get some good advertising by pinning a chunk of paper on the back of Uke's wedding suit. Everyone in church would be aware of his fine popcorn when Uke strolled down the aisle with his bride.

The city had thoughtfully written into the law a note stating "while a permit was required to salt popcorn on the streets, vendors would be denied salt permits." In effect, anyone eating popcorn had to buy a permit. Uke saw the salt shakers Otto had placed on the ledge outside the wagons. If the popcorn eaters wanted salt they would be breaking the law, not him. He also noticed the price of a bag had risen from a nickel to ten cents and guessed Otto was losing a lot of salt shakers.

The city fathers cried long and loud that Otto was not following the spirit of the law. Otto wrote to the newspaper and told them he

would take the salt shakers away. He did not
bother to say why. He added a penny to the
price of the corn and rented the salt shakers
to the customers. By handing the shakers out
the windows he didn't feel responsible for the
use to which they were put. Otto supplied each
popcorn wagon vendor with a photo of all the
city dignitaries. Salt shakers were denied to
anyone with any civic "responsibilities."

Uke couldn't know that having satisfied
himself there was nothing more to be done
around the statue, Otto decided to saunter down
Mainstreet. After a few blocks he became aware
people were noticing him. Some were people he
knew, some were people he didn't think he knew,
and some he was certain he didn't know. Louie
Baumblatt stopped whittling to stare pensively
at him, did Otto let the feeling come to the
surface. Louie was nearly blind.

Higgie, washing windows at Stockwell's Drug
store nearby, listened in on the conversation.

"Howdy, Louie," Otto kicked the shavings
absently.

"Yep."

"Whittling?" Otto dug his hand into his
pocket.

"Yep."

"Seen Uke?" Otto fished out some change and
returned all but a silver dollar to his pocket,
making noise so Louie would know he was getting
paid for the information.

"Yep."

"Where?"

"Over there," Louie indicated the pawn shop
across the street. He began to whittle again,
indicating the interview was complete.

Otto flipped the silver dollar noisily into
the convenient tin cup and waited until Louie
turned back to his whittling before quietly
filching it from the cup.

Louie shook the empty cup. "Bastard," he

whispered as Otto drifted away.

Crossing the street, Otto hardly paused to examine the three brass balls hanging precariously over the door. Himie Nostrov sensed he had a visitor almost before he heard the door open. Himie was following in the footsteps of his older brother, Alby.

The dank mildew odor was overwhelming. Otto paused to become accustomed to the darkness.

The usual wild variety of items lined the shelves and hung from the walls. He noted a silver inlaid cribbage board. He'd like to have if he knew how to play the game.

Himie was perched on a stool behind a glass case with revolvers, their hammers removed. There was no other glass display case in the shop. He was a careful operator. No one could buy a gun, load it and turn it on him, although he probably deserved it. Otto guessed the best revolver was conveniently under the counter within easy reach.

Nostrov slid from his perch and hurried forward peering over his latest pair of glasses for a better view of his customer.

"May I help you?" He tried not to show concern. His brother, Alby, in Middletown, had told him Otto's wife had been over to see him recently. Himie wondered what his fool wife, Mihich, had put into her head with the fortune telling nonsense. It was getting so his wife was bringing in more money than his pawn shop.

"What was Uke, the sheriff, doing in here?" Otto demanded to know. He had never been in the shop before. He did remember a pawn ticket in one poker pot, but he had lost it with the next hand.

"Uke? Sheriff? I run an honest, reputable business," Himie cried. "Been no sheriff in here." He picked up a nickel plated watch fob and nervously laid it on the counter near Otto. "Real sterling silver," he nodded toward it.

Otto picked it up, but was unimpressed with the quality. He put it to his mouth and could taste no silver in it as he bit into it.

"Liar," he tossed it back on the counter, making a mental note to remember the fob if it ever appeared in a poker pot. "Big guy, with a .38 hung on his hip," Otto's voice took on a menacing quality.

"Yah, big fella, no gun." He dug under the counter and fished out an assortment of items. "Pawned this stuff. Had receipts for all of it."

Examining the articles, Otto became aware most of the things were not the property of Uke. A jade figurine, a pearl tie pin, a ster-gentleman---or a crook.

No, Uke certainly hadn't swapped the goods. By the way he hovered over the stuff, some of the items must have had more than passing value. As he left the shop, Otto smiled when he saw Himie biting the watch fob to test its silver content.

Higgie paused with his window washing and called out to Otto from across the street, "You gonna make that court appearance?" What he really wondered was why Otto and Sis Granley were both interested in pawn shops.

Otto nodded, grateful for the reminder. He cut across the square and made his way up the steps of the courthouse. More than the normal number of people decorated the walls and benches in the dimly lit building. The odor in the courthouse was not too different from what he had to tolerate in Nostrov's place.

He had had a notion to tell Nostrov to shut his wife up, but he decided some nonsense in Sis's head wouldn't hurt anything. Besides, it was her money she was spending and once he had the statue in place there would be plenty of money and he'd get his share, you could take that fact to the bank.

"Hear ye, hear ye," the bailiff intoned, "this court will come to order, the Right Honorable Judge Harold Bower presiding."

Judge Bower swept in like a black witch who had lost her hat and broom. He surveyed the scene with obvious distaste before plumping down behind the bench. Wiping his fat, round face with a silk embroidered handkerchief, he advised, "I like to mete out justice swiftly and with expediency." He rapped for order subduing a murmur and glanced at his watch. He should have added "and play golf every afternoon."

Otto noticed the prosecuting attorney, a slight man with shifty eyes, who stepped forward to present his case against Otto. He glanced at his own attorney: he too had shifty eyes. Shaken by this observation, Otto turned to the judge and discovered his beady eyes darting around the courtroom. Probably looking for someone to hang a contempt charge on, he guessed. This was always good for twenty-five dollars and costs.

"Costs" were something maybe a lawyer could figure out. Why costs? Why did it cost anything to take a man's money away from him? The judge's golfing partners had the answer to this one. The judge paid them off at the end of the game and they were not going to tell anyone why there were "costs".

Pink Dardley, who had dropped a load of two-by-fours on Main Street when his horse bolted, also dropped fifteen and "costs" amounting to twenty bucks. The judge had played poorly the day before.

Stud Wilkens, ten and costs, for failing to yield the right of way to a freight train. He lost one arm and couldn't reach his wallet fast enough and wound up with a contempt of court. This added another twenty and costs. But then, it was also because it had rained for two days and the judge was in ill humor. The same string of empty freight cars Nick Jansti had lost his battle with was at the same train crossing.

Uke had cautioned Otto about 'costs' when he discovered Otto would end up in Judge Bower's court. The district attorney refused to try anymore cases in this court and always sent his assistant in case a contempt and "costs" was tossed around, it would land on his assistant, instead of him.

In a secret agreement beforehand in chambers, all the charges against Otto were dropped except the one for transporting unlicensed materials through the streets without a permit. After five minutes of hard thinking Otto came to the conclusion it meant the statue.

It was a moral victory for Otto because the rest of the charges for some unknown reason had been dropped. Otto's lawyer, Will Thatcher, whose law career blossomed after he happened upon a beach party of birthday suit swimmers, knew the reasons. The district attorney had since joined a nudist club two states away in order to keep his reputation clothed in respectability.

Later, Otto told Uke he was surprised to find Father Aloysius in court. The old gent winked and patted him on the shoulder before taking a seat directly behind the defendant. Otto admitted this friendly gesture put him immediately on guard, no one was ever nice to him. The judge hesitated in the pounding of his gavel to note this bit of familiarity. But if the afternoon golf match were to get under way as scheduled at three o'clock, this business at hand must be dispensed quickly. Judge Bower hammered the courtroom quiet.

The assistant District Attorney, Van Gruder, stood up and glared with disgust at Otto while tossing a couple of light jabs at his character. He missed completely with a left hook at

the all night poker sessions. Poker was a gentleman's game and took a good deal of character
and the Right Honorable Judge Bower considered
himself a scholar of the game. In fact, he was
often able to recoup some of his golf losses in
the locker room after a bad round. The judge
frowned heavily at the eager young attorney.

Seeing the frown, Van Gruder changed tactics
and threw a right cross below the belt...a
smirking reference to Grandpa Compton's past.
Uke entered the courtroom with Sis hanging on
his arm and this brought the hair up on the
back of her neck. A restraining hand from Uke
kept her from charging the animal.

Now it was their turn. Uke relaxed and
decided court was better than silent movies.
Will Thatcher, fresh from law school and nude
snooping, stood up and began to shuffle papers
in a deliberate attempt to ignore his
surroundings.

"Your Honor," he paused and noisely cleared
his throat, "I didn't expect my esteemed col-
league to present both sides of the case, but
he has done a remarkable job. His arguments,"
he paused for effect and tucked a thumb in his
vest and jabbed an accusing finger at his adversary before delivering what he hoped to be
the knockout punch, "his arguments should convince each of us the defendant is guilty of
nothing more than raising the ire of the city
council and those who make a mockery of human
rights and civil liberty to justify their own
inadequacies and ring down the curtain of justice upon the heads of the innocent who have
been damned throughout the ages under the
supposition of self government so long as it
satisfies the powers to..."

He paused trying to remember the next lines
of his carefully memorized speech. Uke spell
bound by the oratory, was fully aware of what
the attorney was saying had nothing to do with

the subject at hand. Come to think of it, not
once during the entire proceedings had anyone
said anything about whether they could or could
not haul Sis's statue down the main drag.

"So long as it satisfies the heads of power
from..." Thatcher began again.

Judge Bower's head nodded and the gavel slipped from hand and crashed to the bench top
bringing him up with a start. "Twenty-five
dollars and costs," he shouted pointing his
finger at the one moving thing in the court
room, Otto's attorney, Mr. Will Thatcher. The
time spent chasing two states away to get some
leverage on the D.A. would have to be reinvest-
ed at a later date.

"Judgement for the defendant, case dismissed," the crusty old judge glanced at his watch.
He had no idea he had snoozed that long, he had
twenty minutes to get to the golf course.

Thatcher sat down hard. He had indeed won his
first case. Otto had agreed to pay him twenty
dollars and it was costing him at least twenty-
five. "The quality of mercy is not strained,"
he muttered to himself, "it's diluted."

Uke tried to catch Otto who headed for the
door without thanking his attorney. Mr.Thatcher
was liable to hand anyone a bill for asking the
time of day. Uke had brought the truck downtown, but prepared to get chewed out knowing
Otto wouldn't appreciate his helping himself to
it. If Otto didn't like it: well, tough.

Otto said nothing and apparently had bigger
things to worry about. Now that he was free his
missing gold stock certificate was upper most
in his mind. Sis and Uke silently slipped into
the cab of the truck. Otto drove out to the
ball park and collected the proceeds from the
popcorn wagon out there. Six dollars and
seventy-two cents. He never understood where
the odd pennies came from since the minimum
charge was a nickel. (Sales tax, a form of

legal theft, had not as yet been invented.)

Next he stopped and emptied the till on wagon number two at the children's park. Sixty cents. Uke guessed they would be moving this one. At wagon number three, he gave Uke a dollar and tried to purchase back his half interest in the wrecked wagon. It was fair, he told Uke, since he blamed Uke for wrecking it. A sharp jab in the ribs from Sis and he decided to take up the issue later when she wasn't around.

Sis was impatient to get on home. She had a way of getting Otto to move without any arguments. She had also noted Uke did not kick the tire or for that matter crank the truck. She'd take that up later with Otto, also.

"Today is divvy day," She announced pulling a pencil and note book from her pocketbook and busily began making notations while they bounced along. Each was entitled to a portion after she subtracted their room and board and food bill. Uke took the ten spot she handed him and stared at it. Good thing I'm sheriff, I'd starve if I had to rely on Grandpa Compton. The old duck was leaving less and less each time.

"Divvy Day" happened at unexpected moments. Sometimes they were once a month, then again, once a week. They seemed to occur whenever Sis felt she might be losing her grip on the family. Both Uke and Otto had learned to maneuver toward a "Divvy Day."

The money mysteriously appeared out of Sis's hand bag, never in any great amount, but always better than nothing. It was dispensed due to Grandpa's heroic efforts in years past. Uke never expressed the thought to Sis that there would have been more if Grandpa hadn't admired other people's horses, other men's wives and cheap whiskey.

A number of times he saw Otto rummaging through Sis's purse, and guessed he never found so much as an Indian head penny. Not one red cent. She included Abe when dispensing the money, but where she hid his share, neither had any idea.

"Do you want me to hold yours until tomorrow, so you'll have something?" she asked Otto. She had been asking him the same question for years.

"No, I'll take it now," Otto growled, it was his same answer for years.

"Careful," Sis laughed, "how you talk to me, or I'll give you costs." Maybe it would soften him up, he was concerned about something, but what? The wedding and the statue were coming to fruition, so it couldn't be the problem. She also knew he would never tell her what it was. Possibly the gold stock?

Uke wondered what Otto was smiling about. They both knew she was in a hurry to get home. The smile on Otto's face turned into a broad grin, he was pleased to hear his wife laugh. He was honest enough to know he never gave her much to smile about.

Uke continued to study his divvy.

Meanwhile, Judge Bower rushed up to the first tee and found his partners waiting impatiently.

"What kept you?" Father Aloysius asked. If he had to rely on his parishioners for pin money he wouldn't be able to afford to play golf. Judge Bower had deep civic pockets.

CHAPTER THIRTEEN
THE BIG DAY

The wedding day dawned clear and promised to be another warm one. The house on Devil's Lane bustled with activity shortly after the sun painted the tops of the Elm trees a fiery gold. Uke parted the bedroom curtain and watched thoughtfully as Otto prepared to back the Durant from the shed. He saw him pick two eggs from the front seat and toss them into the weeds before brushing a gaggle of hen feathers from the upholstery.

Uke couldn't remember when the car had last been driven. Collecting eggs was Sis's chore, but she had been busy the past few days getting ready for the wedding. He hated to think he might be served rotten eggs for breakfast. He watched as Otto discovered two more eggs and put them on Sis's balancing scales used to measure canning ingredients. The scales were near the open door by the case of dynamite.

Otto's favorite transportation was the truck so he had to be getting the car ready for the wedding, Uke surmised. Never could tell when he might run onto something and you couldn't haul much in a car, Otto always insisted. He could see from his view that the tires on the Durant were soft and it was probably low on gasoline.

Sis rode in it when she wanted to put on the dog...not too many people had cars. He watched Otto back out of the shed and ease the Durant out onto Devil's Lane, probably headed for Howell's Filling Station, Grocery & Hardware Emporium. Otto liked to see old man Howell hurry out to the curb to fill a gasoline tank while trying to wipe raw meat from his hands.

He let the curtain fall back in place as the Durant stirred up dust. He was worried about the upcoming events. Marriage has to be all right, it seems all right for Sis and Otto. I know a lot of other married people. I never thought of it this way before: these people seem to have been together all their lives like marriage was a part of them. But now I'm faced with it. He wished desperately for someone to listen to him. He studied the new, green suit hanging on the door knob, shrugged and slipped into his fishing clothes.

His stomach didn't feel right, and it was not hunger. It could not have been the third piece of apple pie last night, his stomach had never worried about pie before. Threading his way down the narrow, steep, staircase, he had the strange feeling he should hurry. The urge to run over-whelmed him. Run anywhere, except that his feet were encased in lead.

He came to a frightening conclusion: he had to admit to himself he was scared, but of what? I'm not afraid of nobody. I can beat up anybody in town and in the county including Otto if I have to. Sometimes Sis scares me, but Ruth doesn't scare me. Marriage?

That must be it! But why should it? I'm big and strong and she is tiny and Sis takes good care of me, and Otto looks out for me, I don't have to be scared, but will it all be the same once I'm harnessed? It's the future I'm afraid of.

The kitchen was empty as he pushed open the

creaking stair door. Frustrated, he trowled some peanut butter on a slice of bread and decorated it with a liberal thickness of salami before sitting down. "Not much of a breakfast," he groused, as Sis appeared.

Sis nodded a good morning, "I don't have time for any nonsense this morning." She hurried toward the screen door.

He took one bite from his bread and stared at it thoughtfully. Since when are ham and eggs and toast and coffee nonsense?

"Uke?" Sis turned and shouted through the screen.

He jumped up nervously and a piece of salami slid to the floor.

"Uke, get out and feed the chickens. I don't have time."

He kicked the piece of salami under the stove. He didn't much care for it anyway, and besides, Otto always referred to cold cuts as "floor sweepings."

"And gather up the eggs," her voice shrill and demanding, "and don't forget to check the front seat of the car, they've been taking to laying them there lately."

He didn't bother to tell her that Otto had taken care of the eggs and the car. He grabbed his hat from the kitchen wall peg and stalked from the house. Cripes, you'd think she was the one getting married.

He located the sack of crushed corn and gravel next to the box of dynamite in the shed, dumped some in an empty, tipped over pail on the floor and headed for the henhouse. With a wild sweep of the bucket he sprayed the corn and grit through the fencing into the chicken yard and half-heartedly began to look for eggs. This was a woman's job, wedding or no. Was she so loose in the head that she didn't hear Otto take the Durant?

One hen had the good sense to put her eggs in

a nest. One had laid in a discarded torn shoe box, another had dropped hers on a rock and smashed it. Disgusted, he searched and found more in the darkest recess of the old shed and under things he thought it would not be poss- ible for a hen to get under, like the over turned wash tub and under the cover from an old ice chest.

He had two dozen eggs in the feed pail when he remembered the two eggs Otto had placed in the pans of the balancing scales.

The scales delicately balancing each other looked too much like the slim graceful figure down at the county courthouse holding the scales of justice. She had on a blindfold.

"Hah, justice is blind all right, real blind."

He walked to the door of the shed and care- fully selected the largest egg in the lot and threw it at the cluster of hens milling around the scattered feed by the hen house door. The egg shattered against the chicken wire and sprayed through the fence scattering the squawking beasts.

He studied the frenzied creatures for a moment before striding over to the fence. Raising the feed pan over the top most wire he tipped it until the eggs rolled out. If Sis wants her eggs so bad, she can scrape 'em off the ground, he told himself.

"Damn," he growled disgustly and threw the pan at old Fred, the Plymouth Rock rooster, preparing to challenge him. He pulled downward on the soft chicken wire fencing to allow the rooster to flutter over it. Two hens hurried to join the rooster. Uke felt better.

He heard the Durant returning and stepped behind the corner of the shed. Otto wheeled the car into the drive and parked it alongside the truck. He kept out of sight. Right now he wanted no company.

Otto was studying what appeared to be a dent on the right front fender of the automobile. He smiled as he watched him try to rub some dirt over the scar. Otto hurriedly quit as Sis stuck her head out the door.

"Where is Uke?" she snapped.

Otto shook his head and shrugged while maneuvering in front of the scar on the fender.

Uke knew that even if Otto had seen him, he would never tell her. The wedding was six hours away and she acted like it was six minutes away. What in hell comes over a woman the minute her daily routine is changed?

Otto strolled through the kitchen door ignoring Sis's glare, but not before he stopped to study the gladioluses. He had no interest in flowers, but he had to for ever show her she couldn't stampede him. "Uke is probably eating, sleeping or getting ready to do one or the other," he advised, brushing past her. She was in her usual no nonsense mood.

"Where can that man be?" she wondered, clutching the dish rag in one hand and her wedding dress in the other. "I haven't seen him since he went out to feed the chickens hours ago. Please locate him," she called loud enough that Uke could hear her.

Hours ago probably meant at least ten minutes, "Plymouth Rock rooster probably chased him," Otto laughed a little too loud, "or he shot himself in the foot trying to shoot the rooster." He dodged back out the door before she could reply. The logical place to start looking would be at the hen house. He would sooner do that right now than listen to her hysterics.

Uke peeked around the shed to see Otto studying the overturned feed pail in the corner of the chicken yard and the freshly smashed eggs drying out in the feed. He heard him laugh.

"Uke's showing all the symptoms of a pros-

pective husband about to be brutalized by
marriage vows," he called to Sis.

Uke could hear the hens, clucking and kicking
as they tried to free their feet from the
sticky, yellow, egg yolks. Otto kept prowling
around and he heard him out checking the shed.

"Better have Uke git rida'that case of dynamite, if'n he don't use it all up on the
fourth. Maybe I kin take it down to the river
and set the whole thing off and then run like
hell, who could prove it was me?"

Uke wondered if he always talked to himself
that much?

To Otto it was obvious that for the first
time in his life Uke faced a problem not
concerning food or sleep. He had to think about
what Uke might decide to do. He fished out his
cigarette papers and rolled a smoke before
sitting down on the case of dynamite to ponder
the problem. Lighting it, he watched the blue
smoke curl upward. What would Uke do when faced
with an unknown concerning his future? An
enigma to be resolved by sampling the fruit?
That's it! Uke would run. Plain and simple, he
would run away.

He couldn't run to Sis who had created the
problem. Nor could he go to Ruth, who repre-
sented the enigma. Where then, would he go? Not
to me, certainly. Not to the sheriff's office.
He was enough of a politician not to get caught
in public with a worried look on his face. Then
where ?

Otto returned to the house and looked behind
the closet door on a hunch. Uke's fish pole was
there, so he didn't go fishing. Thoughtfully
closing the door, his face brightened. Uke
didn't go fishing, but he went down to the
river. That's it! More than once he had found
him there.

Uke understood the currents, the tides, the
wind rippling over the water, the angry thrash-

ing of the spring floods, the bleak, wind swept
ice buckling when it expanded from the cold as
it formed in the dead of winter and the break
up and floating ice floes in the spring thaw.

Most of all, Uke understood the pleasure of
stretching out in the sun on a warm day with
bees buzzing around in search of nectar and the
birds searching for bees. In mid-summer, the
river was low and hiding places abounded, but
where ?

Right now the river water was warm and
languid swirls of foam floated about while the
water spiders skated giddily from willow clump
to willow clump. He recalled Uke had a favorite
spot where he and his twin, Abe, used to spend
most of the summer afternoons when they were
children. That had to be it.

The place was a big bend in the river. Over
the years water could not make the turn and
gushed into a low spot, creating an ideal en-
vironment for clumps of willows to proliferate.
It was by far the largest accumulation anywhere
around. The wetness attracted frogs and snakes.
Although they were only grass snakes, the frogs
took care of that problem.

He recalled how upset young Uke was when he
had brought home a gunny sack full of frogs and
Sis had prepared a feast. One of Otto's favorite meals. After the third belch from Uke, he
could restrain himself no longer and told Uke
it was his frogs he had eaten. It was the only
time Uke had ever cried.

From his hiding place near the remains of the
shattered popcorn wagon, Uke watched him climb
into the truck, but had no idea he was headed
for the river. He watched Sis peeking through
the curtain and more than likely wondering
where Otto thought he'd find him.

Like his sister, Uke suddenly became aware
that the tire did not need kicking nor did the
truck need cranking as Otto brought it to life

144

without ever leaving the cab. I'll bet she's
going to nail his hide about that once the
wedding is behind them. He could always tell
when she was getting disturbed about Otto
making a fool out of Uke. The muscles of her
jaw worked hard when she was angry.

Uke could see through the plum trees as the
truck headed down the road toward town. Otto
must be going to see if a poker game is in
progress, he guessed. He ought to drive past
the church and check on the statue. After all,
he reasoned, the city is looking for the
statue, not me. He also knew Otto wouldn't care
much if he missed the wedding or not.

CHAPTER FOURTEEN
THE BIG MEETING

Keeping the shed between himself and the window, Uke hurried toward the river and slid down the bank picking his way through the willows. Allowing his mind to wander from the wedding to the statue, to Sis, and back to the wedding.

His path avoided the potholes filled with rancid water and miniature, oily rainbows. He couldn't help but feel this place had changed. Yet it was no different than he could ever recall. It has to be me. I have a decision to make and I can't make it. But I have to make it.

A freshly broken twig brought him back to the present. Someone had been here recently, maybe they were still around? He moved slowly, and quietly, the senses developed in childhood playing cowboys and Indians were at once alerted.

"Hello, Uke, I've been kind of expecting you."

Uke froze with the willow clump half parted. Before him stretched out in his favorite spot lay a figure mirrored in his own likeness and it sounded almost like he was looking and listening to himself.

Abe raised up on one arm and waved Uke into
the willow clump with a friendly grin. Except
for the tailored expensive clothes, he had
changed little since Uke had last seen him.

"Abe, Abraham!" Uke shouted with mixed
emotions.

"Come on in," Abe invited, moving slightly to
make room. "I expected you sooner."

"How'd you know I was coming?" Uke squatted
down. "I didn't know myself until about twenty
minutes ago." This perhaps wasn't exactly the
truth, but caution was the better part of valor
when dealing with Abraham. And besides, Abe
didn't need to know I made my own breakfast and
had to find eggs and feed the chickens like
maybe I'm a woman.

"You was always slow," Abe laughed, slapping
Uke on the knee.

"What you doing here? And why didn't you come
up to the house? And why'd you go to see Ruth?
And what did you go to the pawn shop for?" Uke
demanded, ignoring Abe's jibe. His curiosity
was genuine.

Abe waved his hand trying to push the questions back where they came from. "I'll answer,
but first, let me tell you in my own fashion
without hurrying." He dug out his pocket watch
and flipped the fob several times before looking at the time. He was proud of the time
piece, but more so of the fob. It had an eagle
embossed on the front of it.

Uke sat down and rested his back against a
burned out cottonwood, the only one in the
willows. A train whistled at McNamara's cross-
ings. Probably the ten-thirty commuter.

"Did ya' get the wedding suit?"

"You sent it?"

"I wanted to do something nice for you, Uke,"
he said softly. "Needed to scratch up some
change to do it, so I pawned some real precious
relics in order to outfit you." He didn't

bother to tell him he had by accident discovered Otto's gold mining stock in the process.
That dumb pawn broker let it slip that Sis had
brought it in. He confided in Abe because Alby
thought he was cozying up to Uke, the sheriff.

"You never did nothing nice before," Uke
argued. He sensed needing to be on his guard.

"Did so. I told you Ruth was too good for me
and you could have her," Abe objected, "course
if you want to change yer mind' maybe got
chicken and turned coward at the last minute,
why, well, maybe, I'd take her off yer hands
for a few days."

"I came down to think things over," Uke
ignored the implications of Abe's thoughts.

Abe continued on, Uke wasn't getting the
picture. "She's a wonderful girl." He gazed
over at the far bank of the river through the
willows, his eyes a watery distant blue. It
would serve the snot-nosed broad right if he
bedded her while she thought it was Uke.

Uke had no idea what he was thinking, but was
aware Abe had become excited.

For his part, Abe was certain he could best
Otto, upset Sis, enjoy Uke's discomfort and
settle a score with Ruth for preferring Uke to
him.

Uke finally realized what Abe was intimat-
ing. "You can't have her back." He tried to
sound firm.

"No, I don't want her back," Abe continued.
He wanted her, but certainly not on a permanent
basis. "Maybe I could do you one last favor before I walk out of yer life forever, never to
return?" He wiped his eyes with a knuckle and
peeked at Uke.

"What's that?" Uke glared, suspicion mounting
once more.

"If yer going to be that way, I won't tell
you." Abe found a blade of grass and pulled it
slowly out of the ground and began to chew on

it looking out over the river drifting past.

Uke studied him. The words of warning rang in his ears, both Sis and Otto had told him Abe was no good, but curiosity prayed upon him. It was because Abe had returned he had been talked into proposing. The fear that dragged him down to the willows was either because of Sis or Abe, he couldn't be certain which. Now Abe wanted something, some one last thing. When Abe had ever offered anything to him he fully expected something in return.

"What brought you back to town?" Uke asked. He secretly congratulated himself in his effort to change the subject and to learn why Abe had returned.

"You," Abe replied, watching a water spider skate behind a rock and then skitter back out again making a miniature wake on the tiny placid pool.

"Me?" Uke watched the spider dart back behind the stone. A frog appeared from nowhere and its tongue flicked out but missed the spider.

"Yep, you," For the first time Abe looked directly at Uke. "You never were the brightest guy around town and I figured you would be thinking of settling down and would need some advice and help." The frog moved closer to the rock and patiently waited for the water spider, confident it would reappear.

"Advice and help got me into the spot I'm in right now," Uke snorted. He bit on his lower lip. "Besides, if you had stayed away, I wouldn't be getting married." Not that Ruth wasn't all right, but he was comfortable with things the way they were. The frog moved slightly anticipating the next try.

"Tell you what I'm going to do," Abe raised up on one arm and searched for a new blade of grass to chew on, "I'm going to fix all yer problems and troubles."

"How?" Uke demanded. He did not want to ask,

but he was intrigued. He knew his brother well
enough to know he didn't want to know Abe's
solution. This was the payoff, whatever Abe
wanted, Uke had given him the opportunity. He
knew one thing: he had no need for more
troubles in the form of suggestions or ideas.

Zap! Slurp! Woosh! The water spider disappeared and the frog slipped silently under
the water and swam toward its private sunning
rock.

* * *

Otto discovered the statue sitting on a
large, flat bed trailer hidden among the lilac
bushes where the priest had said it would be.
He tugged at the tarpaulin covering the statue
and wriggled underneath, to make certain it was
the statue and not some prank the priest may
have decided to play on them. The priest had
played enough games with him and he was not
about to take any more chances.

Satisfied Grandpa was all right, he walked
back to his truck and climbed in. It was about
a ten minute drive to the river so he did not
hurry to make up for the lost time, although
the wedding was now about an hour away. No need
to hurry, there wouldn't be any wedding without
a groom. He wondered where and how his gold
stock had disappeared. He believed it might be
worth a great deal of money.

* * *

"You know," Abe stretched out with one leg
draped over a willow clump, "the reason I left
home was on account of Sis spending all of our
inheritance fortune on that statue. It was a
mistake for me not to have fought it out with
her in order to protect you."

"Naw, she has plenty left an' all you had to
do was to stay home and you'd get yer share
after the statue was finished... I think." He
had no sympathy for Abe, he left home with all
the money he was paid when his chicken job blew

up in his face, but mostly because he also had
no taste for Sis's fury.

"I'm back now an she hasn't given me my
share," Abe snorted, not bothering to tell Uke
he had not been near the house or Sis "An you
know you won't get your share, either. Sis ever
tell you about the stipulation in the will
which says anyone gets married they won't
collect? The proceeds then go for pigeon food."
He added, giving his argument a nice touch.

"That so?" Uke sat up in interest. "She got
married."

"Right, and paid herself fifty a week to make
that damn statue and its taken her near to ten
years to build it."

"That isn't true," Uke stood up indignant,
brushed himself off and rasped, "Sis wouldn't
do a thing like that."

Abe spit the blade of grass from between his
lips and watched it flutter down into the water
before replying. "Did you ever know that bum,
Otto, to do an ounce of work? Does Sis work any
place? Where do you suppose they get their
money?"

Uke slumped slowly down again. True, Otto
really didn't work at any of his popcorn wagons
and he did enjoy poker which really couldn't be
considered work...he enjoyed it too much.

The frog slipped off its rock and surfaced
again and looked around. They both watched the
frog for a few moments before Abe pressed on.

"Here's my plan, its simple," Abe continued.
"We get rid of the statue and I marry Ruth and
then we get a good shyster lawyer to take
what's left away from Sis. It's ours!"

Uke was stunned. So this was what it was all
about. "Get rid of the statue, a shyster
lawyer, and you marry Ruth?" He was dumb
founded. The easiest part to swallow was the
shyster bit. There were plenty of them around.
When a court case came up where he was in-

volved, there were two lawyers, not counting
the judge. Three lawyers ought to be enough to
scare the living hell out of anybody, Otto had
always insisted.

"Sure, we blow up the statue tonight, I marry
her in about an hour and we hire a lawyer right
after the wedding." He hoped Uke would not
realize he had prowled around the homestead and
had discovered the case of dynamite left over
from his chicken gut and outhouse business.

Uke fell silent and tried to digest Abe's
plan. He had no money for a lawyer and he
doubted if Abe would pay for one if he did he
have the money. The only thing around here Abe
owned was the case of dynamite left over from
when he blew up the chicken gut pile and then
hurried over to do old man Cooper's outhouse.
Old man Cooper, people guessed, was in the
outhouse at the time since he hadn't been seen
since.

It would be a way out for Uke, except Ruth
was someone special and if Abe wanted her, then
she must be all right to have around. No, the
wedding would have to stand. GOOD GRIEF! The
wedding!

Uke jumped to his feet, "I gotta go, Sis will
kill me, I'll see you later, can't be late."
He crashed off through the willows toward the
river bank hurrying toward his date with
destiny. Abe thoughtfully chewed on another
grass stem until he could no longer hear the
noise.

The frog peeked out from behind a clump of
weeds. The water spiders had all disappeared.
The frog climbed back on a rock to sun itself.

Uke did not hear Otto pushing his way through
the dense undergrowth. He stepped into Uke's
recently vacated place.

"What's the matter, boy, you got cold feet on
your wedding day?" Otto grinned at Abe. "Say,
who just went tearing up the river bank, Abe?"

Abe studied Otto for a moment."That was my good-for-nothing brother," he replied, imitating Uke almost perfectly.

"Abe?"

"Yeh," Abe responded, and then on an impulse added, "he wanted me to switch places with him at the wedding."

"That louse," Otto growled, this was even more than he could tolerate. "Let's go, boy, you are getting married in a half hour, we got no time to lose." If nothing else, he could enjoy watching Uke squirm at the wedding.

Abe jumped to his feet. He had not expected any help from this source. He eagerly followed Otto through the willows. If I have Otto fooled, and I know I can confuse Uke, all I have to do is back Sis into a corner. It won't be too hard to do, Abe decided, anticipating the pleasure of fooling Ruth in the bargain.

Otto called over his shoulder, "You go straight on home and get ready and I"ll bring the truck around by way of the bridge." The route was a circuitous one and in his laziness, Otto had chosen to drive as close as he could to the river, rather than walk a short way. "You ought to be ready by the time I get there."

Abe calculated his timing. Uke should be clear of the house by the time I arrive and most certainly by the time Otto arrives. He had to walk about four blocks, while Otto had to drive almost three miles, so Otto would be no problem. If he knew Sis, she'd be tearing her hair and pushing on Uke to get him moving. By the time I show up at the house, everyone will be gone. He smiled, if he had planned it, it could not have been any better.

* * *

Uke hurried into the house and discovered Sis had his old blue serge suit laid out for him. Instead of arguing or trying to explain away

the mysterious new suit, he decided to wear the
old one.

"Where in the world did you go?" She combed
his hair the best she could and tied his shoes
and straightened his tie all the while scolding
him for disappearing.

He didn't answer.

"Go up and get a white handkerchief," she
craned her neck to see if she could see Otto
coming down the road. She blamed herself inwardly for ever sending Otto to find Uke. Now
Otto was missing. "You'll have to drive me to
church and Otto will have to use his truck,"
she screeched, "providing he hasn't been side-
tracked by a poker game someplace and forgotten
all about the wedding. Men!"

Sis held the keys out to Uke when he came
down the stairs stuffing his shirt into his
pants.

"Otto don't let me drive the Durant," Uke
backed away holding his hands behind him. He
dearly wanted to drive it, to see if he could.
The gear shift was entirely different than the
truck's and something of a mystery to him. He
also had decided not to tell Sis about his
meeting with Abe, at least until he could
figure out who was on his side and who wasn't.

"It's my car and I'll decide who drives it,"
Sis asserted, propelling him out the screen
door.

Uke took the keys and licked his lips. I will
remember today for a long time, he thought, I
get to drive the Durant!

* * *

Abe opened the screen door and peered with
uncertainty into the kitchen and decided the
house was empty. He proceeded through the room
dragging his hand over the table and chairs
reminiscing, it had been a long time since he
had been here. He shrugged thoughtfully before
pushing the memories from his mind. Climbing

the narrow stairs he wished things had turned
out differently for him.

Opening the door to the room he once shared
with Uke, he stood for a moment drinking it in.
The same tattered bedspread and the square
mirror mounted on the dresser with the crack
high up in the corner, decorated the room. A
yellow stain on the blistered wallpaper design
caught his eye. It was peeling from the walls.
Nothing had changed, yet everything had
changed.

He found the suit of new clothes he had
purchased carefully spread out to press under
the mattress. He searched for any money Uke
might have hidden there. He found none. He
paused and listened until he heard someone
downstairs. Otto was calling out for Sis. Abe
called down to him in answer, "She must have
left."

Although he turned to the task of dressing
quickly, Abe took the time to shake out Uke's
pillow, remembering he sometimes hid money in
it. Nothing. He felt behind the dresser for any
tell tale signs of envelopes or bags with possible valuables. He struggled with the buttons
on the stiff shirt, investigating some old
shoes and an empty tobacco tin high on the
closet shelf, but found nothing of value.

He could hear Otto impatiently pacing
downstairs and brushed a cobweb away for one
last look in the mirror before stepping out
into the hallway buttoning his fly as he walked
toward the steps. He hesitated and then returned to the room and lifted the edge of the throw
rug. Nothing. He straightened up, shrugged and
stepped into the narrow staircase, headed for
destiny.

CHAPTER FIFTEEN
THE WEDDING

Father Aloysius studied the ground where the statue had flattened the earth and thanked the Almighty he would soon be rid of it. The monstrosity was now conveniently hidden behind a clump of lilac bushes. It had been moved next to the ninth station of the cross in order to be nearer the street and the parade route. Yet it could not be seen from the street. It was actually better hidden from view than it was at the third station, (and also from the congregation.)

He paused trying to decide if he had time for a fast round of the stations before the Ladies of the Mission arrived for tea. He pulled his old Elgin from his pocket, but couldn't concentrate on the time. An automobile clanged noisily toward him. He parted the shrubs in time to see Uke wheeling the Durant past his church with Sis perched like royalty on the back seat in her Easter finery.

About all he could really see was the large brimmed hat loaded with fake flowers. He rubbed his watery old blue eyes trying to confirm the scene.

Shaking his head, he began to recite the litany of the first station. It was then he

recalled Uke was getting married down at the
First Congregational Baptist Church of the
Latter Day Saints of Second Street. He paused
on his way to the next station, startled by a
roar greeting his ears. He parted the bushes
again in time to see Otto's truck careening
down the street with Otto hunched over the
wheel and Uke, dressed to kill in a bright
green suit, hanging onto the windshield for
dear life. Father shook his head in wonder,
this was impossible: Uke had just driven past
in the family car with his sister.

Crossing himself, he exclaimed, "To heck with
the Ladies of the Mission." He found his way
out of the maze of stations, lilacs, and shrubs
and hurried down the street toward the First
Congregational, a few blocks away. Either Uke
was one fast change artist, or there were two
Ukes. Either way, this town hardly needed one
Uke, much less two. He tried to assure himself
he was not being nosey, just interested.

Meanwhile, Otto shook his head, "It beats
me," he shouted to Abe above the roar of the
truck being pushed beyond its capacity, "how
come Sis has the Durant, I didn't know she
could drive." A horrible thought crossed his
mind, "Uke, have you been teaching her to
drive?" If he feared the question, he feared
the answer more so.

"Nope," Abe shouted back, without turning
toward Otto. The less he showed of himself, the
less chance of being discovered. Otto let out a
deep breath, it was better in his judgement for
Sis to teach herself than have Uke involved.

In the meantime, Uke eased the Durant expertly into the spot reserved for it in front of
the church and scrambled out. Handling the car
was easier than maneuvering the truck and a lot
easier to park.

Pulling a favorite red bandana from his suit
pocket, he mopped the perspiration from his

forehead before hurrying around the car to help
Sis out. He tucked the handkerchief tightly
away before she could see it and start ragging
on him. She was putting on the dog was all he
could figure...she had climbed in and out of
the truck and the car many times without any
help. Now she insisted on his hand and arm. The
car was a heck of a lot easier than the truck
to get in and out of and the running board was
closer to the ground. Also, she didn't have to
hitch up her ankle length skirt to get into the
car.

He tried to take her hand in his, instead she
accepted a couple of his fingers for help.

Uke saw good, old, Higgie Jones give the high
sign to the organist from his vantage point at
the door and the church organ began to blast
out the wedding march. Sis, now hanging on
Uke's arm, urged him up the steps.

Why, Uke wondered, do you always have to walk
up steps to enter a church? He could never
remember seeing one you could walk straight
into, much less one you could walk down into.
Except maybe a new one down on Center street
which was in a basement, but it wasn't really a
church. It was rented to the congregation by
the guy who ran the dry goods store upstairs,
Holy Hill Baptists, he thought maybe they
called it.

It was probably better than the old burlesque
show the parishioners had been using on Delaney
Street. The walls of the Delaney Street theater
were covered with murals of people in all
states of attire, or lack of it.

The guy who ran the dry goods store pinch hit
as a preacher on Sundays. His sermons, Uke had
heard, were not always about fire and brim-
stone, and he charged them to speak. He also
loaded in plenty of dry goods commercials. He
lost some business when they moved from the
theater to the store basement. Wives no longer

had to poke their husbands in the ribs during
the sermon to keep them from oggling the walls
of the old theater. Since the men were no
longer interested in church the wives had a
difficult time attending.

Uke reached the uppermost step before glancing up. The threatening double doors of the
church were wide open preparing to gobble him
up. He could see all the way down the aisle to
the alter. Although the altar was a decent
distance from the door, it was much too close
for comfort. Higgie stood spread legged in the
middle of the doorway, barring their path, but
this was small comfort to Uke.

The people on each side of the aisle were
twisting and stretching their necks looking
expectantly toward the door and at him. The
church was full of people. Uke did not recognize many of the faces on either side of the
aisle. He had no way of knowing most of the
people were not well wishers, but towns' folk
with nothing to do except to expect something
different.

Uke faltered, was it too late to back out
now? He felt Sis give him a sharp jab in the
ribs with an elbow designed for this purpose.
When she entered the vestibule an usher took
her by the arm and escorted her down the aisle.
She was sidestepping into the pew before she
realized her escort was Higgie Jones, the
window washer and her sometime chauffeur. She
could not remember inviting him to the wedding,
much less asking him to usher.

Uke felt a hand on his elbow and turned. It
was George Wisler, the best man. He didn't much
care for George, a sneaky appearing type. Otto
had contributed him to the wedding party when
George could not cover a bet in a poker pot.
Uke hadn't seen George since he threw him in
the river after George had tripped over Uke's
best casting rod on the bridge, and didn't want

to get his feet wet retrieving it.

George was a big favorite of Sis, probably
because he wore thick glasses and had curly
hair. Sis said he was smart as a whip, but
anybody who would trip over a fish pole and
spend two weeks in the hospital because he
didn't want to get his feet wet couldn't be too
smart. Sis had made Uke promise not to lay a
hand on George when he discovered who the best
man was to be. Otto would have been a better
one in Uke's judgement, but Otto had declined
for his own reasons and Sis preferred George.
Uke had no say on the subject.

He found himself standing at the alter all
too soon with George uncomfortably close to
him. The urge to turn around and see what all
the whispering and exclamations were about
behind him became too much to resist. He turned
enough to catch a glimpse. It was Ruth coming
in through a side door and heading straight for
him. She was all done up in white, almost like
a fairy or an angel, or a short order cook, he
couldn't be sure which.

Uke turned back to face the altar. Something
was clawing at his gut. For a moment he thought
he might throw up all over George. Was it
really Ruth? She looked like something out of a
book. She was beautiful. So why am I so scared?

Ruth and the minister closed in on him at
about the same time. He was having trouble
breathing and his vision blurred and he thought
he might faint. He felt like about the time
Otto claimed it was Herman, the catfish, who
rapped him in the head with the flashlight. He
took a deep breath and it seemed to help. He
was aware of a light squeeze on his arm. He
looked down into Ruth's radiant face. Beneath
her glowing smile he could see fear in her
eyes. He felt better.

Meanwhile, Otto careened around the corner
and ground to a howling halt a moment after Sis

and Uke disappeared into the darkened bowels
where so many men had been led astray,
including Otto.

As the organ bellowed out the last chords of
Mendelssohn's wedding tune, Otto gave Abe a
friendly nudge and shouted, "Just in the nick
of time, you old son-of-a-gun!" He clapped Abe
so hard on the small of his back the duplicate
bridegroom almost fell from the truck seat
where he was glued. The sign stating POPCORN
TEN CENTS was stuck on Abe's back.

Abe was beginning to become unglued. At the
very least, being the wrong groom should have
been funny, in fact, should have been hilar-
ious. What an uproar, what consternation it
would cause to the bride with the wrong groom!
Because of his plan, he was certain they would
never hold their heads up around here if the
bride wound up with two grooms. It was his
great chance to get even with all of them and
especially with Ruth who, in truth, had ditched
him so long ago and wasn't the way he told it.

A thought came to mind. He sat frozen on the
truck seat. What if he let the situation get
out of hand and he became married, legally and
legitimately? He felt Otto peeling his hand
from the windshield frame. The roar of the
organ blasting out into the hemisphere totally
disintegrated his confidence. I can make a run
for it, Abe thought, aware of Otto tugging on
his sleeve trying to force him to move.

"Come on, Uke, ain't nothing to it," Otto
laughed, urging him. "Why, tomorrow it'll seem
like it never happened." If he had the time, he
would have told him it was kind of like going
into business. It was easy to get into, but
tough to get out.

"I can't," Abe cried out in desperation, I'm
not Uke, I'm Abe." He realized the financial
betterment, getting even, and the humor in the
situation was not worth the risk he was taking.

A whining wife and a house full of snotty-nosed kids was not his cup of tea.

Otto made one final tug at him before Abe's words registered upon him. "Come on, Uke. <u>ABE</u>? He released his grip and slowly backed away. "You're Abe? No, you're not, you're Uke. What a dirty way to try to get out of this!"

Abe shook his head desperately. "Uke must be in there getting hitched right now." The organ had shut down, a blessing in itself. The silence was deafening.

Father Aloysius turned the corner. At that moment, Otto aimed a punch at Abe, smashing him back against the side of the truck. The man of the cloth shook his head in wonder and continued to hurry toward them. Abe collapsed, out stone cold. Not so much from Otto's punch but more from the blow he received when his head crashed against the truck's cab.

"Ah, give me a hand with him, will you, Father?" Otto asked, noticing the priest for the first time. He wondered how Uke could possibly make him believe such a story. "I gotta get him into church in time for the wedding."

Otto took Abe under the arms and pulled him away from the truck and waited for Father Aloysius to scoop up Abe's feet and together they struggled up the church steps with the reluctant but peaceful bridegroom.

"Thank the Lord they are not getting married in my church," Father wished he could cross himself, but he did not have a free hand. It was just as well, he, too, began to see the possible humor of two bridegrooms and only one bride. This is delicious, he vowed, what a way to even the score with Otto, he doesn't suspect the truth.

I don't have the slightest idea how this happened, Father mused, but what a spectacle we will present! It will serve Reverend Williams right. He was the one who nailed my golf shoes to the locker room floor last Tuesday.

A black Packard, the finest the taxpayer's money could buy, rolled past while they labored up the steps with Abe's appropriate bottom bumping on each step. The mayor and four of his aldermen strained at the windows of the large sedan. They could hardly believe what they were seeing. They were on their way to try to locate the missing statue.

Otto and Father dropped their goods inside the entrance and stood gasping for breath. They were in time to hear the good Reverend Williams, a ten handicap golfer announce, "I now pronounce you man and wife."

Reverend Williams had an excellent view of the front door and decided it would be for the best to cut the ceremony short. He was certain the priest was trying to square things for the prank he had pulled. He never dreamed he would dump a drunk into his church let alone during a ceremony.

Otto started to bolt up the aisle, intent upon getting the entire mess straightened out here and now. Fast as he was, Father Aloysius was faster. He caught him by the collar and Otto came flying back with almost the same speed with which he had started to leave.

"Otto," he said in a quiet but firm voice, "I saw two Ukes. If she is indeed married to the impostor, the marriage is void. If he is the correct one, no harm has been done."

Once this information sunk in, Otto's shoulders sagged visibly and the priest released his grip.

"Now, let's get this one into the truck and settle this thing quietly...after all the guests have left." The padre was greatly troubled, fate had dropped a double burden upon mankind, there were indeed two Ukes.

CHAPTER SIXTEEN
A NIGHT TO REMEMBER

Otto picked up his respective end of Abe and
began to drag him out of the vestibule and Father
Aloysius grabbed the legs. the bride and groom
were just turning to begin their stately parade
down the aisle.

The black Packard turned the block for another look just in time to see Abe dumped head
first into the back of the truck. Mayor Wendell
Clausen's honorable mouth dropped open in
astonishment.

"Oh, my goodness," he exclaimed to no one in
particular, "I have heard of shotgun weddings,
but I never really believed they occurred."
Abe's feet protruded over the tailgate. Otto
and the priest clambered into the truck and
drove off at the precise time the bridal couple
appeared on the front steps. Father Aloysius
turned in the seat and studied Otto intently
unindful of the Dillinger like getaway of the
truck.

The thought crossed his mind as to why he
likened the episode to Dillinger, the famous
bank robber who had recently escaped from the
Crown Point, Indiana jail using a gun carved
from a potato, soap or wood.

"You know," he said at last, "no matter which

man we have here, I saved you a great deal of trouble and you owe me a debt of gratitude."

Otto cast him a quick glance. If gratitude meant doing something, it was a lot better than paying him. Besides, he wasn't about to pay anyone for anything. "Maybe, what do you have in mind?"

"The mayor and his gang drove past a minute ago and they perhaps are looking for your statue. When that monstrosity reappears in the park, you are going to be in for one of the roughest times since Custer fell asleep in cavalry class. You can't beat city hall."

Otto nodded, but he was not in complete agreement. "Maybe you can't beat city hall, but you can crap on the steps and run like hell!" He drove on, wondering what the priest had in mind. He was beginning to like the old duffer.

Father knew his psychology and allowed the bait to dangle.

"O.K., so what's on yer mind?" Otto finally asked.

"No one has any objections to a statue in the park, or anywhere else...it's the statue they object to." Now he had said it, he avoided turning to see what Otto's reaction might be. He allowed only his eyes to shift.

Otto deliberated upon this possibility. The old coot might be right. He turned the truck at the next corner and headed for home, for lack of a better place to go at the moment. He had to dump "sleeping beauty" somewhere and home would be handy so Sis could sort out the bridegrooms. "So?" he demanded.

"I have an idea for the statue that would be appropriate," Father Aloysius spoke slowly, believing the slower he spoke, the better the chances were Otto would accept the idea and perhaps claim it for his own. "It would be acceptable to everyone, I believe. City hall would forget the whole matter and I'm certain

your wife would eventually get over her
obsession, once the park had a monument in it."
His mind sorted out and cataloged the people in
his parish. There has to be someone for this
job, he assured himself.

Pondering the pastor's last remark, Otto
turned the corner and wended his way down
Devil's Lane toward the house. They were the
first of the expected well wishing vanguard
there.

"Say," Father suddenly said, when the truck
gasped in relief, "I don't want to go to your
house. It wouldn't be right for me to be at
your wedding party."

"Nuts," Otto snapped, he was beginning to
like the good man who would more than likely
get blamed by Sis for what almost wrecked the
wedding. Better Father Aloysius, than me.

"Nuts?"

"Nuts. It's about time I put my foot down and
straightened Sis out on a few things."

Abe groaned slightly when the truck came to
rest in a cloak of dust in the driveway by shed
number two. He tried to sit up, but fell back
clutching his head.

Otto hurriedly scrambled out and reached into
the back and began pulling on his feet. "It's
my woman who has been causing all the problems," he called over his shoulder to Father.
"Me an her is going to have an understanding."

"Your good wife is not the root of your
troubles," Father laughed. "You bring most of
your difficulties upon yourself, but I do not
wish to argue the point, nor be around when you
assert yourself at home." He pushed the truck
door open and jumped to the ground with the
ease of a railroad switchman and began to tug
on Abe's other foot.

"Let a sleeping dog lie." Otto decided,
dropping the leg he was tugging. If the priest
hadn't been there, he would have gone through

Abe's pockets. He had not forgotten Abe owed
him money on that chicken gut job that blew up
in his face.

Abe groaned louder and struggled to a sitting
position. He nursed his jaw and felt the welt
rising on the back of his head. He sat in silence allowing the butterflies, bees and stars
time to take flight. The paper sign from his
back fluttered to the truck bed. He picked it
up and tried to focus on it.

"The best thing for you to do," Otto advised
Abe, "is to pack up and get out, because if I
ever see you around here again, I"ll tell Sis
what you tried to pull, if she hasn't all ready
found out." If this is Abe, he'll take off,
Otto figured. If it's Uke, he'll stick around.
He snatched the popcorn sign from Abe's and
stuffed it into his pocket.

Abe eased himself from the truck silently
nursing his jaw and disappeared behind the hen
house without a backward glance. Otto watched
him leave. He was interrupted by the wild honk-
ing of a horn and the Durant careened into the
yard, with Uke at the wheel. Otto hurriedly got
his truck between himself and Uke.

Ruth and her father were in the back seat and
Sis sat rigidly alongside the groom hanging
onto her flowered hat to keep it from blowing
away. Father Aloysius shook his head.

Sis leaped from the car before it came to a
halt and strode toward the truck. "What was the
meaning of that episode in the back of church?"
she hissed, keeping her voice low so the bridal
party wouldn't hear.

"It was the front of church, and you'd never
believe me," Otto shrugged.

"Try me," Sis snapped, not in a mood for his
games. "Wait, we'll get to the bottom of this
later." She turned and smiled brightly at the
advancing wedding party.

Uke, with Ruth hanging on his arm, had left

her father to fend for himself. The old man was content to stay in the back seat fanning himself with a piece of cardboard he found on the floor of the car. Dried chicken droppings from his fan's breeze flew about.

Emily, the mousey bridesmaid, and George Wisler, the fearful best man, rolled to a stop right behind the Durand in George's new DeSoto Airflow. George did not care for the glowering look on Uke's face when he handed him the wedding band at the altar like maybe it was George's fault he was getting married. First chance he had George planned to clear out, the walleyes were running, he had heard. He was pleased he hadn't lost the ring before the ceremony. If he could get rid of Emily who was hanging on his arm, like he was a life preserver, he'd get clear of this nutty family.

Sis kept a broad smile on her face nervously inviting the guests to the kitchen, "We'll go in and have some upside down cake and punch and then you newly weds can be off."

"Off?" Uke inquired, "we aren't going nowhere."

"No," Ruth promptly agreed, "we don't have any money for a honeymoon, so we are going to move in with Dad and keep house for him."

"We are?" Uke wondered when these arrangements had been made. He couldn't remember any plans having been made for anything more than a wedding, which was enough. The harsh truth struck him. I have to move out of my room, I have to leave this house. After today, everything will be different. This is why Sis wanted to marry me off. Now I can't keep an eye on her and what she'll be doing with the rest of the money. His stomach revolted when he caught sight of Ruth's old dad grinning like a baboon at him from the back seat of the Durant.

Reading Uke's mind, Sis offered, "Uke, you kids will come back real often to see us." She moved toward the house. Clusters of guests were

arriving. She would have to hurry if she was
going to get the wash tub filled with popcorn
in time to serve all of them.

* * *

Immediately after the last of well wishers
left, and the bride and groom had driven off
with Ruth's father firmly ensconced in the back
seat of the Durant, Sis removed her apron and
sat down in a chair opposite Otto who was
nursing a cup of black coffee with an ounce of
whiskey to sweeten it.

"Now I want to know right from the beginning,
what were you up to today?" Her quiet, but firm
voice signaled Otto not try to persuade her with
any nonsense.

He let out an audible sigh for her benefit,
in case she was buying anything. She wasn't.
Her fingers drumming on the scarred table top
indicated impatience. He had no choice but to
begin at the beginning. Well, what the hell,
why not? As near as he could tell, he had done
nothing wrong.

While the story of the mix-up unfolded, Sis
leaned over the table intent upon absorbing
every word. He was surprised she appeared to
believe him. Otto could remember a lot of
stories in the past more plausible and she
hadn't bought them. The thought struck
him...maybe truth is stranger than fiction?

Sis listened, wishing she could confide in
him. The secret burden in the will seemed at
times too much for her. If Otto had any information, it would be difficult to see how he
would use it to his own advantage. But use it
he would, she knew her husband.

Grandfather's will stipulated a statue before
any of the money could be distributed to the
heirs. Her mother had never gotten around to
creating a statue. Mother had money of her own.
Pa operated creameries. When they showed a
profit, he sold them, they packed up and moved.

Ma hated packing up and moving about once a year, perhaps this was why Sis had bought her own home, two old farm houses joined together served them well. She didn't care for moving, either. Otto would never buy a house and if he did it would be in and out of a poker pot several times a week. This was no way to live.

Her mother had sworn her to secrecy. A blood relative had to build the statue. Grand Dad, she said, figured with kin doing it the thing would take on a life of its own. He would not be suitably honored if someone did it for money. The women in her family had a knack of marrying weirdos. First, Grandpa Compton, the horse thief, next was her Pa, a fast buck artist, and now she had Otto, a crooked poker player.

Furthermore, the will directed Sis not divide the money while Uke needed a home. Uke, mother felt, needed the protection of a woman, and had sworn Sis to the obligation. Sis was reasonably certain Ruth would be up to the task of providing shelter for him. Uke needed little care and perhaps being married he might just improve radically.

CHAPTER SEVENTEEN
A NIGHT TO FORGET

If Father Aloysius plan worked out,
tomorrow the statue would be in place and with
Uke married, all the obligations of the will
were met. On the fifth of July Sis would go to
her attorney and demand settlement. What
worried her was the will had resided in the
hands of the lawyers for two generations and
the Blackwells were both driving new Auburns,
very expensive automobiles.

She wondered how much the cars had cost her.
If there was a suitable amount left, perhaps
she and Otto could retire to Florida away from
this tired old town. But then again, why take
Otto along? He was nothing but a free loader
and a scallywag. Trouble was never far from
Otto. She would have to give this possibility a
lot of thought. Getting rid of Otto, she knew,
would not be easy once he smelled money.

Uke had his mind made up. After carrying the
old man from the back seat of the car to his
room and then having to wait while Ruth changed
clothes in private, he sat on the edge of
Ruth's bed and wondered when would be the best
time to blow up the statue. Tonight? Maybe
early in the morning before the parade tomorrow? He had no idea where Abe would meet him

for the bombing. He agreed with Abe that it was
the only way.

In the morning the parade would signal its
official start with a bomb blast and Abe did
say he would help. Two explosions would perhaps
be better. Ruth, doing her best to be alluring,
coyly entered the bedroom and slipped into bed.
Uke glanced at her, immersed in his own
thoughts. He should be excited, but wasn't.

The words and events of the past few days
smoldered in his mind. Sis and Abe both fed him
enough information to make the decision chew at
him until he couldn't stand it. He would have
to blow up the statue and then demand his share
of the money from Sis. It was rightfully his.
He had to take care of the statue tonight so
maybe he could sleep soundly....her bed didn't
look big enough for one, let alone two people.
He sat there for some time. Ruth was taking an
auful long time.

He looked over at Ruth taking up over half of
the lumpy bed, her hair tousled and draped over
the pillow. She was sleeping in peace. He had
never shared a bed with anyone before. Abe had
always pushed him out on the floor.

He made up his mind and turned off the light,
picked up his shoes and tip-toed out of the
room. I will never get used to sharing a bed
with someone else. He did not give her a glance
and carefully closed the door and crept slowly
down the steps in the unfamiliar house. He
eased himself out the front door. Despite being
careful not to make any noise the door squeaked
as he opened and closed it.

Our bed, she had told him. It ain't my bed
and beside it feels real lumpy. A corn shuck
mattress was the best. He paused on the front
porch to pull his shoes on, wishing he had
something more practical than his wedding suit
for the job tonight.

Ruth, meanwhile, opened her eyes from her

pretended sleep when the room became dark. It
took time for her to realize Uke had left. She
had supposed he was about to climb into bed
with her. Once she realized he had slipped out
of the room she became angry.

No, she was furious. Grooms don't slip out on
their wedding night for any reason whatsoever.
Self doubt and then curiosity welled up inside
her. She threw off the covers and snatched her
bathrobe and went in search of the groom. She
felt she had much more to offer than a bed and
a roof, much more.

She reached the front door in time to see Uke
disappearing down the street under the corner
streetlight. He was headed in the direction of
home. Anger and frustration surged up in her.
She turned and stamped back into the house.
Fear and uncertainty laid their hands on her
soft, bare shoulders as she removed the robe.

Aware Uke was not the most eligible man
around, she was determined he could be managed
with some tips from Sis. All any woman could
ask was to be given the chance to do the job a
mother had never been able to accomplish. Uke
did have a few of the qualities a mature woman
would look for in a man. Her mind made up, she
finished dressing quickly and set off in hot
pursuit.

* * *

Otto decided tomorrow would be a better day
to tell Sis about the deal he had made with the
priest. He would like to put the matter from
his mind, but somewhere in a remote corner of
his head a warning light tried to go on. Sis
had gone upstairs a few minutes before so he
decided to climb into his truck and before long
discovered he was driving in the direction of
the church idly wondering what the newlyweds
were up to.

He didn't care about missing Sis's planned
shivaree. Why go pounding on pans and kettles

and making enough racket to scare a politician
when Uke didn't have any money to throw out the
bedroom window? No money - no mock serenade on
their wedding night as far as Otto was
concerned.

The heavy cloud cover made the night dark and
Otto wished the truck had better lights. The
only usefulness the headlights served was to
let someone know where he was, the noise of the
truck served a warning he was coming. He certainly couldn't see much of anything else, much
less the road.

This was the time Sis had been waiting for.
She had changed and hurried back down stairs
unaware Otto had left. Gathering up her wash
tub, a pail and several broken broom handles,
she dumped the remaining popcorn out of the tub
and hauled the tools out by the shed door.

Tossing more tools into the tub, she noticed
the box of dynamite. Otto said he had rid them
of the stuff. Tomorrow he'll get rid of it, she
vowed, and tugged the box closer to the door so
that in the morning she would not forget.

Several of the wedding guests returned and
helped themselves to the noisemakers and drove
off toward Ruth's house intent upon giving the
newlyweds a shivaree. Sis didn't bother to tell
the revellers Uke had no money to buy them off,
custom, or no.

When they gave up and returned to the house
she would dump the contents of the tub and make
more popcorn. Higgie would stick around until
the last and then she would ask him to drive
her over to Middletown first chance to check on
the gold stock. By now Himie Nostrov's brother,
Alby, would have an answer on its value. She
hoped the answer would be a good one.

Uke crept through the shadows near home and
watched the party quiet down. The cars filled
and he wondered where they were all going. He
waited a few minutes making sure the house had

emptied before he moved toward the shed. Hig-
ie and Sis were the last to leave with Higgie
easing the Durant from the drive. In case someone was still there, he had to be careful not to
open the old shed door too fast.

He should have oiled the hinges this morning
when he had the chance. It would be easier to
locate the dynamite if he could scratch a
match. Fumbling around in the dark, he felt for
the wooden box where he remembered leaving it.
The dynamite was not there!

Desperately he tried to remember where he had
last seen it. Absently he felt in his pocket
for a parlor match. Before striking it, he
realized the truck was not in the drive. Otto
was off probably to a poker game. Otto would be
gone all night, but Sis could return at any-
time, he'd have to hurry. He fished out one
long, wooden parlor match and flicked the blue
and white head with his thumbnail. It flared
into brilliance in the coal dark shed. The
light momentarily blinded him. He shaded his
eyes with his free hand.

* * *

Abe pulled himself from the dirty lumpy matt-
ess in Flannigan's Boarding House located too
near the river. He fished a parlor match from
his pocket and absently lit a cigarette to help
hide the odor of fish. It was no use, he could
not sleep. His head was aching like it did when
Otto punched him. Pulling on his shoes he slip-
ed out and began walking, no place in partic-
lar, just walking. The night air helped. He had
to work off his guilt and the ache. His steps
took him toward the house. Home.

Home was a word he had long since dropped
from his vocabulary. He wanted to turn away,
but his feet continued on toward the house. Why
toward home? Why toward Sis? An unknown force
propelled him. That was it, he needed Sis. He
never felt he needed anyone before now.

Now that his need had been defined, he cut
through Evans' vacant lot and pushed aside the
branches of Sis's plum tree and stepped onto
the sidewalk. The maneuver brought him alongside Ruth who by now knew where Uke was headed.
Startled, she gasped, in the moonless night.

"Uke," she demanded, "where in the world do
you think you're going?"

"What're you doing here?" Abe countered, he
needed to buy time after this unexpected
meeting.

"I came after you," Ruth placed her arm on
his trying to turn him around.

Abe allowed himself to be held in check. "I
wanted to walk and think," he replied quite
honestly. He wanted to tell her he was not Uke,
but the words refused to come out. She was a
woman. The law protected them until eighteen,
nature protected them at sixty-five: anything
in between was fair game.

Ruth pushed his arm away and turned back in
the direction from which she came. She hesitated once to see if he had decided to follow.
A pair of dim headlights came down the street
toward them. She increased her pace. It would
be time enough in the morning to get to the
bottom of this. Never would she ever forget her
wedding night!

Abe paid no heed to the frail truck lights.
He shrugged and willingly turned to follow
Ruth. A voice within screamed 'the truth, tell
her the truth. It was not to be, curiosity and
instinct controlled him. Life is strange, he
thought, all my planning and scheming got me
nothing and now by a strange stroke of luck,
here she is, right on a platter, panting and
eager.

* * *

Uke held the burning match high and searched
for the dynamite box. He desperately tried to
remember where it should be. His search took

him deeper into the shed away from the dynamite. The match flickered out. He searched his
pants pocket for another and then remembered to
grind the old one into the dirt floor. He had
to be careful he cautioned himself.

He flicked his thumbnail against the head of
the fresh match and watched the head fly off in
the dark and streak like a shooting star toward
the door. He breathed a sigh of relief when the
missile appeared to die in the dark.

The moment of fear while watching the match
head fly disappeared. He was no nearer to finding the dynamite. He dug into his pocket for
another match. He lifted his leg to tighten his
pants and swept the match head over the area to
build up the necessary friction to light it.
The match broke in two just as it flared and
the head flashed like a shooting star arching
across the dark room.

Unerringly, it arched toward a large wooden
box. In that moment he knew where the dynamite
was located. A whisp of flame appeared. The box
he was looking for was next to the fire.

In another second, his entire personal history flashed before him. The arithmetic book he
accidentally tore the cover off of in the
fourth grade, and the time he cracked his head
open diving off the old Four Mile Bridge and
how he had spiked the punch at Sis and Otto's
wedding. The preacher was the drunkest.

Lord I'm too young, too handsome, too much of
everything to go this way! He rushed toward the
door and leaped through the opening with both
feet moving swiftly toward safety. The box of
dynamite would not last more than ten seconds
at the most, if it was going to blow at all.
He was not going to hang around, about all he
knew about dynamite was it made a lot of noise
and a mess of anything near it.

Fleeing by instinct, he cleared the hedge by
the drive in one leap and dodged between the

peonie bushes and the new chicken coop. When
he arrived at the back door of the house he
paused to catch his breath and watch for the
blast. Flames licked their way up toward the
window of the tinder dry building.

Ghastly orange and yellow tongues hungered
for the dried out shed lumber. The dynamite
would not stand much more heat. Uke could not
believe how quickly the flames soared up toward
the roof of the building.

* * *

Otto felt around on the truck seat for his
flashlight. It was not there, he must have
forgotten it at the house. He never referred to
it as home, since it did not belong to him.
Without the flashlight it would be pointless to
check out the statue on such a dark night.
He was in the act of returning to get it, hoping it hadn't been lost or stolen. It was one
of his prized poker possessions.

He'd been having a gnawing feeling of anxiety
about something but couldn't put his finger on
it. The feeling lasted all day, and it wasn't
about the wedding nor was it about the gold
mining stock. He didn't know what it was.

He drove down Devil's Lane toward the yard,
and noticed the flames for the first time,
dancing up beyond the shanty's window. The glow
did not look like fire to him, but more like
someone in there with a good, intense, kerosene
lantern. He wondered who would be prowling
around in there this time of night?

From the porch Uke watched Otto drive up and
turn into the drive and park the truck. He
wanted to cry out, but his tongue was sticking
to the roof of his mouth. He stood transfixed,
wanting to warn Otto of the impending disaster.
His legs also refused to move. He felt something warm trickling down one leg, he knew he
was wetting in his pants.

Otto hurried toward the shed. Whom ever was

in there, was in great danger if they weren't
careful using a lighted lantern. He reached
the front of the shed and tugged the door open.
For the first time he realized the building was
on fire. "Fire," he shouted, trying to see
behind the wall of flames. The flames were
encouraged by the benefit of fresh oxygen.

Uke managed to find his voice, "Otto!"

The sound of panic in the familiar voice
made Otto turn and try to flee. At this moment
the dynamite let go with an almost soundless
"woosh" followed by a low penetrating roar. The
blast momentarily snuffed out the flames. The
building disintegrated before Uke's eyes. The
noise and the force tugged at his clothing and
tore at his ears. Threatening to suck his eyes
from their sockets. Bits of lumber began to
decorate the yard.

Rudely awakened, Fred took a running start
and flapped his way to the top of the weather
vane, calling for his brood to hurrying and
join him.

The blast almost knocked Abe and Ruth down a
block away. For a moment they stood mystified
and frightened. Ruth recovered first. She
pulled away from Abe who had his arms wrapped
around her and was fumbling with the button on
the back of her dress near her neck. She ran
stumbling in the dark toward the house. She had
no idea what had happened, but was certain it
somehow involved her.

Fire station number three heard the blast and
put down their cards and rushed for their rubber garments and horse drawn fire wagon. Winnings were left on the table, in hopes they
would all come back to continue the game. The
fire wagon came out of the station and rushed
down the street in the wrong direction.

They began to argue with each other, un-
decided on which way the unearthly noise came
from. They continued to push their rescue

vehicle as they shouted at one another.

Knobby Nobloff finally noticed the bright-
ness in the sky behind them. It looked bad, but
he was thankful he had folded his poker hand.
He had been holding second best hands all
night. He was pleased he had no money on the
table right now.

Ruth was afraid to get to the house and yet
afraid not to continue on toward it. She nearly
reached the end of the block before beginning
to doubt two things, Uke was not with her. She
was now alone. The sudden change in Uke made her
aware for the first time that Uke might be Abe.

Uke leaped from the porch and ran toward
Otto's new truck. A new flame licked at the
shed door which had landed almost intact
alongside the right front fender, but unfortunately Otto's head was in the way of the door as
he had dashed for safety.

In the dancing light of the flame Uke could
see Otto stretched out by the rear wheel. Two
of the heavy wooden spokes were broken out of
the wheel and by the looks of things, Otto's
head was involved.

He hesitated long enough to pull the flaming
shed door away from the truck before hurrying
toward Otto. He grasped him by the shoulder and
rolled him over. Otto was beyond help. Now he
became aware someone was running up the drive.
He dropped Otto and rushed into the darkness
behind the chicken yard.

Ruth took in the scene at a glance and saw
the hulking figure lumbering away. She could
not bring herself to touch the still form on
the ground. She was certain it was Otto.

Abe hurried back to his boarding house near
the river. He suspected that Uke was responsible for the blast. It would bode him no good.
He had Ruth for a witness, but how could he
ever explain what he and Ruth were doing out
there on her wedding night? He couldn't. He

scooped up his meager belongings and ran from
the room intent upon putting as many miles
behind him and home as quickly as he could.

When he heard the dynamite go off, he thought
he knew what had happened...especially since he
put the idea of blowing the statue into Uke's
mind. It was enough for him. Somehow the damn
fool had set it off.

* * *

Sis and the shivaree party banged on their
kettles, pails and pans until Ruth's father
answered their summons in his night shirt. Once
they were convinced by the dotty old man the
newlyweds were not there, Sis promised the
party cake and ice cream at the house. They
arrived ahead of the fire department who were
still searching for the cause of the blast.
Two of the better poker hands were demanding
they forget the noise and return to the table.
Nobby Noblock, conscientious fireman that he
was, wanted to find the cause of the blast:
he had lost enough money for tonight.

* * *

Sis pushed her way through the milling crowd
of sightseers to stand at Ruth's side. She
demanded to know what had happened. Ruth trembled as she told her what she had come upon. Sis
stood white faced with her lips drawn thin and
one hand clenching Ruth's shoulder for support.

The excitement hungry crowd pushed and milled
around. It was difficult to get to the outside
of the cluster. Ruth told her in a low toneless
voice she had seen Abe run off into the dark.

"How do you know it was Abe, and not Uke?"
Sis demanded. She knew something was real wrong
with the wedding night, neither the bride nor
the groom were where they were supposed to be.

"Because Uke was with me up at the corner,"
Ruth answered quite simply. She refused to
accept the doubt forming in her mind. She had
hardly allowed Uke out of her view for more

than a few minutes since the wedding. And after all, didn't she know her own husband?

There were too many questions unanswered to suit Sis. Far too many.

CHAPTER EIGHTEEN
CAPTURED!

The Fourth of July dawned hot and clear
promising to be a beautiful day. Fire crackers
popped intermittently and ladyfingers snapped
in answer. Now and then a cherry bomb punct-
uated the air with an oath of authority. Life
went on for everyone remembering other Fourths,
except for Sis and Ruth. They sat up most of
the night waiting for the missing bridegroom.

Hardly speaking, engrossed in their own
private thoughts, they tried to fathom the
events which had torn their lives so suddenly.
Yesterday had started beautifully: a day for
happiness and pleasure before ending in a disaster too difficult to contemplate. From time
to time Sis got up and went through some of the
routine housework motions to keep busy.

Silently Ruth watched her. The truth, or the
possibility of a truth had threaded its way
through her mind during a barren sleepless
wedding night.

Was it possible the man who had been with her
before the expolosion was Abe and not Uke?

She had seen both just before and after the
withering racket There was no way to know
which, other than the difference in behavior on
the sidewalk. She could not make herself

believe Uke was the one she had seen fleeing,
but how else to explain his absence?

The only one she could confide in would be
Sis, but they had never been close. Age and
perhaps some jealousy had played a part. Sis,
because Ruth was younger and in her mind beautiful, Ruth because she thought Sis had everything she never had, a husband, money, and a
home of her own.

She had known Sis a long time, but they were
never what you would call friendly, perhaps
cordial. Opportunities for an intimate feeling
had never existed. She knew Sis well enough to
know she was a determined person, one who knew
what to do and how to get it done. Not the type
one could easily take into one's confidence. In
truth, Ruth admired her and tried hard to
pattern her life after Sis.

Right now the dilemma overpowered the girl.
She bit her lip and watched Sis worrying a bowl
of flowers for the tenth time. She wanted to
tell her she suspected Uke, not Abe, had killed
her husband, but hesitated. Would Sis believe
her or suspect she had a motive of some kind?

Ruth came to realize that when Uke and Abe
were found, one of them would have to be ident-
ified as being with her and one of them a crim-
inal. She could do neither since she was unable
to tell them apart.

It would be painful to admit she was with the
wrong man on her wedding night. Worse, was her
husband a killer? A cold chill flowed through
her...perhaps she had married the wrong one?
Sis interrupted her thoughts.

"Would you like a cup of coffee?" She stood
poised with the coffee pot in her hand,
waiting.

Ruth nodded and watched her pour. She really
didn't want coffee. "Mrs. Granley?" She cleared
her throat.

"Call me Sis," she smiled, mopping up spilled

coffee from the table with her sleeve.

"Sis," Ruth whispered, "I didn't tell you everything last night."

Sis studied her for a moment before asking, "Like what?"

Ruth pushed her chair away from the table and picked up the coffee cup. Her hand trembled. She was forced to place the cup back on the table and began to pour out her thoughts.

To keep from crying she sucked in sobs from time to time confiding her fears, withholding nothing. Uke had not come to bed. Instead, he dressed when he thought she was asleep and sneaked out of the house. She had dressed and followed him, but lost him in the dark. When she stumbled on him near the house it took no convincing on her part to get him to return to the wedding couch with her. She wondered why he had so abruptly changed his mind. Why had he so easily agreed?

While Ruth talked, Sis slowly slumped down in a chair opposite her and gazed intently into the frightened pair of eyes. It had been a long time since she had heard anyone under this roof tell her a story with any sincerity, or for that matter, truth.

Ruth finished by saying, "Whatever I do, I must tell the truth. If Uke blew up the shed it was an accident, if Abe did it he probably had a reason."

"Yes," Sis agreed, "If Uke blew it up, he'll be forgiven, if Abe did it, he'll be lynched." What fools we mortals be, she thought.

Ruth searched the words for a hidden meaning and found none. Resting her elbow on the table she placed her chin in her hand. Sis's words made her shudder, although some of the weight had been lifted from her shoulders by her confession. Knowing she had added weight onto Sis's shoulders didn't make her feel better.

* * *

Father Aloysius, along with a number of his more trusted parishioners, worked through the night along with Edgar Hughes and his older children, preparing the statue for entry into the grand parade. They had heard the blast and the furor of the evening. They had joked about a huge firecracker and then forgot the it.

At ten in the morning a cherry bomb inaugurated the parade festivities. The float was ready. Grand Dad's left hand now held a staff remarkably similar to one a shepherd held in biblical scenes. The upraised right hand no longer held the bird house, instead, a magnificent gold cross glistened from on high. The priest fought to restrain tears. He had upon occasion visited the holy land and Rome and had seen all there was to see, but their work during the night moved him like none other had. Perhaps he was weary?

He regretted not having time for a quick tour of his unadulterated stations. Without any idea of where the Comptons or Granley might be, he had to take command and supervise the final portion of the big move. It did not surprise him they had not shown. People were like that. He turned to the task of inspecting the float for last minute changes.

He approved the remodeling of the long hunting coat. It had been hammered and pieces had been added until it resembled a vague looking robe reaching almost to the ground. The broad brimmed hat was unchanged, but the inscription on the base of the statue had been altered. It no longer said, "Pioneer and Founder of Rootville." Instead, it was entitled, "Moses Compton finds the promised land."

A statue of a child was placed behind it and off to one side. At least it looked like it might be a child. Father Aloysius could not be sure his emotional reaction was due to the alteration of Grand Dad, the religious appeal, the child or weariness.

The child had been riveted and welded from old auto parts and the original sculptor, Amos Van Duet had claimed it was a child. Father Aloysius had accepted the donation graciously, shortly after he arrived at his new parish many years ago and had promptly hidden it in the vestry. Now was a good time to be done with it. He was pleased the child now had a permanent home, but more so that he had rid himself of it. He was proud of how his parishioners had rallied around. They had spent the entire night working over the float.

Never in its history had the Fourth of July parade begun on time. However, a large truck backed up to the flat bed wagon at five minutes to ten and a hitch pin fell into place. The statue was ready to move toward its final rest-ing place, or so Father hoped. He certainly didn't want it between the stations of the cross any longer. He stopped the truck driver long enough to have him climb on the wagon bed and straighten the comb under Grand Dad's nose.

The volunteer fire department's float moved from its assigned side street location into position in the parade, manned of course, by Father's parishioners. A gap opened between the fire department and Eli's Department Store float manned by loyal souls of the church. The truck and wagon filled the opening smoothly and efficiently. The gap closed and only par-ishioners at the beginning of the parade route were aware an extra float was in the parade.

Confused spectators wondered about the strange contraption and dismissed it, preferr-ing to concentrate on the other floats fed into the parade from side streets with regularity. The parade would take several hours and end across the street from city hall.

Few people saw Father Aloysius cross himself before hurrying off on foot to lend moral support and supervise the tricky effort when next the statue touched ground. If he had it figured correctly, the few people in favor of the statue and those who were not influenced, might possibly exert enough power to make this caper stick.

No one was aware he was the guiding light behind this entire venture. He almost enjoyed the thought of sitting in at the next city council meeting.... if they didn't try to hold a secret meeting in an attempt to put the statue to rest in the local garbage dump.

Almost as if it were a miracle Grand Dad Compton had appeared in his garden and now he was taking the junk yard child away. Such were the marvelous workings of the Lord!

He felt it strange none of Grand Dad's heirs had as yet arrived to observe the wondrous workings. He would have bet next Sunday's collection plates that Otto and most certainly Sis would have arrived. Uke would be busy.

The volunteers manning the fire department float were too busy discussing last nights excitement among themselves to tell anyone else about it. It would be later when Father Aloysius discovered Otto was no longer a problem.

The cannon announcing the start of the parade let go with an enormous blast, but nothing at all compared to the one last night.

* * *

The screen door rattled when the officer in a broad brimmed hat hammered on it.

"We got two guys," Ruth heard the state patrolman tell Sis who was blocking the doorway.

"I'll go to the county jail," Sis agreed. "Will it be all right for Ruth to come along?"

"I don't know why not," Ben Hibbs agreed. The local state trooper twisted the ends of his walrus moustache while explaining his views as they drove toward Uke's office, "It don't take nothing a'tall to figgur' both these stupes is lying. What baffles us is why they'd be trying to claim to be the same guy when neither one seems to be much of a bargain."

Ruth let out a muffled snort while Ben continued to ramble. She had a husband and she intended to stand by him and be proud of him, but she was awed by the wide brimmed hat on this officious looking man with the brilliant red and royal uniform. When things settled down, she'd see to it Uke fancied up his sheriff's uniform.

"Ya see," Ben went on, "we caught one them down by the river hiding in the willows and the other one we nailed in the freight yard trying to jump a humper."

"Do you know which one you caught where?" Sis demanded. She knew a humper was an unattended freight car moving through the switch yards, but wasn't sure, and was in no mood to encourage Ben's ramblings.

"Naw, the dumb deputy got 'em mixed up," Hibbs replied, "so's we don't know which is which." After a moment he exonerated the deputy, "Ya see, both deputies thought at first it was the sheriff they had."

Sis interrupted. "You don't know where you caught which one?" She was incredulous. Men, she thought, no wonder everything in the world is such a mess.

"All we know fer sure is one is dumber than the other," Ben retorted.

"He is not!" Ruth spat, twisting in the back seat of the squad car with fire flashing from her eyes. She jerked her head around and looked out the window. Some of the parade moved slowly through the next street intersection off to her left. She thought she may have briefly seen Grand Dad on a huge farm wagon. However, it hardly resembled him.

Perturbed, Ben laughed, "Which?"

"My husband is the sheriff," Ruth realized it
was the first time she had used the word. She
allowed herself the luxury of bathing in the
thought for a moment hoping she could handle
being married to a none too brilliant political. She was going to have to manage Uke's
every move to keep him from these ridiculous
situations.

"Which one is he?" Hibbs asked with interest
watching her from the rear vision mirror. He
had been wondering what part this girl played
in the scheme of things. She was nice looking,
certainly more favorable than his old lady.

"I don't know," Ruth admitted miserably.

"Boy," Ben whispered, "Boy, oh boy!" He
shook his head and looked at her with renewed
interest. This could be a delicate situation
seeing how one of his prisoners was apparently
the sheriff. He did not relish trying to find
the county coroner to make the arrest stick
until he knew which was the sheriff.

The sheriff apparently didn't know he could-
n't be legally hung out to dry by anyone other
than the coroner or he'd be screaming by now.

Ruth sank down deeper in the seat and continued looking out the window. Yes, it was Grand
Dad escorting them intersection by intersection. If this man doesn't know where he found
which, she thought, how does he expect me to
tell them apart? Abe would head for the
freight yards, Uke would head for the willows,
of that much Ruth was certain.

CHAPTER NINETEEN
THE POKEY

Apprehension welled up in the sister-in-laws
arriving at the jail with their escort. They
were ushered into the corridor between the
cells immediately upon arrival. Only two cells
were occupied. One jail bird occupied a cell
hastily marked 'Willows' on a piece of cardboard and crayon and the other across the aisle
a crude hand lettered a sign marked 'Humper.'
   The jail had an unwashed odor of old cigars,
cigarettes, and very stale beer in the dimly
lighted area. Sis nor Ruth cared to touch anything for fear of becoming contaminated. Since
Uke did not smoke, they both wondered why he
allowed such conditions in his jail.
   Probably because he hardly spent any time at
the office. How could he be expected to control
this filthy vice much less supervise the
cleaning when he was never there?
   "Hello, Sis, hello, Ruth," the two of them
called out almost in unison. They were both
obviously happy to see them.
   Ben turned to Ruth, "All right lady, which
one is your husband?" Waiting for an answer, he
drummed his fingers on the wall while she helplessly studied them.
   Eventually Ruth turned toward Hibbs and began

to weep. She desperately picked in her purse
searching for a hanky.

"You don't know him by sight, or mannerisms?"
Ben shouted at her, "An yer married to him?"
Ben Hibbs was beginning to suspect someone was
pulling his leg. Frustration turned to anger
since he didn't know, either. Both of the
prisoners were busily trying to convince Ruth
of their faithfulness to her. They both pinned
their hopes for release on the prim lady.

Sis stepped forward and took Ruth by the
shoulders and gently moved her aside. "I know
which one is which, but to be sure, I'll ask
each one a question. One of them won't know the
answer." Since she had cared for them both from
birth, she was confident she could sort them
out.

She turned to the one on the outside wall
with the small window high up. "You," she
demanded of Abe, "how do you start the truck?"

Abe paused for a moment before replying, "Ya
climb in, fiddle with the spark lever, then the
gas lever and pull out the choke and turn on
the key and then swear at it before stepping on
the starter." He knew Otto well enough to know
about the cursing.

"You," she wheeled around satisfied, but it
wouldn't hurt to be positive, "how are we going
to get the statue down to the square today?"

"I ain't supposed to tell, it's a secret."

"Not any longer, it isn't," Sis insisted,
"not if you want out of here."

"Haul it on a wagon in the Fourth of July
parade." Uke responded quickly.

Sis pointed at Uke, "That's her husband. You
found him down by the Willows and the other one
knows how to start all Model-T's except ours."
She wheeled and strode from the foul smelling
room into the office in need of fresh air.
Even Mihich's dark parlor smelled better than
this place.

Ben Hibbs scratched his head. He owned a Model-T himself. He could see nothing wrong with what either of them said. He turned to Abe, "How else would you start it, unless by cranking it once in a while?"

"I know Otto would swear at it, say, where is he?" Abe asked.

I sure ain't going to tell him, Uke vowed silently.

In reply, Ben shrugged and left the two prisoners and followed Sis into the next room, leaving Ruth with the two prizes. Trooper Hibbs looked at Sis expectantly awaiting an answer. He had been having trouble starting his squad car lately. She seemed to know more about the law business and automobiles than he did or at least when it came to grilling suspects. Further, she was not a woman to cross, he suspected.

Sis turned to him, "The problem is determining which one killed my husband."

Hibbs nodded in agreement. At least now he knew which one was the sheriff and which one may have killed Otto. He was the law around here until the coroner showed up.

"We gotta figure out why he did it," he pulled a pencil stub from his pocket along with a pad of paper. "Knowing which is which isn't helping much. Both of them is lying about everything."

Ruth entered the room and he studied her for a moment, as if seeing her for the first time. "I can sure understand both of them claiming to be yer husband," he leered. Compared to his own dumpy wife sitting at home eating chocolates and waiting to tell him how hard she had worked today, this lady was a prize.

The office was cleaner than the cell block. Sis helped herself to a chair and rested her head on her hand while she tried to review the events leading up to the present. The facts brought her to one conclusion: Uke had left the bridal suite and returned home hunting for something in the shed. The dynamite? Somehow he had started the fire. Certainly he would not have the ability to plan anything like this, so it had to be an accident.

At any rate, this was better than the other alternative. Abe would have no reason to destroy the shed or to get Otto. The element of chance involved in a planned motive was far too great and Abe was too smart, anyhow.

Satisfied with her conclusions, Sis jumped from the chair and strode to the big steel door separating her from the prisoners.

"Open the door and release the prisoner on the right," she demanded. For emphasis, she held her hand high and pointed to the right. "He is innocent of any crime and the other," she lowered her voice and dropped her hand to the horizontal position with the palm upward, "is at the mercy of all who know him."

Hibbs started for the cell block and then checked himself as he swung the door open. Sis was on him in a moment. She had him wavering and she had no intention of allowing him to change his mind.

Stepping close to Ben, she lowered her voice and explained that Uke had lied out of fear. Abe, she continued, lied, thinking he could pass himself off for Uke and at least temporarily lead a new life.

Abe hung on the cell door frame watching Sis put on her magnificent act for he was the one on the right. He had no idea Sis would point the finger of guilt at Uke instead of him. Sis ain't all bad if she can get this door open, he thought.

Ben Hibbs debated the issue. In an hour he would be forced to charge one or the other with something or other and would have to release the other one. It was illegal to hold a prisoner more than twenty-four hours without charges. The district attorney was fighting tooth and nail to change this law: it interfered with his golf game and midnight beach parties.

One thing was certain, Ben wasn't going to charge both of them with the same crime, although he would like to let someone else make the decision. He did not want to spend time in Judge Bower's courtroom. The less he saw the "contempt and costs" judge, the better.

The last time he appeared it cost him two weeks pay for three "contempts and costs" when he had supposedly brought in a bank robber single handedly. He learned why two other state police and an F.B.I. agent had refused to take any credit for the capture.... they didn't feel they could afford to testify.

A happy thought occurred to him and he studied it in detail. Free both the prisoners and report it was an accident, wasn't this what Sis had claimed? I can let it go at that. This will keep me out of court. Old Bower can always get a grand jury together if he doesn't like it. He smiled recalling Judge Bower had once held a grand jury in contempt and made a mint of money until the state Supreme Court decided he had no jurisdiction in shaking down juries and made him give the money back.

He turned to Sis, "I'm inclined to agree with you, Mrs. Granley. I'm going to free both prisoners immediately and turn them over to your custody."

"No you're not!" Sis objected. "Uke has a wife, turn him over to her custody."

"I wouldn't turn any man over to his wife's custody." Ben retorted, "Either you assume responsibility or they stay here." He watched her struggle, hoping his bluff would work.

Sis rolled a burned parlor match back and forth under her foot, feeling the corrugation in the match stick when she did so. Uke would be no problem, but Abe would be out of town in an hour. But what would be so bad about that?

"All right," she said at last, almost reluctant to stop feeling the vibrations of the match stick, "turn them loose."

The two prisoners came through the door blinking in the bright lights like two white mice released from a shoe box. Uke stood by Sis until she pushed him towards Ruth.

Abe warily circled the group and made for the door. He was almost to the rooming house to pick up his gear before the other three left the jail house. He had had enough of this town and his relatives. He would have just enough time to get to the pawn shop and then to the freight yards before anyone thought to look for him. He wondered where Otto was. Otto was one of the few people in this world to whom he felt kinship. At the moment he knew nothing about the gold mining stock, but was about to.

Once Uke realized he was free, he pulled his badge from his pocket, polished it on the seat of his pants and pinned it to the lapel of his wedding suit. He strode over to Ben Hibbs and hovered over him for a moment to make him understand how things really were.

Sis and Ruth refused a ride home from Hibbs and walked toward the house in silence leaving Uke to trail along behind them. It was a long, warm walk from the courthouse to the homestead. The ladies both jumped nervously when fire crackers exploded close by. Otherwise the walk was relaxing. The strains of music from several different bands and a drum and bugle corps belting it out in the parade drifted through the air, but they were not of a mind to celebrate.

Uke had almost caught up to them when they turned down Devil's Lane. They were in time to see a truck liberally advertising "Hobart's Furniture and Funeral Company" on the side,

delivering new furniture onto the front porch
of the homestead. Sis broke into a run despite
being warm and tired.

"What's going on here?" she demanded. "I
haven't ordered any new furniture." She ran her
hand in appreciation over the arm of a horse-
hair stuffed leather chair.

Jewels Felstrap, the larger of the two
movers, edged forward and fished into his
coverall pockets and retrieved a piece of
crumpled paper. "Lady, we got orders to deliver
here." He paused and unfolded the sheet for
her to look at. "This is the right address,"
he insisted handing it over, pleased with
himself.

Sis took the paper. She scanned it and shook
violently handing it to Ruth. She turned away
in the same motion opened the front door,
struggling to control herself.

Ruth, in turn, glanced at it and looked up at
Jewels. Her lower lip quivered. Uke reached for
the paper, but Ruth pulled it away and waved it
under Jewels' nose.

"This paper says nothing about furniture, you
fool, you are supposed to deliver a body." She
trembled trying to control her anger.

Jewels took the paper and studied it. He
removed his hat and scratched his thinning
hair. "I'll be darned," he murmured. "Henry,"
he turned and called to his red haired helper,
"load up the furniture and drop the stiff off
here, instead."

Henry spat into the peony bushes in disgust
and snorted, "Twice't this happened. Last week
you pulled the same bone head stunt." Disgusted,
he picked up a small table and started back
toward the truck. He squirted another shot of
tobacco juice at the peonies and satisfied he
had knocked several ants off the flowers,
climbed into the back of the van where he was
out of the hot sun.

"Don't tell Mr. Hobart," Jewels pleaded, "he gets awful mad about things like this, an I got three kids to feed."

"I'll tell you what," Henry grinned, pushing a table out of his way, "you load up the furniture and I'll keep quiet. I'll wait in the truck. Geeze it's hot today."

Jewel had to forget about taking his kids to the parade today: it would be over before the furniture could be delivered.

Abe hurried from the grimey building with three globes hanging over the front door...it was easy to get the proprietor to hand over the gold mining stock, without even having to flash his stolen deputy's badge.

CHAPTER TWENTY
A CEMENTED RELATIONSHIP

Mayor Wendle Clausen, honorary chairman of
the Fourth of July parade, guided his prancing
white charger through the downtown section of
Rootville. Doffing his freshly cleaned and
blocked white Stetson hat to the crowd, he wore
his best smile which was as phony as the freshly cleaned white cowboy outfit he donned for
the big parade.

Except for the fact that he and the city
council had been unable to locate that awful
statue, he was pleased because a huge crowd had
formed and the street was lined three deep with
constituents. This was going to be the biggest
and best Fourth of July parade he could ever
remember. No one could hope to obtain cheaper
political exposure. Children had grown up and
remembered him from past parades. They voted
for him. Their children would do the same.

The white stallion danced at an angle to the
direction of the parade, keeping time to the
beat of the marching band two floats in front
of them. Mayor Clausen had to hold a tight rein
when they passed the square where an excavation
had recently been in progress. A huge crane
parked next to the curbing forced voters to
find another spot to enjoy seeing him. A tiny

warning bell tinkled in his head, but he could not connect it to any kind of a political threat. He could not dismiss the vague feeling.

"Darn it," he muttered, all the while keeping the huge smile printed on his face. Vaguely contributing to his unease was that someone had not obeyed his order to get all heavy equipment off the streets on the parade route. This folly could cost him a dozen votes. Through his three terms, his popularity had steadily declined, every vote was important.

He wiped his forehead with a white silk handkerchief. It was beginning to get warm and the parade had hardly begun. He would rather be sitting in the shade of inviting trees in the small park behind the heavy equipment. He couldn't, it was just one of the high prices a mayor had to pay for being an elected official.

Voters were the high cost of any of his con- siderations. Right or wrong was secondary. Why, if the contractor who left the stuff out on the parade route doesn't come through with a good sized campaign contribution, I'll make him wish he had. The election was not too far away and best of all he was certain there were no strong candidates on the horizon to oppose him.

The mayor turned the corner at Fourth and Main and led the parade towards its destin- ation three blocks further down the street. Grand Dad Compton, resplendent with the junkyard child, followed the mayor at a re- spectful distance, swaying majestically to the beat of the national award winning Boy Scout Drum and Bugle Corps two floats in front.

From the shade of the trees in the park, a man stepped out in work clothes and climbed into the huge crane and began to warm up the engine. It could not be heard above the Boy Scout bugles playing "The Monkey Wrapped its Tail Around the Flag Pole" for the tenth time.

Parishioners swung into action once the

statue came abreast of the park. Edgar Hughes older children caught up to the wagon and climbed up next to the statue. The boom on the crane swung around to hover directly over the patriarch with a rope dangling in the air. A wave of Edgar's hand and it was fastened around the statue's neck. The more fortunate of the parade watchers gasped in disbelief.

The statue, with the child dangling helplessly from it, seemed to leap from the wagon bed. Grand dad and the orphan disappeared with a mighty bound over the tree tops.

Those who witnessed the Miracle on Main Street broke out in applause at the totally unexpected performance. Children screamed in delight and clapped their hands allowing their balloons to created Easter eggs in the sky. The balloon vendor with an eye for business hurried in their direction.

Grand Dad found his final resting place in a pool of freshly setting cement, with the junkyard child at his side. The local Catholic high school band paused at that juncture of the parade and struck up 'When the Saints Go Marching In'. The band director smiled. He had fulfilled Father Alolysius strange demand.

Women dressed for the Fourth in shorts and halters and not much else except sun burn, laughed and pointed and asked their escorts to go and see what happened in the tiny park. The men scratched their heads, nudged each other knowingly and laughed, but few had the courage to investigate.

Edgar Hughes, dear and trusted parishioner that he was, lifted his youngest and tenth child, a girl, onto the wagon. He jumped up beside her on the wagon bed where they assumed the pose of the missing figures.

Before the float disappeared from view, few spectators were convinced they had witnessed the event. When the parade stalled for a few minutes, which it frequently did, some of the more daring souls slipped into the shrubs to convince themselves they had actually seen a minor miracle.

The mayor veered up Water Street after the parade had passed the imaginary finish line. He trotted toward the rendezvous where his long suffering wife, Eunice, had parked the horse trailer behind the park on the back street running parallel to the route in a spot marked "No Parking," just for that purpose. She couldn't lift the sign so she tipped it over and rolled it under the trailer out of sight.

As on Fourth of Julys past, his honor planned to rest his magnificent stallion in the little park and let the horse munch grass while they enjoyed a picnic away from the hurley-burley of city life. He considered the park his personal property and had plans for the tiny area.

Some day a statue of the Right Honorable Mayor Wendell M. Clausen, the third, would look down on the good people of Rootville from this enchanting nook. He looked forward to letting his horse graze while he stretched out in the shade to cool off and enjoy their cold turkey and potato salad lunch and hoped the beer he had poured into the Nehi pop bottles was cold.

The magnificent stallion remembered the park and could smell the grass. Before long it would soon be shed of its fat burden. Picking up the pace, it trotted faster and then broke into a lope. The mayor pulled on the bridle and began to saw away at the bit in it's mouth to keep the horse from breaking into a gallop. Each year the huge animal did the same thing. Each year it became more difficult to control it.

Approaching the park the mayor had the horse's head almost turned back against its neck trying to control the beast. People leaving the parade scattered after seeing the run away horse rushing toward the park and the

mayor now desperately hanging onto the horse's
neck. The horseshoes slipped and skidded on the
brick pavement. Sparks flew with each clip clop
when they struck street car rails. The white
prancer skittered over the tracks toward the
best grass in the county, continuing to ignore
the steel bit tearing at his bleeding mouth.

Five of the aldermen in their Sunday finest
stared at the statue. It was not possible. It
was standing in the park! The mayor had drawn
each one aside and charged him with orders to
keep the statue out of the park, but there it
was! Each wondered if it would be appropriate
to etch his initials in the soft cement?

Their black suits made them look like blackbirds lined up on a telephone wire. Each one
approached and tapped a toe into the fresh
cement to test it and then tried to decide
which one would be forced by the other four to
inform the mayor about this horrific deed.

The horse charged on, unmindful of the demands upon his raw and bleeding mouth. The
mighty steed felt himself losing his balance
and scrambled across the sidewalk. The soft
earth in the park was more to his liking. The
beast managed to break into a full gallop ex-
hilarated by the fresh, damp smell of grass.
The line of flight brought the stallion into
the opening behind the aldermen with a burst of
energy. In desperation, the mayor gave one
final heave on the reins and the horse felt the
steel cut deeply into its torn and bloody lip
and decided to obey.

His honor tugged furiously on the reins trying to brace himself. Unfortunately, he lagged
one reaction behind the horse. The inertia had
now reversed itself. Adding to the problem the
last band in the parade struck up "The Stars
and Stripes Forever". The mayor had spent weeks
training the animal to fold its front legs on
the ground whenever it recognized the melody.

The aldermen wheeled like one to find the cause for the commotion behind them. At this moment the Right Honorable Wendell Clausen, Mayor of Rootville, raced into view and slid over the horse's neck as the animal reacting to the melody, began to kneel.

The mayor tried desperately to fall with his feet under him, but he could not free them from the stirrups quickly enough and succeeded in making a swan dive. His flying block into the aldermen with his outstretched body would have done justice to Nitsche. The blackbirds, resplendent in their freshly cleaned and pressed suits, plunged backwards in unison into the cement. The mayor collapsed on top of them unhurt, but badly shaken.

Mayor Clausen slowly raised himself to a sitting position testing each muscle. His eyes traveled from one city elder to the next. They were desperately trying to clamber out of the goo. Next he saw Grand Dad's legs behind them and his eyes slowly traveled up to the torso and then up to the head and followed on up to the out stretched hand. He did not notice the half hidden junkyard child in his smoldering fury. His white cowboy suit and hat were ruined. His beet red face made a nice contrast to his glaring white cowboy suit.

The blackbirds managed to scramble out of the mire once his honor finished trying to use them for a sidewalk and desperately sought methods to remove the rapidly settling concrete from their clothes.

Mayor Clausen half in and half out of the mess, sat transfixed. The red in his neck changed to purple and crept upwards like a thermometer until it reached the level of his mouth and then to his eyes. It only stopped when it reached the top of his bald head. By now they all knew he wore a toupee. It was disappearing along with a crop of sweet, red clover into the horse's mouth.

Blackbird number two tried to cleanse his fingers by snapping his arm. The gob of setting cement struck the mayor in the chest. His Honor's neck bulged and his eyes spat fire, but not a word from the right honorable gentleman. He wanted to bellow in rage. But with a mouth full of cement, he couldn't. The rest of the blackbirds glared at number two. They continued to try to wipe the glop from their Sunday best.

A lone reporter, Ewell Jason Paine II, following the parade route, sensed a story when he discovered the crowd near the park buzzing and pointing. Should he bother investigating? He already had a front page story. He had captured the switch of statue with his camera and now he moved the film to the next setting. His nose and sixth sense told him another story was unfolding in the little park.

The great white stallion turned away and continued to crop grass, satisfied he had done a fine job in the parade. This grass was the best around and much better than the weeds in his pasture.

He had earned this reward. However, he kept watch on the mayor out of the corner of his eye when the honorable one lifted himself to a sitting position and then rose to one knee. Moving like a run down clock, the mayor finally managed to stand and then crept up behind the horse. Using his last ounce of energy he gave it a swift kick in the south end.

Ewell Jason Paine II hurrying in the direction the crowd had pointed, burst onto the scene at this opportune moment.

The animal had been savoring a juicy mouthful of clover and alfalfa. The unexpected blow startled the beautiful animal and in surprise and instantaneous reaction, kicked back. There were two things in this world the mayor knew he could not be assured he could control: one was his wife and the other was the stallion.

The left rear hoof caught him in the bread basket and he flew backwards into the picnic lunch his wife had placed in the arena.

Two of the aldermen made a frantic lunge to save his honor, but fate decreed otherwise. They missed in their grab for honors and landed back in the cement at Grandpa's feet. This time the two heroes landed face first. They scrambled up together while the mayor, in his rage, jumped into the mire and tried to lift one foot to give Grand Dad Compton a swift kick, but the weight of the cement restrained him.

The earth trembled and shook and the leaves fell from the trees garnishing the potato salad with twigs, leaves and cement.

"Get me the police, get me the fire department, get the mayor and the recreation department and the park board," the mayor screamed, wiping his face with a muddied hand. "I'm going to personally hang anyone responsible for this. I'm going to sue them for all they have, I'm going to....I'm," he paused for breath. "Tarnation and fidgits," he shrieked, giving up. He desperately tried to remove the remains of another mouthful of cement.

"Why, Wendell," Mrs. Clausen, returning from getting the marmalade and fly paper from the car, surveyed the scene. "get out of that mud this minute and put the horse in the trailer. The very idea! We must eat and then get on home. The Reverend Bixby is coming for tea later this afternoon." She hoped to divert his thoughts. It was bad for his blood pressure. She noticed the newspaper man for the first time and began to fluff her hair and straighten her blouse.

Mayor Clausen raised himself to one knee and reached for a glop to throw at her. He thought better of it when Officer O'Clancy appeared from the far side of the statue. O'Clancy was

not in his pocket. "Officer," he shouted, "Go
and arrest the Comptons and the Granleys."

"Whoever they might be," O'Clancy retorted,
"but right now O'im jist interested in the
people defacing this foin park who'll be
getting jailed."

"I'm the mayor," Clausen raged.

"I'm his wife," Mrs. Clausen declared. She
immediately wondered why she had admitted it.
She suppressed a chuckle at the sight of her
desperate husband and his cronies.

"I'm Alderman Jensen," Blackbird number #1
snapped, "you are addressing the mayor, and
these," he paused to make certain the words
would sink in, "are aldermen Hansen, Jensen,
Andersen and Poploski." He nodded darkly toward
the others.

"Sure an yer tellin' me you didn't put this
foin puddle of mud on me beat?" O'Clancy, ad-
justing to the turn of events, recognized the
mayor's voice. He watched his honor pawing at
his face before he added, "I'll bet it was some
of the dirty O'Grady clan that be doin' this."
He wished he had added "or those Danes from out
on the west side."

Mrs. Clausen quietly caught up the reins of
the horse when it moved near, nudging her for
sugar cubes. She led it willingly into the
trailer and then climbed behind the wheel of
the car and locked the doors. She waited until
his honor finished scraping off hardening
cement. It was a hopeless task and the quorum
of the city council soon squeezed into the
trailer along with the mayor and allowed
Officer O'Clancy to close the gate on them.

"Do hurry," O'Clancy called to Mrs. Clausen
with a wave of his hand, "sure an the cement
will be setting up quickly unless they get
scrubbed!"

O'Clancy waited until the trailer was out of
ear shot before appraising the incident.

"Indeed, 'tis the first time I've seen one
horse's head and all those other ends in one
trailer." He shook his head, laughed and
helped himself to the picnic basket before
stalking out of the park, but not before he
paused to inspect the statues. He patted the
junkyard child on the head. "Nice."

He nodded and tipped his hat to a workman,
who with trowel in hand, was about to repair
the mess the city council made.

Ewell Jason Paine II hurried toward his off-
ices. He knew tomorrow morning's paper would be
filled with his sequence of statue shots and
the picture of the mayor kicking the horse. He
hoped a pay raise would be coming: the publish-
er had been trying for years to find a way to
rid Rootville of that pompous horse's patute.

If his car had been closer, Ewell Jason would
have jumped into it and followed the mayor hoping to catch him and the council scrubbing
themselves. He doubted Mrs. Clausen would allow
them into the house until clean. She did agree
to call the city attorney as he requested from
the depths of the horse watering trough.

* * *

After soaking and scrubbing, the mayor
charged into his sitting room where the city
attorney and his three assistants fretted
silently. The mayor was spoiling their Fourth
of July. Each one had responded to the guarded
request from Mrs. Clausen and was missing the
beer and watermelon cooling in each respective
back yard filled with constituents.

Trying to keep the wet towel from slipping
from his middle, the mayor demanded the immed-
iate arrest of those concerned with the statue.

"Your honor," the city attorney, Fred Fred-
ricksen tried to reason, "we know all the
people connected with this and some of them are
powerful in politics." (By powerful he meant,
contributors to the mayor's campaign fund).

"They are?" the mayor asked, drying a leg. "Like who?"

"O'Grady, for one and Father Aloysius. We can't afford to get the Catholic faction angry." (He always felt it necessary to caution his Lutheran brethren of this fact.)

"Well, then who can we crucify?" the mayor demanded, dismissing his financial benefactors from consideration.

"Well," the attorney hesitated, the best man to get who has no political pull, and won't stir up the newspaper on his behalf, is Otto Granley.I have a warrant all made up for his arrest. Sign it right here." He pointed to the appropriate spot. "I'll get the sheriff to honor it today."

* * *

After Hobart's Furniture and Funeral Company had delivered Otto's remains into Sis' front room for the customary visitation of friends and relatives, Mr. Hobart waited out of sight down the block until the truck left before driving up to the house in his big maroon Duesenburg with chrome wire wheels. Tiny purple pennants fluttered from the front fenders. White lettering on the flags announced his profession, but said nothing about furniture.

He was a slight man with tiny spectacles on the largest nose Uke could ever remember seeing. Mr. Hobart had on dark trousers with faint gray pin stripes in them to match his cut-away coat. His black shoes had gray spats covering them. The spats were for funerals, he could quickly remove them to sell furniture. He had an annoying habit of sniffing the air like a white rat.

He would tip his huge nose up in the air when each new odor strained through his Andy Gump moustache. Uke smiled and tried not to laugh. He was not concerned about Mr. Hobart, but he did not want to offend his sister.

"I came to finish preparing the body," he
sniffed through the screened front door. It did
not bother him that today was a national holi-
day. What did bother him was the dumb mistake
his furniture movers made delivering furniture
instead of the body he had patched together.

"Come in," Uke grinned, "I think you'll find
him waiting for you in the drawing room."

Hobart sniffed the room with a habit reserved
for unsavory locations and conditions: it was a
sniff suggesting his funeral parlor would be
more appropriate.... and certainly more financially rewarding. Next he opened the lid and
busied himself straightening Otto's necktie and
coat. It was difficult, much of Otto was missing and he had stuffed him with old newspapers
to make him look proper.

Uke kept his distance. You sure wouldn't
catch me touching no dead person he vowed to
himself. On the rare occasions when he had to
deal with a body he saw to it a deputy handled
the task.

"You know," Achibald Hobart turned to Uke,
"the real modern and up-and-coming thing is to
have the viewing at the funeral parlor. It's
the real modern thing."

"I want him right here," Sis snapped, entering the room with another arm full of peonies.
The flowers all leaned heavily to the west.
They had not had time to recover from being
flattened by the dynamite blast.

"Maybe he wasn't president nor mayor, he
was my husband with just two more nights
under this roof."She reminded them.

She saw a lot of good in Otto and felt he
was a better man than most mayors, or presi-
dents for that matter. No one could deny he had
many of their traits!

"You can't have a good old fashioned Irish
wake in a damn furniture store," Uke agreed.
He really had no idea what a good old fashioned

wake might be, but it had to be better than a funeral or standing around in a furniture barn.

"Oh, was he Irish?" Hobart inquired. He could see Sis was no one to fool with, and changed like a chameleon to appear sincere and almost friendly.

"Heck no!"Uke exploded. "He always thought he was, up till about a year ago when he found out he was Welsh."

Hobart inched his way toward the front door.

CHAPTER TWENTY-ONE
LAST RESPECTS

Despite darkness, Mayor Clausen ordered a crane, a city truck and floodlights poised around the statue when the last of the reluctant councilmen arrived, their Fourth of July ruined. The mayor's foul mood hardly helped the situation. The unpleasant task of finding all of his loyal aids had been trying.

It was a beautiful, cool evening. They all had looked forward to spending it with their families watching the fireworks, the culmination and high light of a year's effort on behalf of the citizens of Rootville. For them it was not to be.

The expensive fireworks display began just as the mayor began his tirade. All that the council could see were the last vestige of the higher flashes of brilliance struggling to expose themselves over the tree tops.

"I wanted you all here to see this ridiculous monstrosity," the right honorable Mayor Wendell Clausen shouted in his best political voice. "Otto Granley is responsible for this!" "He is going to pay for the cost of removing this thing," he grimaced, pointing a finger skyward at the imposing and most distinguished of the Compton clan. "He is going to be prosecuted to

the fullest extent of the law." A compulsive
shudder ran through him when his eyes came to
rest on the junkyard child for the first time.

A dented Essex hubcap face grinned up at him.
The child, he discovered, had two flat washers
for eyes and a valve stem for a nose. The mouth
had been sawed or chiseled into a grin.

A murmur of approval sifted through the
blackbirds who had lined up for a better view.
Blinking at the bright lights on the heavy
equipment, they nodded vigorously in agreement.
Those who could see the junkyard child shuddered along with him. If the mayor ever retired,
they would want his endorsement for mayor.

Bill Gorden assistant city attorney, (and
gopher) arrived with his boss, the city
attorney, just as the mayor ended his tirade.
The city attorney, Fred W. Wessley, spelled
with two s's, drew the mayor aside and whispered in his ear the tale of his assistant's woe.

When he had finished, the mayor shook his
head in disbelief and asked him to repeat it.
Fred, with two s's, went through the story
again, leaving out none of the bizarre episode
Bill Gorden had confided. He couldn't resist
adding a few embellishments to Bill's story.

"Mayor," Wessley advised him, scuffing his
toe in the grass, "we'll be the laughing stock
of the county, serving a warrant on a dead
man."

His honor's mouth dropped open with this
shocking information. It took time for him to
allow the blood to settle down below his ears.
His mind raced. His political success had
always hinged upon turning defeat into victory,
no matter what the costs or who was hurt in the
process. "I believe you're right," he conceded.

However, his ego preserved. "Gentlemen, an
unfortunate incident has occurred." Briefly he
recounted what the assistant city attorney had
told the city attorney, all the while polishing

up the story.

Fred W., with two s's, nodded his head at each word. Bill Gorden listened in wonder, the story he told his boss hardly sounded like the story the mayor was telling the aldermen. One true fact was now divulged to the group by his honor. The warrant was in the hands of a dead man!

"Perhaps we should go over and pay our last respects to the dear man," the mayor suggested with an evil grin before adding, "and see if we can't get the warrant back."

The blackbirds nodded their collective heads in unison when the meaning of his statement be- came clear. Bill Gorden wondered if he would get fired for not personally serving the warr- ant. It should have been handed directly to the offending individual, but the ice was melting on the beer at home and he knew the sheriff, Uke, would only be too obliging. He now real- ized why Uke had laughed so hard at the time...and all the while he thought it was because he'd be serving it on his own brother- in-law, Otto.

The mayor ordered the lights shut off and told the work crew to go home. They were on overtime and important things had to be done. Overtime pay of an extra twenty-cents per man could add up in a hurry for three men.

He led the council from the park. The last blackbird to leave turned for a final glance at the park's newly acquired addition. He couldn't be positive grandpa didn't wink at him. For sure, the junkyard child's fender for an arm, waved goodbye in the gloaming, if not, then the auto door body did a hula, that was for certain.

No sooner had they left the park than Father Aloysius, stepped from behind elderberry bushes and shook his head slowly. The Lord certainly works in mysterious ways, he muttered to him-

self. He called to his well hidden parishioners
nearby.

Motioning to his faithful crew he said, "You
fellows patch up this mess before it sets up.
I'm going to drop over to the Granleys and pay
my last respects". His problems with Granley
were over, the Lord certainly works in
mysterious ways, he mused.

He arrived almost on the heels of the official delegation. When Sis caught sight of the
priest standing at the back of the group of
politicians now crowding into the kitchen, she
seemed pleased to see him.

With Fred W. Wessley, spelled with two s's on
his right, and Bill Gorden on his left, the
mayor explained their mission. "We thought it
right and honorable to come over and pay our
last respects to this fine, loyal, leading
citizen, a pillar of strength in our fair
community."

The good priest rolled his eyes heavenward.
The mayor shook Sis's hand vigorously and tried
to see past Uke who was blocking his view in
the doorway. "My deepest, er, sympathy," he
boomed. The aldermen strained to see past the
group. The paper delivered by Bill Gorden
should be in Otto's fist. It was!

The clutch of blackbirds lined up in single
file and moved slowly passed Uke and Ruth
expressing their condolences. Uke tried to
squeeze each hand slightly harder than he had
gripped the last. Each blackbird held Ruth's
soft hand longer than necessary and poured out
their sympathy to her while caressing the
small hand.

Sis received a nod of the head from each
dignitary and an unintelligible murmur of
condolences. Her rough working hands filled
with callouses contrasted with their dainty,
unsoiled hands. After all, people who worked
with their mouths weren't apt to get callouses

on their tongues.

Father Aloysius received a gentle handshake from Uke and did not tarry by Ruth. He somehow made it to the head of the procession and into the front room where Otto and the last of the peonies leaned, slightly fried from the blast. He edged between Sis and the casket.

Catching sight of the good Father for the first time, Mayor Clausen paused, uncertain which of them held the prestige for the moment. Should he allow the pastor the respect of the cloth, or did his office make him more important?

Father Aloysius had no compunctions about protocol, he moved into the room and knelt before Otto's remains and in a louder voice than necessary, began to recite a Hail Mary.

Everyone in the house quickly knelt and bowed their heads in prayer. Ruth joined in saying the beads: she was the only one in the room who knew the prayer. Her mother, rest her soul, who believed in covering all the angles, taught it to her.

"Oh, Lord," he exclaimed finishing, "judge us not for what we are, but for what we try to be. Amen." He immediately regretted saying this about Otto, anyone else, and it would be all right. He looked quickly about to see if heads were properly down.

The mayor on his knees now had to struggle to get back up. By the time the aldermen had followed suit, the priest had crossed himself, scanned the room for a head count of others doing the same (Catholic brethren). He was the first back on his feet, and smiling broadly.

Few in the room were Catholic, but he knew when in Rome: they would do as the Romans do. He winked at Sis while the mayor, stiff and sore from the parade adventure, managed to rise and step toward the silk lined wooden box.

Mayor Clausen sighed audibly in relief, and

quickly snatched the paper from Otto's hand.
When the last alderman and the assistant
district attorney (lowest man in the pecking
order) had filed past, Uke gazed into the
coffin. The warrant was no longer between
Otto's fingers!

He hurried over to Sis, breaking up a conversation between her and the good Father and
whispered excitedly into her ear. The mayor had
all ready stepped through the door, holding it
open while counting the aldermen and motioning
them to hurry.

"Mr. Mayor," Sis called softly as she stepped
toward him, "I don't know what you intend to do
with that old insurance policy. Father Aloysius
tells me it ran out on him years ago."

"Whatever are you talking about?" Mayor
Clausen blustered.

"You, or one of your people, tried to steal
the warrant for my husband's arrest, but
instead took an old insurance policy."

The mayor fished the policy from inside his
coat and examined it briefly. A former insurance peddler, he immediately recognized the
twenty pay life policy, and handed it back to
her, the redness rising up his neck and above
his ears served as a comment. Sis closed the
door gently behind his honor and returned the
papers to Father Aloysius. He handed the
subpoena back to her.

"I didn't serve Otto with an insurance
policy," the baffled Uke insisted.

"I understand you're having a good old
fashion wake tonight," Father smiled at Sis.
"Do you mind if I stay?" These people met his
jabs and parries and came back with more fight.
He was becoming genuinely attached to them.

Sis nodded, "I'd like that." She turned to
the stove, tossed more wood into it from the
pile on the floor and put on another pot of
coffee, overwhelmed by the show of respect for

her and the family. Sandwiches and pie came with the coffee.

Uke and the priest sat down, while Ruth took a seat across the table from them wishing she had the courage to take over Sis's chores. Uke wondered if he should get the wash tub out and throw some more wood into the stove. Sis always made popcorn when she expected a lot of people. It had been his job to haul in wood.

CHAPTER TWENTY-TWO
THE WAKE

Uke could sense the feeling of being lost and
the shock of losing Otto began to lift from his
shoulders. Sis also seemed to have resigned
herself to the event. It wasn't anything that
had been said, but the fact these people took
the time to sit with them and enjoy the food
and casual conversation. The laugh over the
trick played on the mayor eased the tensions.

Father laughed and related his version of
Otto's attempt to get even with the ducks...he
did not tell them about his last laugh with his
game warden, nor did he tell them the warden
was his brother. At length he pushed his chair
away from the table and found a used cigar in
his coat pocket.

"You know," he studied the freshly lit end
of the stogie, "the art of getting along is
compromise."

They helped him watch the blue smoke waft
toward the ceiling for a moment until Sis
pushed herself away from the table and began to
collect the dishes. Father Aloysius reached out
and gently restrained her.

"Compromise," he continued, "is the way to
get along. You compromised with your husband.
He never compromised with anyone." He smiled

saying it, hoping no one would take offense.

"I compromised by letting the statue stand in my garden," he went on, looking deeply into her eyes. He didn't see fit to add he had also rid himself of the junkyard child in the process. "Some people never learn this trait, Otto was one of them. We must all learn this secret to a greater or lesser degree, none of us practice the art nearly enough."

"I have the feeling you're trying to tell me something," Sis interrupted. She leaned forward, almost pleading. This man was different from any man she had ever known and she felt her reserve melting.

"Yes, I am trying to tell you something." he sighed, "due to the events of the last day, you are not aware the statue is in place and cemented down. By the time the mayor decides what to do about it, it'll take all his resources to remove it."

"Do you think he'll try?" Sis asked anxiously. Uke and Ruth were also surprised and pleased with the news.

"No, but I have to tell you the statue doesn't quite look like it did when it left the house." He spoke quickly, explaining the statue would be more acceptable because of his professional touches. Unfortunately, he pointed out, the statue had lost its importance and the real issue was a matter of principle. "It's yours and on your property, so you can work it over, if you like."

Almost an afterthought, he added, "Oh, by the way, don't worry about Clausen removing the statue, the city clerk is one of my most faithful and reliable parishioners, he assures me he can throw enough roadblocks up to keep the mayor busy until doomsday."

"Yes, I suppose I could work it over," Sis agreed. It was in place and that was most important. She glanced at Uke who nodded in

agreement. A flash of insight gave her pause:
in that moment she felt perhaps Uke might be
coming of age. She began to see her brother in
a different light.

"The mayor and council weren't going to let a
statue into the park sculptured by Michelang-
elo, much less you, Otto had them so riled up."
Father waved his arms in the air in a forceful
rendition of anger and emotion. He wanted to be
certain he was convincing these people he had
done the right thing for the good of all
concerned.

"Why do you think they'll allow it to stand
now?" Ruth wondered. She gave Uke a scowl for
pushing an entire slice of cake into his mouth.
Much work would have to be done to mold her
husband into a gentleman.

"First of all," the priest smiled, "you
people have them over a barrel. They issued a
warrant for a dead man, and secondly, they
don't know what to do about it...for the
moment." His words were cold and icy.

The effect wasn't lost on Uke, "Then let's
not worry about it," he suggested, in his mind
the conversation had ended. Besides, the cake
plate was empty, not a sizable crumb was left.

"Wrong," Father snapped, "they'll run your
popcorn wagons off the streets, raise your
taxes, make you get out a license for each
chicken you own and generally make life
miserable for you."

He pushed his coffee cup out of the way and
crushed out his cigar on the edge of his
saucer. "There's an old saying, 'you can't beat
city hall', and you'd best believe it." He
refused to encourage these people by adding the
rest of the phrase. For his money they had city
hall all but white-washed. The cities' efforts
stunk like his crushed out cigar.

"What do you think we should do?" Ruth asked
in alarm.

Father Aloysius leaned forward in his chair,
looking intently at Sis before speaking, "Let
me compromise with them on your behalf."

"No, we'll fight it out," Sis snapped. Her
hands clenched the sides of the table and her
knuckles whitened. "I'll sell the house and
move away before I'll allow them to cheat us."

"Yeh," Uke growled. He searched for his big,
red handkerchief, blew his nose lustily and
wiped his face before putting it away, unaware
of Ruth's grimace.

"They'll throw up all sorts of legal roadblocks to keep you against the wall," Father
retorted, trying to get them to see the futil-
ity of it all."Even with a real estate agent,
who do you suppose issues the license to do
business as a broker, and who do you suppose
sells the license to the broker?" He was not at
all certain of this information, but right now
he felt the need to invent obstacles.

Sis started to get up from the table, but sat
down weakly. Perhaps he was right, maybe a
compromise would be better? "How would you do
this?"

"Well, if Otto left a couple hundred dollars
to the mayor's campaign fund," he smiled, gaz-
ing off into an empty corner of the kitchen,
"it would be a start."

"A bribe, you mean," Sis nodded wiping her
perspiring hands on her apron. "That's the way
the game is played, isn't it?"

"All up and down the line," Father smiled
sadly, "with the councilmen who are members of
my parish, and the money, I should be able to
get things to quiet down." Otto, he thought to
himself, is now on the lay-away-plan.

A thought suddenly occurred to Sis. "And what
do you expect to get out of all this?"

"I owe you something," Father Aloysius replied. "I remodeled your statue, got Otto into
a peck of trouble with the game warden and

frankly, I like all of you."

Sis stared at him. He was sitting there,
willing to square things and apparently for no
good reason. Thus, a decision fashioned itself.

"Why not try it? Things can hardly get any
worse," she concluded, absently brushing crumbs
from the table onto the floor. "See if you can
smooth things over."

A knock interrupted any further conversation.
The first of the real mourners had arrived to
pay their respects to Otto. Sis pulled off her
apron and hurriedly smoothed her hair with her
hands in a futile gesture before going to
answer the door. Ruth hurried from the room,
feeling her hair and straightening her dress.
She hunted desperately for a mirror.

Uke laughed at them. Women, tough as nails
most of the time, get so flustered over nothing. He rose from his chair and pulled open the
lower kitchen cabinet and began to remove
whiskey bottles and brandy and rye canisters.
Otto had won all of it at one time or another
in a poker game.

Father Aloysius took the cue and hunted
through the cupboard until he found the good
glasses up high on a shelf. He rinsed and
polished them to a high sheen, wondering if the
goods were acquired before or after prohibition
came into effect. And this is a dry county, he
mused.

"Ya know, padre," Uke pronounced, "you're a
hell of a nice guy."

A warm smile creased the preacher's face.
Uke knew he had scored a direct hit. The priest
continued to smile and raised a glass to inspect his polishing job on it before allowing
Uke to fill it with cheer.

"Yes," Father readily agreed, pulling off his
black coat, starched white dickey and collar to
reveal a brown cotton sweater beneath, "in case
the people out in the front room wonder who I

am, tell them I'm your friend Ike, from up
Nakooska way."

Uke's mouth fell open at the contrast in
appearance. Now he don't look no more like a
preacher than I do, he thought. He understood
what Ike was saying. After all, how could he
have any fun, or anyone else, with a priest at
the party?

Uke finished filling a tray with glasses.
Ike grabbed it and made for the front room.
"Hi," Uke heard him shout above the rising
din, "I'm Ike, an old friend of the family, and
this is my calling card."

Ruth smiled helplessly at Sis and helped herd
the women out to the kitchen, but not before
they saw Father place a glass of whiskey in
Otto's hand resting on his chest. Then he
offered the rest to the guests. This marked the
official beginning of the wake.

Uke greeted the steady stream of mourners at
the front door while Ike kept the glasses
filled. Uke could hear snatches of the conversation in the room.

O'Rourke, the bricklayer, regaled them with a
story about the time Otto loaded a pile of his
bricks onto his truck when he thought no one
was looking. He waited until Otto was in front
of his next project before stopping him. "Got a
free haul job out of him," O'Rourke laughed.

"He was a good guy," Maloney shouted back in
Otto's defense. "He beat me out of the deed to
my farm and then gave it back the next day."
In the kitchen a smile played over Sis's face
as she heard.

"Remember the time a hold-up man came rushing
out the door of Sweeny's Drug Store?" Notonski
asked. "It was an accident Otto fell over him,
but by the time Otto got to my place, he had
changed the story six times. He made a real
genuine hero out'a his self."

"He was a guy who knew the southern part of

Wisconsin," Stuart broke in, ramming his thumb over his shoulder at Otto. "Or anyway he knew all the trout streams and catfish holes in this part of the state." He laughed loudly, several others nodded in agreement. The whiskey was having the desired effect.

Uke saw Wiseman going through Otto's pockets before Otto was lifted from his final resting place by two of his poker playing cronies and stood up in the corner, making him seem like one of the crowd. He started out to collar Wiseman, but then recalled that he had tried every way he knew how to get Otto to pay him the five dollars he owed him. Otto had told him he'd rather owe him the money than beat him out of it.

By now the noise had risen to a din. O'Rourke and Notonski stepped outside to settle a dispute and when they returned Ike bathed O'Rourke's cheek with whiskey to disinfect the wound. Nottonski asked Ruth for some of Sis's "Irish gasoline."

"What is that?" puzzled, Ruth had to ask.

"Ah, dear girl, that's Sis's coffee."

With the first traces of morning painting the eastern sky, few of the mourners were able to continue singing the Irish tunes Ike kept leading them in. One by one, the women entered the room and coaxed, wheedled or dragged their husbands home. All except Mrs. Johnson, who lived on the far end of Devil's Lane. She went home and returned with a wheelbarrow which she kept handy for most Saturday nights.

"Why don't you stay?" Sis asked Ruth when she noticed the girl making preparations to leave. "I don't think Uke is in any condition to walk all the way to your house."

"I would prefer to take my husband home," Ruth confided, "we haven't as yet begun our honeymoon."

Sis thought it best to change the subject.

"What are we going to do with him?" She pointed
to Ike who had a lamp shade on his head and was
trying to play Yankee Doodle on a washboard
with two clothes pins. Ruth took the board and
clothes pins away from him and retrieved his
Roman collar which Otto was now sporting.

Realizing the party was over, the good padre
stood up experimentally. He grunted in satisfaction. The test proved a success. Sis steered
him gently toward the front door. The cool
early morning air would do wonders for him.

He turned and directed his smile at Ruth,
"Thank you for a wonderful evening," he beamed,
feeling for his collar to see if it was in
place.

"Uke and I will walk part way with you," she
responded.

"Why don't you stay?" Sis half pleaded, half
demanded of Ruth.

"We have our own place," Ruth replied wear-
ily, "and we've been married two days and,
and...."

"Oh, yes," Sis forced a smile in resignation.
She stood at the door watching the three of
them move down Devil's Lane with Uke holding on
to the other two for support. Long after they
had passed from view she continued to look.

When the funeral is over, she decided, Uke
will have to do something about the smashed
truck in the yard. The easiest way to get the
problem off her hands would be to give him the
ruined vehicle. Parts were scattered over the
entire property. The explosion had damaged it
almost beyond recognition.

* * *

Otto was laid to rest the next day on a knoll
under a big Oak tree. A squirrel sat on the
lowest branch and chattered nervously watching
the family pay their last respects. Ruth cried
and wiped her eyes. Uke kicked at the fresh
stones scattered about the family plot,

wondering if anyone else had a hangover.

He wondered where Sis had come up with this preacher and where he had ever found so many nice things to say about Otto? Sis stood quietly, mixed with her grief was the feeling Otto was holding all the cards in a no limit poker game somewhere. The gathering was very small, not more than ten.... including the squirrel.

CHAPTER TWENTY-THREE
THE REVELATION

Uke was determined to repair the truck. By
tomorrow I should have a good start, he figured. I'll need most of today to find the tools
for the job. He spent the time tramping around
in the high weeds checking out the sulky and
the old truck cab for tools. He found a hammer
and a wrench in fair condition in the dog
house. There were teeth marks on the wrench,
looked like maybe from a badger, he decided.

"This here project is going to take a while,"
he advised Sis. She didn't tell him where she
was headed this time of day, and he refused to
ask. He turned back to the job at hand.

The skin on the truck was all but a total
wreck. The cab, fenders and hood were either
torn or bent beyond use. His eyes followed Sis
down Devil's lane. She turned toward town.

He debated following her, sensing her errand
was important, but the truck was more so. He
dismissed her from his mind. Probably going to
find Higgie or that crooked old hag, Mihich.

"Seen Higgie today?" Sis asked Cumber, who
was inspecting Higgie's job on his store windows. "Cuke" jerked his thumb over his shoulder
up the street. She saw no one else on Main

street. Some days all she had to do was examine
the condition of the business windows. If they
were dirty, Higgie hadn't been there. If they
were fairly clean she looked for nose prints on
the glass, Higgie's trade mark.

* * *

Uke again debated following her, but decided
against it. There was a lot of work to be done
on the truck and the sooner he had it running:
the sooner he would be driving it.

He resumed his search. A crowbar up in the
rain trough where it had slid when he had
helped Otto fix a leak in the roof about four
years ago was the latest find.

The new truck had the gasoline tank under the
hood in front of the windshield, unlike the old
one where the gas tank took up all the space
under the seat. Most of the wrenches were there
making the hunt easier. If his guess was right,
borrowing tools from someone would be difficult. Those he found, he suspected were borrowed items never returned by Otto when he had
finished using them.

Sis appeared to have rebounded after Otto's
demise, and was almost her old self. He could-
n't be sure. It seemed Sis was quite happy.

He turned back to his task. Sometimes with a
wrench, at other times with a hammer and chisel
and often with the sledge hammer he managed to
collect replacement parts at Axel's Junk Emporium. A wheel, fender, then the hood were loaded
into the wheelbarrow and pushed down to the
junk yard to be matched up with better parts.

It would have been easier and faster to dump
the parts into the back seat of the Durant, but
Otto had warned him he was not allowed to use
the car...evil things could happen to him. He
couldn't argue the point: he had driven the
Durant once and it was to his own wedding.

Sis didn't offer the use of the Durant. Uke
would have refused for reasons he could not

tell her. He was not about to divulge Otto's
threats to her.

It seemed to him that Sis seemed almost
satisfied to have had the disaster happen. She
had commented vaguely that it would prove to
anyone Mihich Nostrov's predictions were true
and nothing to fool around with. Mihich had
foretold the future with uncanny accuracy, she
insisted to anyone who would listen.

Uke had no urge to discover the power of
Otto's threats, much less become involved with
the old witch's predictions about the future.

He made trips up town pushing the wheelbarrow twice a day under the July sun to ex-
change parts. Repairing the truck was exciting
and when each part was successfully replaced,
his pride and enthusiasm reached new plateaus.
He discovered a new respect for himself.

It took the better part of two weeks to
complete the assembly job, Uke was pleased with
his handiwork. The hike uptown in the midday
heat for parts worked miracles on his weight
and confidence, for the first time in his life.

Sis didn't hassle him and Otto couldn't ridi-
cule. Life couldn't get much better. He was
married and with no more responsibilities than
he had had before. He did wonder how Ruth was
getting along since the funeral.

* * *

Every morning before the July day grew hot,
Sis hunted high and low for Higgie without
success. No one could remember seeing him
around. Store windows were getting dirty and
Sis was getting frustrated. If worst came to
worst, she'd have to ask Uke to take her. With
the truck laid up, she was at a loss for help.
She did not tell Uke how terrified she had been
with him at the wheel on the wedding day.

Each day Uke watched her walk up town. It had
to be Higgie she was searching for, Michich was
once or twice a week visit, so it couldn't be

her Sis was looking for. It had to be Higgie.
She didn't put on her walking shoes and head up
town all that often. He had no idea what she
might want with the slippery rascal. It wasn't
official business so he refused to inquire.

No one seemed to know much about Higgie and
had no idea where the man lived or if he was
married. His privacy had to be protected with
a good deal of effort and zeal. Prying into
someone else's business was the towns way of
life. Higgie was successful, in that no one
seemed to know much about him.

Uke put the final touches on the truck and
invited Ruth home to see the results. She came
eagerly, partly because she did not believe he
could accomplish such a task and partly because
it was an opportunity to see her husband.

Life had been no different since she had
married than it had been before. Uke stayed
with Sis who was too busy to notice him. In
all, Ruth had spent one night of her married
life with Uke and it was the night she had
taken him home drunk, over two weeks ago.

But now walking into the yard, she forgot her
pent up anger and held his hand and skipping
alongside him like a school girl. He urged her
to go up to the house and get Sis. She laughed
at his eagerness and danced along the happy to
do his bidding.

Uke pulled the heavy canvas cover from the
truck and stood back to admire his handiwork
one more time. When the two women emerged from
the kitchen door, he hurried around to the
front wheel and kicked the tire. Next he
reached into the truck and fiddled with the
choke and spark adjustments located on the
steering column and waited until they were
standing beside him before spinning the crank.

The truck started immediately and settled
down into a gentle purr like a happy kitten.
The two women stared in astonishment. Neither

were aware Uke had not touched any of the
internal workings of the engine. It had escaped
unscathed in the explosion, protected by the
heavy sheet metal skin.

"Why Uke," Ruth exclaimed, clapping her hands
in delight, "that's tremendous!"

"You did a real fine job," Sis agreed stepping back to take a better look. "I have no use
for a truck, so it's all yours."

"Gee, thanks," Uke shouted, "Ruth, I can have
the truck!" All he ever hoped for was to drive
it. Now it's all mine!

"That's wonderful," Ruth agreed, but with a
note of hesitation. "But don't you think it
should be painted?" Uke looked at her puzzled.
"Why the paint is in A-1 shape. Not a scratch,
not a dent, no nicks or rust anywhere on it."

"Yes," Ruth agreed, "but with a black body, a
red hood, three green wheels and one yellow
one, a violet front fender and a blue one?" She
laughed pointing at the rainbow of colors. The
puzzled frown on his face added to her mirth.

"It should really be one color," Sis advised.
"Only one?" Uke objected. "Wouldn't hurt to
have two colors, would it? Or maybe three?"

"Black is the color the new ones came in,"
Sis recalled, "it's your truck now, you can
have it any color you want." She didn't want to
tell him a trim color would be all right. Three
colors made it look like a circus wagon.

"I'll paint it orange with pink wheels and
maybe a purple pin stripe around the middle,
them's my favorites."

The color drained from Ruth's face, "Don't
you think black with yellow wheels would be
better?" She was furious. If she was going to
ride in it, it would have to be more subdued.
Uke should be consulting her, not Sis.

Sis turned away, it would be best not to
become involved, stupid things like this cause
family fights. She did not care to become a

part of the one now brewing. Reaching the kitchen door she could hear Uke raising his voice. Moments later he stormed in.

"Women," he snorted, heading for the stairway.

"Uke."

The tone in Sis's voice brought him up short. "Where are you headed?"

"Up and lay down for a while before supper."

"No you're not."

"Why?"

"Uke, you have a home and a wife now." She waved a wooden mixing spoon at him, the same one she used to use to spank him with.

"Your place is with her. Where is she?"

"Don't know an don't care. I ain't going to see her no more. Not even on Wednesday date night." He had repaired the truck and running better than Otto ever managed and Ruth had laughed at him and made fun of the paint job.

It took a moment for Sis's next words to sink in. "Well, you can't stay here, that's final."

"You've been staying for weeks now. I was wrong letting you stay here while fixing up the truck, it's worse since you're angry with her."

Uke felt like he had lost his last friend. He took his hat from the door knob and ambled from the house fighting the urge to scratch under the red handkerchief pocket.

He kicked the front tire on the truck and spun the crank. Climbing in, he backed slowly out watching the kitchen door, hoping Sis would appear and call him back. Deep in his mind he knew she would not, things had changed. He drove aimlessly through town.

The truck took him past the Catholic church and Father Aloysius looked up from puttering in the garden near the stations of the cross. He tried to flag Uke down to tell him the good news. If the warrant was returned, the city would allow the statue to remain in the park

providing shrubs were planted in front of it.
He ignored the priest. He was in no mood to
talk to anyone. He kept going. He wanted to
drive and think things out.

Full of angry thoughts about Ruth and now
Sis, he continued past one of the popcorn
wagons and ignored the frantic signaling from
Jeff Benson to stop and relieve him of his full
till. The money resulted mostly from the Fourth
of July celebration and this wagon was near the
parade route.

He was on the far side of town and almost to
McNamara's crossing. Idly, he wondered what
would happen if he let the truck go on up the
hill without making a run for it?

Bouncing over the railroad tracks at the
bottom of the hill, he cast a sidelong glance
at the huge boulder and made a mental note to
stop sometime and pick up the remains of the
popcorn wagon. It might be handy for something.
If nothing else maybe spare parts for the other
wagons? I can dump it down in the weeds behind
the old shed, Sis won't care. I'll sound her
out first, if she objects I'll haul it in at
night and she'll never know it.

The truck slowed noticeably at the midway
point of the hill. Uke worked the pedals to
shift gears. The truck slowed, but continued to
creep up the hill. The engine labored, but did
not quit. He bent over the steering wheel
watching the road in front of him, pushing on
the steering wheel to help urge it along.

He was at the top of the hill right near the
spot where Otto used to wait for him. He pulled
the truck off to the side of the road, stopped
and looked back down the hill.

The results of this triumph troubled him.
Otto always had to turn the truck around and
back the rest of the way up the hill.

Perhaps it would have bothered him less had
he known gasoline cannot run up hill on a

gravity flow fuel system. The difference
between the old and new truck was simple: the
old truck had the gas tank under the driver's
seat and the new one had it mounted under the
hood, in front of the windshield. The tank was
considerably higher than in the old truck,
making the difference.

Instead, he thought he must have done a real
fine job, Otto was never able to do what he had
just done. He stretched out in the shade of
Otto's favorite Maple tree where he had fallen
asleep shortly before he had fried Otto's old
truck. He was not about to fall asleep and have
it happen to his truck.

He rested until he judged the amount of time
it used to take him to walk up the long, steep
hill had passed. It was good to be alone and
have the chance to do some thinking.

The beautiful part was with the truck he
could get up here instead of going to the willows to think. Sis used to raise cain when he
came home all muddy from the river. Silently he
gave thanks to Otto for two things. No more
tirades from Sis and no more mud.

He stood enjoying the slight breeze washing
over him before ambling to the truck. He
reached in to set the spark, choke and timing
and then dropped his hat on the seat before
heading toward the front wheel. Leaning heavily
on the front fender, the violet one, he looked
far down hill through the heat waves shimmering
on the concrete before raising his foot to kick
the tire.

With his foot in mid-air, he hesitated before
placing it back on the ground. Once again his
gaze followed the glimmering heat waves. He was
always intrigued by the water appearing to
cover the road in several places. He knew none
was there. Without taking his eyes from the
view, he bent over the crank.

He hesitated, almost afraid to touch it.

With a deep breath, he wrapped his huge hand
around the handle and gave a tug on it. Nothing
happened. He began to straighten up to perform
the ritual on the tire, but some unknown force
kept his grip on the crank handle.

Taking another breath, he spun the handle
again. This time the engine caught hold with a
roar. The truck danced in anticipation.

He grabbed his hat from the seat and jammed
it down tight on his head. Pushing his lower
jaw out until it hurt, he felt the familiar
lurch of the truck when he put his full weight
onto the running board. Elated, he slipped
behind the wheel and released the clutch.

The truck spun around hard. He pressed his
foot into the floor board over the gas pedal
narrowly missing Otto's "resting tree". It was
the tree Otto had always waited under in the
shade while Uke walked up the hill.

The engine howled in protest and then in
anger, picking up speed on its screaming,
downhill journey. There were things he needed
to tend to and the sooner the better. If the
tire kicking was unnecessary and a farce, so
were a lot of other things in his life.

It would be sometime before he would learn
the small round knob on the floor near the
accelerator was a self starter. The crank was
nothing more than a back up system in case the
battery went dead or the starter wore out.

Catching sight of a slow freight chugging
toward McNamara's crossing belching smoke from
its stack, Uke snarled his satisfaction.

"This time that damn train's going to stop
for me," he shouted above the noise of the wind
and held to his course, continuing to pick up
speed. He leaned over the steering wheel urging
his mighty steed faster.

Intent upon staying on the road, he didn't
notice a brakeman in the middle of the long
line of freight cars lean out over the box car

rung holding on with one hand and put his thumb and first finger to his nose, indicating a hot box. A bearing needed grease.

The engineer, ever alert to this emergency signal of an over heated wheel bearing on the verge of putting the train out of action, pulled on the Johnson bar to slow down. It would take a mile to stop the slow moving freight. Uke continued his headlong race down the hill.

The locomotive ground to a hissing, screeching halt inches short of McNamara's crossing none too soon. Uke careened past and put his thumb to his nose and waved his fingers, the sign of the times telling them to "kiss it."

The engineer and fireman in the cab scratched their heads thoughtfully. The Model-T disappeared into the heat waves. The brakeman several cars back, put his thumb to his nose and waved his fingers in response to Uke's "kiss mine" too late for anyone to see it.

Uke pounded both hands on the steering wheel and shouted in delight, "I can even stop freight trains!"

The truck tipped precariously up on two wheels making a sliding turn into the cemetery, skidding on the loose gravel. He guided it to Otto's freshly covered plot. The squirrel disturbed by a visitor, held forth in the gnarled oak tree swearing at Uke in squirrel chatter.

Jumping from the truck, Uke stood over Otto's wounded mound of dirt for a moment with his hands defiantly placed on his hips. With a slow, deliberate action he bent over and picked up a handful of the larger stones within reach and threw them at the angry squirrel.

The animal ducked into a hole in the tree and then scrambled back out ahead of an upset blue jay and quickly found the right hole and did not reappear. Satisfied, with the stone throwing and the Blue Jay's action, Uke climbed back into the steaming truck.

"First thing tomorrow morning I'm going to drive her damn Durant all over town," he swore under his breath. "It's my car, too."

Forcing the truck from the cemetery, careful not to run over any tombstones, Uke aimed it in the direction of Ruth's house. My house, too, he growled. The truck panted to a halt at the front gate. Uke vaulted the fence.

Ruth was pouring a cup of coffee for her unsteady father when Uke stormed into the kitchen. He grabbed her by the wrist and spun her around, hot coffee flew through the room.

"Let the old man get his own coffee, if he wants it bad enough," he snapped, pulling her toward the bedroom.

Ruth struggled momentarily in the powerful grip before realizing her husband had under gone some violent reaction changing him at least for the moment. Whatever the reason, she followed along almost eagerly, as anxious and fearful as any new bride would be. Whatever happened it was about time, they had been married now for over two weeks.

Uke slammed the door shut almost before she was through it and shoved her roughly down on the bed. She sat looking at him, her eyes wide and uncertain not knowing what the next move should be. She had not long to wait. Uke threw his hat on the floor, whipped out his red handkerchief and mopped his face.

He hung his holster on the door knob and putting his hand on his hips snorted, "You aren't strong enough to move the rock over by the popcorn wagon at the city park," he shouted, stuffing the handkerchief back into his pocket. "And furthermore, the truck went up McNamara's hill by itself. I don't have to kick the front tire to start it, I made a freight train stop for me at the crossing, I threw a rock at a noisy squirrel and I spit on Otto's

grave." The words flew out of him like a
torrential downpour.

"First thing tomorrow morning I'm going to
drive the Durant whether Sis likes it or not,
and I'm going to get the money I got coming
from her and then I'm going over to the Rock
River and catch old Herman, an then I'm going
to put my uniform on and raid the next smoker
Father Aloysius has, and, and," he paused for
breath," and right now I'm going to..." he
inched forward toward his wife, but a light
knock came to the door interrupting his tirade.

"Who is it?" Uke demanded. He picked his hat
off the floor.

Ruth's father answered timidly, "A fellow out
here wants to see you."

"Well, what's he want?" Uke demanded, "I'm
busy." "He didn't say," the old gentleman
replied tiredly, "says it's official business."

Uke lifted his holster from the door knob and
strapped it on. If it was official business:
the gun had to be hanging on his hip. Careful
not to touch the trigger, he felt the butt of
the .38, reassured he reached for the door
knob. "You," he turned to Ruth, "stay here."
No longer fearful, she nodded in agreement.

He started through the door, paused and then
turned toward her. She looked up, uncertainty
in her wide blue eyes. On an impulse, Uke
returned and kissed her softly on the mouth. It
took the startled girl a moment to respond. She
watched him charge out the door.

Jim Atwell stood in the middle of the small
front room. He greeted Uke with an overly
friendly smile holding a thick sheaf of papers.
As Uke approached he held them out to him.

"I'm running for mayor and I thought maybe
you'd want to sign up, everybody is doing it."
Jim waited expectantly. Uke's name on the
petition papers would be an endorsement.
Besides, most of the people in the county

didn't really know the sheriff which Jim
thought was probably a good thing, too.

Uke took the papers and nodded. Jim was
always running for some office. It was about
all he was good for.

As he spoke, Jim wiped saliva from his mouth
with the back of his hand. "Ruth and her dad
have signed. Most of the people in town have
signed, including all the aldermen. I guess
nobody's got much use for that old fossil,
Wendle Clausen."

Uke figured Jim was partly right, but he
doubted any of the aldermen had signed. If the
mayor ever stopped quick: the whole passel of
them would have broken noses!

He took the papers over by the window where
the light was better. He sat down and unscrewed
the cap from Jim's pen. Only a fool would lend
his whole pen to someone: always hang onto the
cap Otto had advise him, the rest of the pen is
of no value without it.

"Ruth," he called loud enough to wake all the
voters in the graveyard, "Get Jim a cup of
coffee." With after thought he added, "please."

He looked the papers over carefully. Yep, the
place for him to sign was empty on almost all
the sheets: like it had been on the papers for
sheriff last election. Well, why not? He began
scribbling his name. Who knows, some day they
might hand me papers to sign for U.S. Senator,
or maybe President? He labored through the
sheaf. Jim Atwell sipped contentedly on his hot
coffee and admired Ruth who had slipped into
her sheer pink wedding negligee in anticipation. Instead, she was serving coffee to a
stranger.

The day after I'm elected mayor, Uke vowed,
that statue is coming out of the park. Might be
a good place to install a popcorn wagon?

Or maybe a statue of me?

CHAPTER TWENTY-FOUR
HIGGIE'S FATE

Uke noticed the store windows were getting
dirtier by the day, the merchants were whining,
and he could only come to one conclusion:
something terrible must have happened to
Higgie. Sis began hounding him to drive her
over to the pawn shop in Middletown.

She was adamant in her refusal to tell him
why the trip was so important. Worse, she would
only tell him Mihich Nostrov could tell her
nothing about Higgie. He was aware Sis's trips
had come more frequent to see the old phony and
guessed she was at a loss to invent a good
story about Higgie. When he had tried to hit
Sis up for a "divvy", she snapped and snarled
at him.

The truth as Uke saw it: she had plied the
old woman with half dollars these past two
weeks and the fortune teller was either unable
or unwilling to tell her anything. Her remarks
about Mihich pleased him: her confidence in the
woman's ability to foretell Otto's demise had
dwindled with no word on Higgie.

"I'm running for mayor," Uke excitedly told
his older sister, hoping she would share his
enthusiasm.

"Would you please drive me over to

Middletown?," she asked. He noted her previous
quests had been in the form of demands.

"Maybe next week," he replied. No divvy, no
service.

"If you want campaign money I will need your
help." She would have had better luck if she
told him that finding the stock and getting the
will consummated according to her lawyers
should come first, now that the statue was in
place.

He wondered if the gold stock wasn't another
excuse to keep from settling the estate?

* * *

Higgie had listened intently to Uke's fish
story. Uke had explained to him in great detail
how he had captured Herman and without prodding
on Higgie's part, exactly where. Right below
the electric company's dam on the east side of
the Rock River.

"To hell with the windows. If I get Herman,
I'll present him to Otto and then maybe he'll
like me enough to let me put some more money
into the popcorn wagons," Higgie decided.

Along with some documents he had seven
dollars tucked away in the sole of his shoe.
The wagons were a good investment and in the
meantime his filing system kept the wet from
seeping through the hole in the sole of his
shoe.

Higgie much preferred the old silver certif-
icates. These Hoover dollars said "there was on
deposit," instead of "there is on deposit." He
had buried a tomato can full of good ones someplace. He couldn't remember where. Now with
this new president, they were talking about
taking that legend off the money all together.

He ranted about this to anyone who would
listen, but never offered any information on
popcorn wagon stock. It was too good. He knew
the movie theater sold big kernel popcorn in
order to fill the bag with less corn and more

husks. Otto's corn was tastier by far, with no
husks. Movie goers were eating lots of popcorn
hidden under their coats when they came into
the theater.

Higgie didn't buy the story about Herman
taking the flashlight and cold-cocking Uke with
a blow to the head. But all the same, Higgie
left his flashlight at home: there was no sense
taking chances.

From Uke's description of the fishing hole he
found it with no trouble. He cared not a lick
for Otto's camp site and planned to tell him
about its lack of accessibility when he got
home. Instead, he armed himself with a fishing
license and set up camp under a large oak tree
right out in the open on the nearby hillside
by the dam.

Meanwhile, Herman hurried over to size up the
new comer and swam around right below Higgie
and his old cane pole grinning to himself. With
his one good eye he had trouble recognizing the
fishing tackle for what it was. He hadn't seen
a cane pole in years. He felt kind of sorry for
Higgie, unlike those other two urchins who
showed up now and then.

Those guys were noisy and boisterous and in
no way would he allow them to catch and keep
him. This one might be different, he'd have to
think about it.

Higgie worked some baker's bread into a nice,
good sized lump of waterproof dough and placed
it carefully on the hook. He had no desire to
ferment clams or chicken innards in a glass jar
by letting them sit in the summer sun until
ripe like Otto always did. He tried it once at
Otto's insistence. It was terrific bait and he
had caught his limit, but lost his breakfast
whenever he baited the hook.

His carp bait worked nearly as well. The
dough ball hung out over the water for a moment
while Higgie settled himself into a comfortable

position with his back resting against a rotting tree stump. He was at peace with the world, no windows out here to wash, no wife nagging him, no children under foot and no sign of rain. What more could he ask?

Herman waited patiently for the juicy delicacy dangling out of reach over the water. In his prime, Herman would never consider leaping out of the water like some foolish trout or black bass. Let the goodies come to me, I'll wait.

The line, however, became tangled in an over hanging tree branch. Higgie worked long and hard to free it. Herman waited patiently for a time before swimming away in search of other food. He felt sorry for such an inept creature.

Eventually, Higgie determined he had no other course but to cut down the tree limb. Herman heard the bait splash into the water and returned in time to see Higgie grasp the fish line and wind several strands around his finger for a better grip before pulling it toward shore. Herman hadn't much luck finding breakfast and this food was in the water for the taking.

Higgie's concern was for the fish hook, heck, he had lots more bread, but no more hooks large enough to land a big fish.

Herman moved quietly toward the wad of bait. With his one good eye he could see by the size of the bait he wouldn't be hungry again for a couple of days. He knew it was baker's bread, one of his favorite foods, other than old chicken guts or clams left to stew in the sun for several days.

Intent upon retrieving his property, Higgie did not see the big catfish swoop in on the prize. He had the fish line wrapped firmly around his finger with a couple of half hitches. He drew the morsel carefully toward shore hoping he had enough fish line left to tie it back on his cane pole.

The closer he got to his feast the faster Herman streaked toward breakfast. Higgie was hardly concerned, he knew catfish didn't like their food to be moving, they much preferred it on the muddy bottom of the river.

Herman opened his mouth wide and sucked in the baker's bread as he flashed past the creature on the river bank. He caught Higgie by surprise, who tried to leap backwards, but Herman had the bait firmly in his mouth and raced away from the scene of the crime.

Higgie's backward leap lifted both feet from the ground. The line tightened around his finger. Any resistance he had was completely lost. The fish line came taut and propelled him toward the river.

The line pointed like an arrow into the water and Higgie plunged head first into the murky swiftly moving water that had spilled over the dam.

He had only enough time to catch a fleeting glance of Herman swallowing the carp bait.

The fishing hole was about four feet deep. Anyone with good sense about him could have stayed calm and stood up in shallow water, but Higgie had one thought as his life flashed by him. He couldn't swim!

With his finger tightly wrapped around the line and the hook firmly imbedded in Herman's mouth, Higgie could feel himself being towed out into the swiftly flowing deep water right below the dam.

In desperation, he tried to get his feet under him. He had to take control of the situation. He had to! But his feet no longer touched bottom. He was being towed further from shore!

In panic, Higgie opened his mouth to call for help. The roar of the water falling over the dam drowned out any chance of being heard.

He gasped as he swallowed a large mouthful of
black, muddy water. The swiftly flowing current
tugged at his clothes and swept him into a
whirlpool and then into an undertow, the one
great fear of excellent swimmers. In that
moment he knew he'd never wash another window.

About a week later, several of the game ward-
en's children discovered Herman and fished him
out of the eddy where he was floating belly up.
A wad of carp bait in his mouth had apparently
strangled Herman. They discovered a body on the
other end of the line. It was obvious the
fisherman had drowned rather than let Herman
go free, he had a fish line firmly twisted
around his finger.

* * *

Uke had listened impassively while Sis
pleaded for help to get her gold mining stock
returned. He wasn't sure that was her real
problem since she unloaded a day by day account
about the hens taking to hiding eggs in some of
the most ridiculous places at the same time.

"I found two eggs under that old rusty
lawnmower near the abandoned dog house in the
weeds, and one on the back seat of the Durant."

He knew about the eggs that used to be in his
room, two chicks now occupied it. He had forgotten to take the eggs out of his shirt pocket
and when he noticed them he had put them on the
dresser near a window where the warm sunlight
streamed in.

"I have no idea how they got up there or how
they existed upstairs," Sis declared.

Uke knew, but was not about to tell her he
had been feeding the cute little dickens
porridge and table scraps.

She also mentioned that her egg hunt took her
down among the high weeds and sun flowers where
a new contraption peeked out at her. Upon in-
vestigation it proved to be the remains of a

popcorn wagon. Instead of popcorn in the show box it appeared to be coal dust. Uke shrugged and walked away when she demanded an explanation. Sis made his decision to move in with Ruth easier.

Determined to confront him, Sis hiked across town hoping Uke would be home. A telephone would save time, but it wouldn't be of much use since few people around town had one and seventy-five cents a month was an awful lot of money.

Ruth answered the door in a maternity dress. "Uke is not home. No, I don't know where he is. I haven't seen much of him since he began running for mayor and talking about how next time he'd go for governor."

"You have no idea where he is?" Sis found this hard to believe. She eyed the maternity dress.

"No, I don't," Ruth replied for the second time. "May I ask why you want him?"

Sis was reluctant to answer the question, it was really none of Ruth's business when it came to personal things. Once more she cast a glance at Ruth's dress.

Noticing the look Ruth grinned, "No, I'm not pregnant, but I'm trying to give Uke the hint."

Sis groaned inwardly, gosh, we have another flake in the family. Impatiently, she explained to Ruth she would probably have to entice him in order to get any results. She rose to take her leave.

"You don't want to tell me why you want Uke," Ruth accused her, "but perhaps I can help you anyway? What do you need?"

Sis restrained a shrug. "I need someone to drive me over to Middletown. I haven't been able to find Higgie."

"I saw a new guy washing windows when I was up town," Ruth volunteered. "If it's a ride you need, I can drive."

"You can?" Sis was amazed. Women, especially ladies, didn't drive.

"Yes, I can," Ruth asserted. "Before long women will be driving all over the place. It isn't hard to do, especially since all you have to do is push on a thingy on the floor to start a car. You don't have to crank the new ones by hand anymore."

Sis was astounded. "Does Uke know this?"

"Why certainly," Ruth was getting angry. What did Sis think her husband was, a fool? "In fact, Otto didn't know about it, Uke discovered the starter all by himself."

Pressed, Sis decided to accept Ruth's offer. She was willing to wait until Ruth changed clothes and saw to getting lunch prepared for her father. The old man had seemed to age considerably since the wedding. Idly, Sis wondered if having Uke under the roof had anything to do with his failing health.

They walked along quietly on the way back to the homestead to get the Durant. Sis was lost in thought and Ruth had her own problems to be concerned about. Her concern was about driving.

She had fibbed to Sis about it. She watched Uke and Otto a number of times with the truck and once had seen Otto with the Durant, but it didn't look too hard. Otto had indicated he would be glad to teach her how to drive.

A few days before his demise, Ruth accepted Otto's offer to give her lessons. With the first lesson she quickly learned Otto wanted to start teaching her about cars from the back seat. When his hand arrived on her knee, she slapped his face. He offered no more lessons.

Arriving at Devil's Lane, Sis tugged open the heavy old doors to the shed and stepped back to allow Ruth to admire her mighty steed. The two women stood for a moment peering into the darkness before Sis gave Ruth a nudge toward the vehicle. The old Durant awaited. Sis fished

through her purse hunting for the keys with no
success.

Ruth hesitated before approaching the car.
It looked larger and different from what she
remembered. The royal blue color and black trim
intimidated her. She took a deep breath and
approached the vehicle trying to hide the fear
strangling her, aware of Sis standing nearby.
Swallowing a pound of terror, Ruth climbed into
the front seat and reached for the ignition.
Relief flooded over her when she discovered the
keys were missing.

"No keys," she managed, hoping she sounded
calm. Sis had not found any in her purse and it
took a minute to remember she had given a chain
of keys to Uke. She frowned and her shoulders
slumped, but suddenly she recalled a trick Otto
had always used.

She reached past Ruth and felt around under
the curve of the dashboard, fishing a key out
along with a long over due egg. She studied the
egg a moment before throwing it against the far
wall of the shed. Ruth realized Sis meant
business and was really in a foul mood.

Quickly she studied the dash and the floor
trying to remember what little Otto had taught
her about driving. She found the small round
starter knob on the floor right near the
accelerator pedal. Stepping on it, she felt the
car leap forward and quickly stopped pressing.
Ah, I have to push down on this big pedal with
the left foot like Otto would do. She stepped
on the clutch pedal and pushed it to the floor.

Taking a deep breath, she tried the round
floor knob again. This time the engine roared
to life and for a moment she relaxed, but she
had to get the thing out of the shed.

Let's see now, I remember, he did something
with this long stick in the floor while he
tried to feel my knee. It looks like it is in
the right position, but a long way from my

knee. Ruth released the peddle on the left.

The clutch engaged and the Durant lunged forward. Being the oldest shed, the wood in it offered no resistance. Had the boards been in better condition, the shed perhaps would have collapsed on top of the car, instead, it teetered for a moment. The car plowed through the back wall.

Ruth's right foot leaped for the brake pedal. The Durant ground to a halt far too long after the incident to help matters other than to show her how to stop the automobile.

Two eggs rolled off the roof, down the windshield, down the hood and then off onto the right front fender and then along the running board toward the rear of the car without breaking.

Sis reached out, picked them up, and put them into her purse and climbed into the back seat. She did not seem to notice the damage the car had done, nor did she seem concerned the auto might need some repairs, she had other things on her mind.

Ruth shrugged and pushed the long stick into the position marked with an "R" and backed out of the wreckage, running over several of Sis's tools left on the ground after the statue had been built.

"Stop at the post office, will you?" Sis asked, as they tooled down Main Street. "I need to get some two cent stamps, I have to write some letters."

Ruth nodded and took the opportunity to study the controls when Sis went inside. She quickly discovered how the automobile was managed. If the engine began whining and bucking, she had to push the long stick into a different position except "R" when it was going forward, remember to use the left foot pedal. The clutch, she remembered Otto calling it, and it had something to do with the long stick.

Sis hurried out and climbed into the front seat. She had in mind to learn how to drive this contraption and become independent. It did have its advantages over a horse and buggy. Probably the biggest advantage was no more cleaning up after a horse. Horse puckey was good for the garden, but not much else.

Ruth gave her a sidelong glance and pointed to a little round window behind the steering wheel, "I think it's the gas gage and it's near empty."

Sis nodded and Ruth drew up to the curb in front of Lou's Hardware and felt important when Lou came out, stuffed the nozzle into the body of the Durant somewhere in back and asked how much.

"Fill it up," Sis called out.

"Please check the oil," Ruth added.

CHAPTER TWENTY-FIVE
THE GOld STOCK

In retrospect, Uke wondered if things might
have turned out differently if he had known
about the journey Ruth and Sis had in mind.

Their trip to Middletown proved uneventful
other than two stops for water. Steam boiling
out of the radiator blanketed the windshield.
Their first necessary stop provided water from
a creek trickling down McNamara's hill and the
second one at a farm pump near Middletown.

Fortunately the small spout on the tea
kettle Sis discovered on the floor of the rear
seat could not replenish the over heated engine
fast enough to crack the block.

Sis solved the over heating problem. She
encouraged Ruth to move the long lever sticking
out of the floor into a different position and
the engine stopped racing and became quieter.
Their engineering prowess elated them. Ruth had
been driving with the knob on the stick indicating a "1". The auto leaped and lunged until
she recalled that Otto had moved the stick
around. She guessed that sequencing the stick's
movement from one through three satisfied the
Durand's demands.

"Ya know when those two guys are gonna' git
the rest of that popcorn wagon?" The farm lady

demanded.

"No," Sis lied, replying to the farm lady's question. "I don't know a thing about a popcorn wagon." She nudged Ruth in the back, urging her to hurry back to the car.

Sis's had Ruth draw to a stop in front of a pawn shop. "Wait here," Sis ordered. She avoided Ruth's inquiring glance. Ruth knew what a pawn shop was, but had no idea why Sis might have business there. Her eyes followed as Sis disappeared into the dim, cheerless recess. After the door closed, she climbed out of the Durant and strode to the edge of a filthy plate glass window and used Higgie's small clear spot in the grime to peek inside.

Sis was arguing with a small, round man with a green visor pulled low over his eyes. A breeze caused a brown spider to swing from its web right in front of her face. She brushed it away. Engrossed with watching Sis, it didn't occur to her she was afraid of spiders.

He pointed to the front door and Ruth realized he was ordering Sis out of the place. Sis was shaking a piece of paper in his face. The man snatched and crumpled it before tossing it to the floor. Sis picked it up and stormed out.

Ruth had no chance to hurry back into the Durant and was standing flat footed on the sidewalk when Sis came out of the building. Unobtrusively as possible, she climbed back under the steering wheel and avoiding looking toward her new sister-in-law.

Let's go home," Sis snapped.

She was furious, of that Ruth had no doubt. Did she dare ask what was going on between Sis and the man in the store? A glance at Sis's face told her if Sis was upset before she went in: she was angry now.

Rolling away from the curb Ruth ventured, "Can Uke be of any help?"

"That's exactly where we are headed." Sis

declared. She half turned in the seat and looked long and hard at Ruth. "Do you believe in astrology or fortune telling?"

Ruth shrugged.

Sis respected her ignorance. Upon an impulse, she decided to confide in Ruth and unfolded the story. Otto had won some gold mining stock and she had taken it to Mihich Nostrov's brother-in-law to see if it had any value. He said it was worthless and would not give it back to her. He said he had thrown it away.

"He was lying, wasn't he?" Ruth guessed.

Sis nodded her head vigorously, pleased Ruth understood. She told her about Mihich and her psychic predictions of the future. Mihich said a great disaster would befall Sis and then she would become wealthy.

"Disaster?" Ruth wondered aloud. "Could she tell Otto would, ...would?" She could not utter the fatal word.

Sis nodded in agreement. Ruth was guessing the truth, helping Sis unravel the net work of lies.

"Wealthy?" Ruth led her on. "Did she mean the inheritance? Uke told me about it. It was why he went home to....blow up the statue, wasn't it? Abe convinced him to do it."

This bit of information surprised Sis she hadn't known Uke was anywhere near the shed. She held her tongue and encouraged Ruth with a nod. Perhaps between her and the girl they could solve the mystery. Did Mihich mean the wealth would come from the stock or from her inheritance? Or both?

When they returned to the house, she would find Uke and Mihich and get to the bottom of this. She was not at all certain what part Uke played, but it would take nothing to find out. Did he blow up the shed on purpose?

The car rapidly approached McNamara's Hill and Sis placed her hand on Ruth's arm, "Please

slow down, this hill is long and dangerous.
Wait, why don't we stop right here and rest?"
Sis pointed out the inviting cove where Otto
and then Uke learned to goof off.

Ruth was happy to oblige, her forearms were
tired from the strain of steering the car. She
had muscles she never knew existed. However,
she expertly eased the Durant off to the side
and shut it down, driving it was not such an
difficult feat after all. If Uke came into some
money she'd get them an automobile and to learn
to drive the truck, too.

"It would be nice if someone invented a way
to help turn the steering wheel," Ruth rubbed
her forearms to ease the strain.

The inviting nook out of view of the road
allowed the two ladies to feel comfortable
stretching out on the grass. Robins saw them
hitch up their dresses a modest amount. They
were comfortable in the afternoon heat.

"I don't know what to think," Sis mused. "The
stock must be worth something or why else is
everyone trying to get their hands on it?

"Would there be any other reason the stock
would have some value?" Ruth wondered aloud
while casting glances about the pleasant little
cove for spiders. She had no stomach for
another encounter with a spider, but would
squash it if one made the scene.

Sis was quiet for a long spell before answering. "The reason, no, that couldn't be it."
There could be no possible connection between
the statue and the gold stock, or could there?

Ruth waited wondering how to encourage Sis to
divulge her thoughts.

"No, Uke would never do that," Sis decided.

This brought Ruth upright, she demanded, "Do
what?"

Sis shook her head firmly and announced,
"Let's go."

"Do what?" Ruth did not move. It was a good

walk home for Sis since she couldn't drive.
Ruth intended not to budge until hell froze
over, if need be. She had to know, she had a
right to know, surprised at her own grit and
determination. Uke was her husband and she
intended to defend him.

Sis stood up and stared at Ruth before she
realized this girl was showing more spunk than
she had ever given her credit for having.

"Let's go see the statue," Sis decided. "It
may explain a few things. The priest, Father
Aloysius, put the idea into her head when he
said, "The statue doesn't look the same."

Ruth relented and picked herself up making
mental notes about this lovely little nook on
the way back to the Durant. She fixed it firmly
in her mind. It was quiet and peaceful and
perhaps with a picnic lunch and a blanket
spread out on the grass and the privacy from
the road it would be an ideal place to bring
Uke and see if she could light a fire in him.

The Durant headed for home like a weary horse
smelling oats in the stall. The car behaved
delightfully. Ruth careened down McNamara's
hill, around the blind curve and whipped over
the crossing moments ahead of a freight train
hauling a long line of coal cars and raced past
a red Essex that a cat had finger painted paw
prints all over. She found the wind blowing
through her hair and the thrill from the speed
was a new and delightful experience she had
never known before.

Sis caught sight of the shattered remains of
the popcorn wagon when they careened past the
big boulder beside the road. It took a few
moments before she put together the strewn
parts and the remains of the wagon hidden among
the weeds and sun flowers at home.

Perhaps this was why Uke had been absent for
several days and then returned filthy with coal
dust. I'll have to query him, she decided. It

seems to me there have been a lot of things
going on around here I don't know about. (She
no longer had Otto's pockets to search for information....or money.)

One concern she had was who really owned the
gold mining stock? Otto, she knew, did not come
by it from the results of honest labor. Asking
any of his poker player pals who owned it
wouldn't do, either. They would all claim it.

Sis was at a loss other than go to the park
and commune with the statue. Her confidence in
Ruth's driving increased by the time they
arrived. The Durant did not jerk and pitch anymore when she started up or stopped it. The car
sailed up to the edge of the park and snorted
slightly as it came to rest.

Ruth shut off the engine and looked at Sis,
letting her decide if she wanted company.

"Come along," Sis invited, "I guess we're in
this together." Her confidence in Ruth's driving spilled over into taking her into her
thoughts.

Ruth was aware of Sis's change in attitude,
but was not certain she wanted to become involved. However, curiosity made her slide out from
under the wheel and join the disappearing
figure. She had almost caught up to Sis when
she heard a shriek.

Startled, Ruth looked around desperately for
something to use for a weapon. She picked up a
piece of rotted tree limb with some effort and
staggered into the shrubs to help Sis.

***

Uke was having problems with his mayoral
campaign. The mayor threatened to sue him for
calling him a dumb Swede, he claimed he wasn't
a Swede, he was a Dane.

Uke went to see Mihich, the psychic. He had
never been to see her before. George Wisler,
his best man, insisted he saw her after Uke
asked to be his campaign manager.

George was smart. He never refused Uke anything since he had thrown him in the river. Uke
walked hesitantly into the dark back room of
the Nostrov residence. The place smelled musty
and Uke could not be sure, but he thought he
saw a bat fly past him when the oil lamp
suddenly dimmed without the help of anyone
turning the wick down. The room was rank with
the smell of kerosene from the lamp.

Once his eyes adjusted to the darkness, he
saw a curtain part and Mihich glided in and
motioned him toward a chair by a small table
with a large glass ball on it. She began by
waving her hands over the ball. Uke sank into
the chair, thinking, boy, I wish I had this
ball for a marble when I was a kid...I'd take
everybody's megs.

"Clear your mind, boy," the gravely voice
instructed. It did not sound like Michich
speaking, but there was no one else in the
room. "I need your fullest concentration."

Uke quelled the impulse to get up and leave.
He would have except she had his five dollars
tucked away somewhere in her God awful red and
purple skirt.

"My crystal ball is cloudy," she offered,
rubbing her hands together before extending one
hand palm upwards. Another five dollars might
clear it up.

"Wipe it off," Uke laughed, "afore I turn you
upside down and shake my five bucks out of
you."

"Ah," Mihich offered, hiding her fear of his
threat, "I see clearly now. A tragedy will
befall you before you come into a lot of money.
You have taken on a lot of responsibility," she
hesitated, glancing at his wedding ring. "Your
wife is in a peck of trouble."

"What kind of trouble?" Uke demanded. She
must mean Ruth?

"The ball is getting cloudy, quite cloudy,

maybe you will come into the money before
having the tragedy?"

"You ain't getting no more money out of me,"
Uke snorted. This he knew for certain: he was
flat broke and payday from the county was three
days away.

There was a sudden rustle and whirring noise
and Uke could see bats skittering around the
dimly lighted room. He hurried out the door,
these flying rodents made him uneasy.

Mihich screamed after him as he gained the
street, "Go to your loved one, hurry, and then
return tomorrow, I am certain the ball will
clear by then." She berated herself: she had
misjudged her mark. Almost always the promise
of money coming into the patron's life produced
at least another fifty cents.

Uke tried to decide who his loved one might
be. Not Herman, he was in last week's Clarion,
the county's leading tabloid. They claimed it
was the biggest fish on record.

A photo showed a badly torn up human and the
headlines on the front page claimed the fish
had caught the man.

Uke knew it was Herman, and suddenly he knew
what had happened to Higgie Jones, a cleaning
towel was visible in the victim's back pocket.
He had led Higgie to his demise and for a moment felt sorry for him. He was thankful Herman
had not treated him this poorly. He felt regret
that Herman was no longer around, now he had no
excuse to go fishing. As for Higgie: it served
him right: poaching on my fishing hole.

"Gosh", he suddenly realized, "Herman, then
Otto, and now Higgie, and I caused it all!"

The truck was his first love. He climbed into
it. Mihich must have meant Ruth was in trouble.
If Ruth was in trouble, then so was Sis. Sis
had told him she was going to Middletown and
the two must be together.

A feeling surfaced that he had never felt

before. A real concern for Ruth. A sense of
urgency came over him as the truck careened
around a corner by the park as he urged it
toward Middletown. He did not notice the Durant
parked on the far side of the street.

One person would know about Ruth or Sis.
Frenchy, the official town drunk and gossip.
His information was reliable, more so than
Higgie's. Middletown was a big place. Neither
Sis nor Ruth were known over there.

Mainstreet was the logical place to begin
looking. Methodically pushing open swinging
doors, he peered inside looking for someone who
had seen Frenchy. The odor of stale beer,
spilled whiskey and up chuck made the job
distasteful. The saloons smelled worse than the
county jail.

After several tries, Uke decided there were
too many taverns in Rootville, what with pro-
hibtion in full swing. He decided it might be a
good idea to shut some of them down. Hey, I can
make it part of my campaign. He wondered which
ones would pay him to let them operate?

The mayor of Middletown had to be taking
bribes, was Mayor Clausen getting paid to let
them sell booze in town, also ? It would be
difficult to prove, but he could suggest it was
happening. Newspapers would take up the hue and
cry and both mayors would have an awful time
denying it. It would make a great campaign
issue. Those I close down can always open again
after the election.

Finally, at the eighth place, Big Jim's Pool
Hall and Refreshment Emporium, he found George
Wisler, his reluctant best man, busily trying
to keep the bar from tipping over. Rather than
take another river bath, George hurriedly told
him where he had last seen Frenchy, but not
before getting Uke to agree any past due debts
were now paid in full, including best man.

Luck was with him. Frenchy was part of the

furniture in Mike's Lube & Eats joint.

"Frenchy, I need some information," Uke ventured. "My wife is missing."

"Uke, eh? I need a drink." The saturated souse tapped his nearly empty glass.

"I don't have no money," Uke confessed.

"Then I don't have no information," Frenchy asserted, rolling his blood shot eyes toward the grime and tin tiled ceiling.

"Got no patience, Frenchy," Uke growled picking up the oiled man up by his shirt front. He shook him enough that a couple of shirt buttons flew to the floor.

The bartender, a new man in town fresh from the freight yards, reached for the baseball bat under the bar and then thought better of it when he caught a flash of Uke's badge. Uke did not have his gun. First of all, it was to be used on official business, secondly, it always slapped against his leg annoying him, thirdly, he didn't want to wear it when he was over by Mihich, fourthly, he wasn't at all certain his missing wife was official business.

"Ready to tell me?" Uke growled at Frenchy, allowing his toes to make contact with the floor.

Frenchy grinned at him and began jabbering in what Uke supposed was French. When he quieted down, he held out his hand. "Honest, I ain't seen either of them."

"Pour him a drink," Uke turned to the bartender knowing he had heard him tell Frenchy he was broke. In a flash, he had an inspiration, "and charge it to the county." He released Frenchy and watched him slither up to the bar.

The bartender was not at all sure if he should comply with Uke's wishes. Uke made up his mind for him, he strode toward the bar,

"What will it be, boy, the bat or the booze?" Surprised at himself, Uke wondered if Ruth or Sis gave him the courage to act so tough. Not

my problem the barkeep decided, he filled
Frenchy's glass. Jobs were hard to come by and
he was lucky to have found this one.

Uke put his hand over the glass of Devil's
Juice and looked at Frenchy.

"Ain't seen them," Frenchy insisted.

Uke knew he was lying. When he had asked
about Ruth, Frenchy had indicated more than one
person was involved.

Disgusted, Uke started to pour the whiskey on
the bar.

"Wait," Frenchy tugged at his sleeve to stop
him. "You know the little park where yer Sis
put the statue?"

Uke waited.

Frenchy hurriedly downed his shot and skidded
the glass toward Uke who advanced toward him.
He thought better of trying for another free
drink before offering, "try the park, they
might be there." It would be the end of his
using the park for a home at least for a while,
Frenchy knew. Well, it was too crowded in
there, anyway.

Since the county was paying for the drinks,
the barkeep poured himself a stiff one as he
watched the big guy stride out the door.

* * *

Ruth rushed into the small opening. Sis was
leaning against Grand Dad, her head resting on
his arm, sobbing. The shoes of the junkyard
child remained and Grandpa's head and half his
torso were missing. How could she know that
with copper selling for twenty cents a pound
and Frenchy's insatiable thirst, the statue
would not withstand commercial interests?

Ruth dropped the tree branch and put her arm
around Sis and led her quietly back to the
Durant, opened the car door and waited. Sis
hesitated before climbing in and took one last
look at the tiny park. The destruction was
hidden from view.

In silence the car stirred up dust on Devil's
Lane and slipped into the drive. The trailing
plume of dust caught up to them and past by
before they saw a man through the bug coated
windshield. The well dressed man lifted himself
up from the kitchen steps, brushed off the seat
of his pants and strode toward them.

"Mrs. Granley, I've been waiting most of the
day." She knew Fred Studey, partner in Studey,
Studey, and Lieb, law firm.

The older partner in the firm eyed Ruth in
appreciation before continuing."All the demands
of the will have been met, and I have checks
for the remaining balance." He fished around in
his vest pocket and his eyes lighted up. He let
out an "ah," and brought the small envelope
out. "A check for each of the remaining heirs,
I trust you will see your brothers get theirs?"
He handed three checks to her face down.

Sis turned them face up and looked at the
amounts. Ruth edged closer. The blood drained
from Sis's face and she straightened up and
called to the rapidly retreating back of Mr.
Studey. "These are for a thousand dollars
apiece, where is the rest of it?"

Mr.Fred Studey paused, turned around and
fished out his handkerchief and in a delaying
tactic, wiped his glasses, before replying. "My
good woman, taxes, costs of administering the
estate, and so forth, took up the rest."

"But a million dollars?" Sis was shocked, she
could not believe him. This bunch of ambulance
chasers had stolen all but three thousand
dollars!

Wow, Ruth thought, Uke is going to get his
hands on a thousand dollars! She began to make
out a mental list of things to purchase. New
dishes, a new rug for the front room, medicine
for pa and maybe a new dress... after an
automobile.

Mr. Studey retreated to his new Auburn. His

one armed chauffeur, Stud Wilkens, impatiently
drummed his finger tips on the steering wheel.
He wanted desperately for the day to end so he
could get out of this new suit of clothes and
take off this white shirt with the starched
collar. His neck was rubbed raw. At sixty-eight
dollars an hour, it was the easiest and best
job he had ever had.

Being Mr.Studey's brother-in-law had absol-
utely nothing to do with the pay. Nor did being
married to the ugliest beast this side of
Heaven have anything to do with the job.

Mr.Studey climbed into the rear seat and sat
back in the plush cushions to enjoy the aroma
of burned gasoline. He would have to find
another inheritance soon. He was wondering if
he should tell his chauffeur he no longer had a
job, or wait until the end of the work day? One
of their best accounts had just ran dry.

Uke gave up looking for the women and went to
his office to see if his deputy had produced
another stack of campaign posters on the
mimeograph machine. He hadn't. Disgusted, he
turned down Devil's Lane before realizing he no
longer lived there. Well, maybe Sis has some
sandwich fixings laying around?

He saw the Durant parked in the yard and
wondered if he could get the sandwich before
the two women got to him?

CHAPTER TWENTY-SIX
WE WIN!

Over in Webster City, near the state capitol,
an event took place of no consequence or interest to anyone other than the two people involved. Well, almost no one. After a fight with
his wife, State Representative Schuster Skyler
Summers III, looked up to see her pointing his
favorite shotgun at his molars. Before you could
say "cavity", he didn't have any.

An intensive search was on for a new state
representative even before SSS III was laid to
rest. Someone had to serve on the Special
Interest and Accounting committee.

The back room brain trust had their collective heads together at the church, then the
cemetery and at the sumptuous free dinner after
putting S.S.S.III to rest. Webster City had no
"qualified" candidates. Qualified meant the same
as money.

These two committees were charged with the
responsibility of helping "distressed" people.
These were the most lucrative, and of course,
the most sought after political posts in the
state. Many wondered how a new, novice cong-
ressman always got on this committee. Those in
the know knew how. He had to be wealthy.

A likely candidate was one Honorable Wendle X. Clausen, mayor of Rootville who was in the midst of a tough mayoral battle with an up-start politician named Ulysses S. Compton. The mayor was trying to defend himself against a charge of destroying a statue in a private park for personal gain. (He lost a lot of voter confidence by trying to put the blame on Frenchy, the town drunk.)

The Rootville rag, alias: The Clarion Bugle, reminded the voters of the Fourth of July episode by reprinting their choice photos of the mayor. They were backing the local sheriff, Ulysses Sampson Compton, for reasons best left unsaid.

The sheriff, Uke for short, won the hearts of the good burgers by a nose in several debates with the mayor. It was said he was no match for the mayor when it came to lingo bingo, but at the end of each debate the sheriff would pick his nose and flick the bugger at the mayor.

When the votes were tallied, the local politicians were at a loss as to why the mayor lost the election by such a goodly margin. Which was a relief to Frenchy since no one else knew what happened to the copper sheeting from the statue. Frenchy's campaign efforts brought him into every saloon in town at least twice before the election, stumping for Uke.

Immediately after the swearing in ceremony of the new mayor, the Webster City back room brain trust were in the waiting room of the Rootville mayor's office. Wendle Clausen was surprised to find all his cronies from Webster City waiting outside the door. None of them acknowledged the fallen city chief, his political life had expired, instead, they were intent upon swarming around the new mayor, Ulysses Sampson Compton.

After the dignitaries left the mayor's office and Uke had a few minutes alone, he cautiously tried out the big over-stuffed expensive horse

hair filled chair covered in genuine cowhide,
paid for by all the people who could never
afford one of their own. He grinned in satisfaction and resolved to spend more time at the
office than he had when he was sheriff.

His new office was on the third floor with a
nice view of the little park. His old office
was down in the basement. Boy, oh boy, if Otto
could see me now! Tired, he leaned back to rest
his eyes for a moment.

He awoke with a start. A group of people,
strangers, all, were arrayed around his desk.
"Oh, sorry, I guess I fell asleep. Tough
campaign and all."

The Webster City group, their intentions upon
selecting Clausen, knew immediately they had
their new state representative. The candidate
appeared pliable and did not seem too insulted,
maybe eager when they suggested he could become
wealthy by following a few directions. Doggone
it, Uke determined, Mihich did know what she
was talking about. He would soon become rich.
With enough money, I can hire her to advise me
along with Sis and Ruth.

Resigning the mayor job created no problem,
the boys in the back room simply discovered a
seldom enforced glitch in the law forbidding a
sheriff from getting paid for two jobs at the
same time. Since Uke had not resigned prior to
being sworn in as mayor, a special election
would have to be held for mayor and sheriff.
Rootville's cemetery was busy supplying voters
for the upcoming election. All eight aldermen
were vying for the job. Not one asked for the
ex-mayor's endorsement...or from Uke.

Uke liked the idea that state representative
paid three dollars a month more than mayor and
free breakfast and haircuts were thrown in to
boot. A shave was a dollar and twenty five
cents. Travel expenses would be paid by the
state.

First thing Uke planned to do was to talk to
people over on the Rock River about improving
the campground. Old Herman, the patriarch of
local catfish, would have children in the Rock
River.

The right honorable Ulysses S. Compton, Uke
for short, was appointed state representative
and sworn in three days later. "I do solemnly
swear to honor and uphold the office of....,"
what was I supposed to say next? He mumbled a
few words, grinned, and reached out to shake
the hand of the Chief Justice. He squeezed the
old duffer's golf hand a little too hard. A
politician's worst mistake.

Sis and Ruth stood happily beside him on the
capitol steps and neither could be certain if
they had seen Abraham, Uke's twin, among the
crowd of nosey people milling around on the
lower steps of the capitol building.

Uke rapidly settled into the routine with few
problems. With the guidance of the "Advisors"
things moved along well and he had no complaints. The pay was significantly better, he
had a nice efficiency apartment, hot water and
carpets on the floor. Ruth was writing letters
daily, it seemed like, asking to join him at
the capitol. When the "Advisors" got wind of
this, they promptly brought in a girl for Uke's
approval.

She reminded him of Ruth. About the same
size, same shape, except with a quick brittle
laugh and her hair was a bright blonde, too
bright, it seemed to Uke. She wanted him to
call her "Goldie." Uke showed no interest, made
no comments and had the "Advisors" scratching
their collective heads. Another girl was
brought in, this time a red head, Uke thought
she was nice, but she wasn't Ruth.

Uke kept occupied scratching his name on some
pieces of paper and raising his hand while
sitting at his personal desk in the state

capitol building exercising his responsibilities
properly. Before raising his hand, he would look
toward the balcony where one of his "Advisors"
was sitting. Depending upon which hand he lifted: Uke would raise a matching hand. When a
voice vote was called, it took a bit for him to
determine "Aye" and "Nay" meant yes or no.

It troubled him slightly when he half understood what was going on at the meetings. It
bothered him a whole lot more when he saw his
name in the newspaper and people complaining
about his voting record. Any lost sleep quickly
disappeared after he complained to the
"Advisors" about the nasty things being said
about him.

Each time this happened, he would find a
white envelope slipped under his apartment door
and a hundred dollars in small bills were
always in it. Uke quickly learned to do a lot
of profitable complaining, until one of the
"Advisors" advised him to cool it.

"Yer gittin' a little greedy, and yer kind
are a dime a dozen," he was advised by the
states largest paving contractor.

"We can always get another candidate," a
gentleman who owned a chain of retail stores
advised him, "and the elections are coming up
again soon."

Uke took the month off from the arduous task
of sitting at a desk for several hours a week
and keeping his mouth shut.

Keeping his mouth shut was one task he could
handle, sometimes.

It took several months before he found no one
questioned his absence. In school, he had to
raise one hand with a finger extended in order
to visit the bathroom or slip outside. If he
was gone too long, he could plan on being
grilled upon returning. This was one of the few
differences between being a state representative and being in the fourth grade. When

missing: no one at the capitol seemed
concerned.

An advisor found him sitting on a park bench
tossing peanuts to the pigeons. "Git back in
there and git ready to vote," the man snarled.
Uke shrugged and did as he was told. After all,
he now had cash in his pocket before the next
payday.

Right after the principal, or what ever he
was called in the House of Representatives,
took the roll call. Uke was never quite certain
what had happened, all of a sudden all eyes
were focused on him. He had been day dreaming,
wishing things were like they were back in the
good old days, me an Otto going fishin', me an
Otto roaming around in the truck, me an Ruth
going to the free band concert down in the park
on Wednesday date night, Sis always fussing
over me....

He jumped to his feet and almost forgetting,
cast a quick glance up in the balcony, no one
was there! He tried desperately to remember
what he was to say if this ever happened, but
the words were not there.

"The Right Honorable Ulysses S. Compton,
Representative from Root County, what is your
deciding vote on this matter?" The goof with
the wooden hammer in his hand was demanding an
answer! No one in his right mind would use a
wooden hammer-you couldn't pound nails with
it...only salt.

Answer to what?

This was worse than not being able to add two
plus four in fourth grade. In fact, this was
one of the reasons he quit school. But this guy
was behaving like a school teacher. Uke studied
his fat belly and big red nose. An answer, to
what?

Uke looked to the balcony, did he see a hand
go up? He couldn't be sure, but time was running out, a decision had to be made. He thought

a moment, "Nay" meant no, "Yea" meant "yes".
That was what he was supposed to vote when he
wasn't certain,
   "Yea!" he shouted hoping to quiet the rest-
less throng squirming in their fourth grade
desks. "Yea, Yea, Yea"!
   "One 'yea' is sufficient, Mr. Compton."
Uke wilted back into his chair and brought
his hand up with one finger extended.
   "Representative Compton? You may have the
floor"
   Too late Uke realized he was asking permission to go to the bathroom and this guy wanted
him to stand up and talk about it. He was about
to wet his pants and this guy wanted him to say
something. Life was suddenly getting too
complicated.
   "I recognize the guy... the one from Rock
county, Mr.Herman", he couldn't remember
anyone's name. He jumped to his feet and
hurried from the chamber, that's what they
called it, the "chamber". Uke knew nothing
about chambers other than the chamber pot he
was hurrying to service.
   When he arrived at his apartment in the
evening, two envelopes were tucked under the
door. He recognized the one and opened it to
find the usual hundred dollars tucked in it. I
must have voted right without being told how,
he smiled in appreciation of his talents.
   The other envelope had a smell of flowers
about it and he hesitated before opening it. It
was in Ruth's handwriting. Ruth. He had promised to come home and had forgotten all about
it. Ruth had been threatening him for the past
six or eight months. She was going to do
something if he didn't come home and be her
husband.
   He hurriedly packed a bag and buzzed for his
personal chauffeur and car. This was one thing
the "Advisors" had warned him about after they

failed to find a girl to his liking. Stay on the good side of your wife, a divorced politician was no longer a politician, he was toast, burned, finished, done.

Uke brushed aside a fellow with a basket of apples outside of the legislative building. It annoyed him to see people selling apples on the street. These people didn't vote, either. Sure, times were tough, but they always had been. The thirties promised to be better everyone insisted. So far, they weren't.

On the one hundred mile trip back to Root-ville, Uke debated whether he should resign his job or continue sitting around doing nothing. While the pay was better and the work was easier, he was bored, and while most of the guys sat around thumbing comic books in the chambers, he didn't enjoy reading. He read Peter Rabbit enough times and now had it memorized.

As his chauffeur whipped down McNamara's hill it didn't appear to Uke that Rootville had changed much since he had left, near as he could tell.

"Drop me off right at that little white bungalow," he order his driver, pointing at Ruth's house. "Wait for me." Uke hesitated when he reached the front door. Do I knock? He wasn't certain. Well, he did live here. He looked at the porch swing where he and Ruth sat while he proposed to her. He reached for the door knob, twisted it and pushed. The door was locked.

He reached into his vest pocket searching for the front door key. He remembered he didn't have one and never did. Doors in Rootville were seldom locked. He had no choice but to knock. He hesitated a moment. The chauffeur was lean-ing against the front fender of the black Chrysler Airflow limousine watching him in-tently. In a rare moment it flashed before him:

this guy was on the "Advisors" payroll also.
The door trembled under the pounding before Sis
opened it.

"Wot you doin' here?" Uke stepped back in
surprise.

If she was surprised to see him, Sis didn't
show it. She took in his expensive suit, the
big black car and the driver in one quick
glance and stepped aside silently to let him
in.

"Something wrong?" Uke twisted around once he
was through the door way. He saw nothing of
Ruth.

Sis said nothing, but nodded toward the back
bedroom door.

Uke put down his suitcase and strode toward
"their" room. He pushed open the door and saw
Ruth on the bed, her hair a mess, her face a
pale white and she was breathing heavily. She
turned to look at him with no recognition.

"Hello, Ruth, I'm home," he managed.

She turned away, tears began to stream down
her face.

Sis demanded, "Why haven't you written, why
didn't you come home for her dad's funeral?"
"Why haven't you answered any of her letters?"

The answer was the same for all her questions. He hadn't opened any of the letters, they
were too hard to read. Ignoring Sis's demands
for an answer, he asked, "What's wrong with
her?"

"You fool," Sis snapped, "she's wasting away
because she is lonesome for you and she wants
to be pregnant."

How can she possibly blame me? He wondered.

CHAPTER TWENTY-SEVEN
EPILOGUE

Ruth, a willful girl, carefully kept records on the family's genealogy. Uke's grandfather was not hung as a horse thief: it turned out the horse belonged to him. This may or may not be a pretty good argument against the death penalty.

Uke had turned up his toes while fishing on the Rock River at his favorite catfish hole. Five of Herman's progeny stretched out on the bank near him drawing flies. Uke had an huge smile on his face.

A generation later, Uke's granddaughter, Ruth, found the receipt for the gold mining stock stuffed in one of the old geezer's shoes in the upstairs closet.

How or when Uke recovered the receipt is unknown to this day. Some suspected that he may have found it out in the dog house among the weeds and sun-flowers. Then again, perhaps it turned up in Father Aloysius' Sunday collection or as collateral in a poker game that Uke may have raided in honor of Otto?

Little Ruth took it over to Alby Nostrov's grandson who could not find a record of it and attempted to discard it. Young Ruth would have none of it and retrieved the stock from his waste basket and stormed out of the dump. She hid it in a hat box, the one with wild flowers on it. It was missing after a visit by one of Abraham Compton's grandsons.

The wrecked statue stands in the tiny park unattended, but the junkyard child was reincarnated by the same fiend who donated it to Father Aloysius' church in the first place.

The property in the park is now worth millions. The city wants to build a large, commemorative bureaucratic mausoleum to honor their bungling efforts, but the park is in the way. Ruth and Sis refused to consider selling it. Abraham's sons tried to hire a lawyer in their efforts to steal it. They soon dropped the idea when the lawyer told them "we are all friends and gentlemen: ya can tell me why."

Ulysses S. Compton's ten sons and twenty-five grandchildren are busily running for office on Uke's reputation as a United States Senator. The back room boys would have none of Uke for a presidential candidate. If nothing else, Uke was too honest.

The odds are one of his progeny will soon be president if they can find the gold mining stock to finance (buy?) an election. That is if the matriarch, Sis, approves.

Sis never bothered with a tombstone for her dear, departed husband, Otto. Instead, she hammered out two poker hands in a memorial resembling a cross. One hand was aces and eights, the other jacks and eights. She mounted both poker hands on a lightning rod over Otto's grave.

Perhaps Wild Bill Hickock never held either hand when he was shot in the back of the head in a Deadwood, South Dakota saloon, but poker players to this day shudder and look over their shoulder when a "dead man's hand" is dealt to them.

Abe was shanghaied and wound up in China. The Chinese are hard on fast buck artists. (They don't like competition.)

Sis promptly began a petition to change the name of the city to Compton.

Ruth is drawing up a petition to have Devil's Lane changed to Angel's Alley.

On the second Sunday in May, a bolt of lightning struck the lightning rod on Otto's grave and melted it all to hell. The squirrel was fried during the event.